VIGILANTE: INTO THE DARKNESS

VIGILANTE: BOOK 1: INTO THE DARKNESS
Book Two of the Vigilante Series by Cliff Deane
Published by Creative Texts Publishers
PO Box 50
Barto, PA 19504
www.creativetexts.com

ISBN: 978-0-578-49759-4

VIGILANTE: INTO THE DARKNESS

BY CLIFF DEANE

CREATIVE TEXTS PUBLISHERS
Barto, Pennsylvania

This book is dedicated to faithful Medical Alert Dog Katie Deane
for never finding complaint with my musings. She sleeps curled in my
arm as I type. I hope you enjoy reading my book as much as I enjoyed
writing it.

A Few Notes to My Readers

In an apocalyptic environment, only the lucky one in ten will survive. Our hero does have a bit of luck and puts it to good use. I guess it is just a matter of being in the right place at the right time. Don't forget the adage "You have to be lucky to' be good." If he were unlucky, I would have no story to tell…

The science behind the premise of this book is factual.
I sure hope you enjoy

Vigilante: Into the Darkness

Clarification: While a Coronal Mass Ejection striking the Earth is at some point an absolute certainty, other than The Carrington Event, we've done well, so far. Just remember that not a bit of this story is true…yet, could happen though…js.

A vigilante is a civilian or organization acting in a law enforcement capacity without legal authority.

TABLE OF CONTENTS

PRIMARY CHARACTERS

Levi L. Levins – Retired U.S. Army, Sergeant First Class (SFC/E-7), Captain, then Colonel, Troop A, Defiance Militia

Sarah C. Levins – Married to Levi, no children, Supervisory E.R. Nurse

Ralph M. Basset – Owner Patriot Arms Gun Shop, Mayor of Defiance

Ben Smith – Manager of Patriot Arms Gun Store, Levi's Executive Officer (XO), a quintessential manager

Bradley Cobb – Combat wounded in Berzerkistan and medically retired from Army as Staff Sergeant (SSgt./E-6), promoted to Troop A, First Sergeant (1st Sgt., Top)

Mike Guyardo – Combat wounded in Kandahar, lost a foot, Sergeant (Sgt.) / Lieutenant / Captain, Marine Force Recon assigned instructor duties for Afghanistan (Berzerkistan) Army.

Scott Eldridge – Former Army Ranger Sergeant, Sgt. / SSgt. / Cpt / Major / Lt. Col. (whew), Walmart Store Manager

The Doctors Monroe (Tom and Faith) – Defiance Medicos

Jordan Daniels – Worshipful Master Masonic Lodge members of The Widow's Sons motorcycle club…good guys.

CHAPTER ONE

Nothing but Blue Skies do I see

28 March
Main Gate, Ft. Benning, GA

The morning dawned bright and sunny, with spring temperatures in the mid-seventies as Sergeant First Class, Levi Leonard Lewis, U.S. Army, Cavalry and Military Intelligence (ret), smiled at his wife and with an obvious heavy heart said, "Well, Sarah, 21 years in the Army, and now retired. I look back on my career and think, where did the years go?"

"Sweetie," said Sarah, Levi's wife of 18 years, "if it's going to make you miserable, let's turn around and you go right back in there and reenlist. You know I'm with you, always have been, and always will be."

I know, I know, but it is time for a new beginning back home. Still, I will miss it, though."

Sarah smiled now and softly said, "I know, hon."

"Sarah, I know all those deployments to Iraq and Berzerkistan were hard on you, too, and I don't think I ever really made it clear what your support and strength truly meant to me. I hope I can make you know how your love got me through some scary tough times. I look at you and wonder how you have stayed so beautiful, why, you look better now than when we got married."

Sarah began laughing, "Flatterer, so what is it that you want, as if I didn't know?"

Turning his head and looking directly at Sarah, Levi said with the sincerity of a mature and lasting love, "You punkin', just you."

"Hey Romeo, watch the road! Dang, now you just get those big puppy dog eyes back on the road and off my chest!"

"Sorry, babe, what can I say? You drive me crazy! But seriously, you know Sarah; the whole world is open to us. I just feel that the future looks very bright. Two weeks from now I start a new career as a Detective with the West Virginia Criminal Investigation Division, and you're your new job at the hospital...wow, it seems like we'll finally have the kind of life in retirement we could have only dreamed of when we were younger."

Sarah smiled, "You know, Levi, I was thinking just last night how awesome it is that I was born at Thomas Memorial Hospital in South Charleston, and now I'll be running their E.R."

"I'm proud of you, honey." Levi said.

Now, smiling and becoming more relaxed, both felt at peace with the future when Levi said, "You know Sarah, I'm glad we decided to take a couple of weeks in Kill Devil Hills. It will be like our second honeymoon, making love like a couple of young'uns, and then, just sittin' in the mornin' sun, toes in the water, ass in the sand…"

"Cute, Mr. Levins, but I think you have your song lyrics spliced together," laughed Sarah. "Still, it does sound very nice."

"Yeah, well I'd bet you're the only one who'd pick up on the Otis Redding thing. Ya' know, I think things are going to work out just fine."

8 May
Room 269, Days Inn Kill Devil Hills Oceanfront
Kill Devil Hills, N.C.

Levi awoke with the sun, as another beautiful spring day dawned almost glaringly bright and clear. The sun's reflection seemed to toss a million diamonds floating upon the surface of the Atlantic Ocean. A slight breeze stirred the curtains through the opened window, and the salty sweet smell of the Atlantic Ocean lapping gently along the shore set a mood that Levi was simply too happy to give up.

He lay back on the mattress remembering their first night in Kill Devil HIlls. Inhaling deeply, he could still smell Sarah's perfume. It made him want to cuddle some more, but when he reached out for her, he found only empty space. He smiled thinking that Sarah must have gotten up early and gone out for fresh pastries from that bakery they passed as they drove into town.

Sitting up, Levi reached out to the bedside light and pushed the button. He was surprised when nothing happened, but assumed the bulb had burned out. Turning on the TV brought the same result.

Well, damn, the power is out. He thought, *I hope it hasn't been out for too long or the donuts won't be ready.*

Guess I'll get a shower…

Levi grabbed a quick shower and began to become a bit concerned that Sarah wasn't back yet. Of course, the power outage probably caused her to be longer at the bakery than she had planned. Personally, he was not happy that the power was still off, and he decided that showering in absolute darkness was now off his bucket list.

He toweled off, got dressed and decided to call Sarah to see how much longer she would be.

Oh, crap, he thought, the battery is dead. *Damn, now what?*

After waiting for approximately another ten minutes with no change in circumstances, Levi decided to go out and meet her at the bakery. The hallway was in total darkness, as the emergency lighting had also failed. Levi was forced to feel his way down the hallway to the stairs. A feeling of unease began to creep down his spine.

The door opened, and a couple came onto the landing. Upon stepping through, they jumped back in shock and surprise at the shadowy figure in the darkness.

"Sorry, folks" Levi said. "It's kind of hard to see in here. Any idea what is going on?"

"Oh goodness, you scared the daylights out of us", the man said. "No, we went out for our morning walk and things got kind of crazy. There's no power in town and everyone's vehicles just rolled to a stop. Hopefully, it won't be long before the power company straightens this out."

Knowing better, Levi replied "Yeah, hopefully is right. Well, good luck to you both". Levi continued on and arrived to bedlam in the lobby of the hotel. Everyone was screaming at the hotel staff at once. Several people were milling around waiting for someone to tell them what to do, but there was no one in charge.

Levi scanned the crowd for Sarah, but she was nowhere to be found. Stepping outside, he scanned the parking lot, now full of non-working cars, and decided he may as well check on his own vehicle for clues to his wife's whereabouts. Always thinking ahead, Levi had backed his vehicle into his spot as he usually did in a spot further away, but nearer to the exit. As he approached his parking spot, he felt a wave of relief when saw that the trunk to the vehicle was open and someone was bent over, rummaging around inside. *Sarah!* he thought.

Just then, a disheveled looking man leaned over and looked at Levi from behind the trunk and exclaimed "What do you want? Get out of here!"

Initially shocked, Levi did a double take to confirm he had the right car before saying "Hey Jackass, this is my vehicle, what do *you* want?"

Without responding, the man stepped from behind the vehicle with a tire iron in his hand, swinging it violently towards Levi. Although surprised, Levi's instincts kicked in and was able to evade the blow, which continued past him, smashing the right rear passenger window and cutting up the man's hand in the process. Seizing the opportunity, Levi stepped in and smashed a hard right directly to the man's nose, knocking him backwards and onto his rear into a sitting position.

Levi lunged forward only to abruptly stop himself... *What the?*

What he had seen out of the corner of his eye had stopped him from jumping on top of the man and beating the hell out of him. There, behind the car on the grass, lay the crumpled form of a woman.

"Sarah!" he yelled. Running to the body, he rolled her over to see that it was indeed Sarah, and she was obviously dead, her head crushed by the same tire iron that had smashed his car window.

"I told that stupid bitch my car wouldn't start..." a voice from behind him began, "all she had to do was give me her jumper cables and give me a jump, but she kept on walking and ignored me. When I grabbed her purse and got her keys to open the trunk, she attacked me. It was self-defense and her own damn fault for not helping me to begin with."

Levi felt rage explode within him as he rose to face the man. "Jumper cables won't do a damn thing, you moron. And besides that, was it self-defense when you came at me with a tire iron just now?"

The contradiction was obvious and the man knew the only way out of this situation was to get rid of Levi. Still holding his bloody right hand with his left, the man bent over and reached down. Levi thought he was going for the tire iron, but instead he attempted to pull a knife from his right boot with his left hand. As he bent over, he felt a horrible pain as Levi's knee came up into his face, again smashing his already broken nose and causing the man to cry out in pain as he again fell to the ground.

The knife fell to the parking lot as the man screamed and held his face with both hands before attempting a second time to fumble for a weapon, this time in his pants pocket. Very quickly Levi retrieved the tire iron and smashed the killer's remaining good hand. The man screamed louder and attempted to shield his mangled hands as he scooted back against the car.

A white rage warped Levi's mind as thought of his beautiful wife's dead body behind him on the ground, murdered by this maniac. His eyes became a steely gray which betrayed a hatred coupled with an unrelenting desire for vengeance.

Levi stepped up to the crying man who began begging for his life. "Please don't kill me, I found her this way, I swear to God."

"Oh, well now, that makes all the difference," said Levi as he brought the tire iron down upon the young man's knee, adding it to the shattered bone list.

He screamed in pain and pleaded, "Oh, God, don't hurt me again. Please, mister, please, I beg you. Oh God help me."

"Is that what she said to you?" as, bang, the left knee joined the list.

Now realizing that the man with the tire iron was not going to stop, the man begged Levi to finish the job. "All right, come on man, get it over with."

Levi squatted in front of the man and asked, "What did the woman you murdered this morning say?"

"Just kill me already!" the man screamed.

Levi sighed, stood, and smashed the man's right elbow. "Now I don't believe she said that. Listen to me, if you want me to put you out of your misery, you will answer my questions. I might even see if I can get you to a hospital; after all, nothing is life threatening here."

"Really? Oh, please help me." This piece of human trash began to cry and plead, "Please, I swear to God I'll tell you whatever you want to know."

"Now, that wasn't so hard, was it? But, since you will be meeting God soon enough I would suggest you leave Him out of this little encounter, and stay where you're more comfortable.

Okay, here is how this is going to work. I ask you a question, and if I believe you then I don't break anything else, deal?"

"Yes, yes, hurry, I need help, what do you want? Oh God, I'm hurt."

Levi broke the man's ankle with his weapon. "I told you, leave God out of this. Mention His name again and what you are going through now will seem like a picnic. Dang, did you know your nose is all flattened out? Man, I bet that hurts like hell."

"Oh G…, wait, please don't hit me again."

"Okay, you see how easy I am to talk to? Now, what did the lady you murdered this morning say before she died?"

Beginning to enter shock, the pain began to fade as the man finally spoke, "She said she would be glad to help, but needed to drop off some pastries to her husband because he would know what to do and then they would both come back, but I didn't want to wait and grabbed her purse. Then things got out of hand…"

Barely able to restrain himself, Levi said, "I'm the husband she wanted to come and get and we *would* have gladly tried to help you. She was my wife of eighteen years, and I loved her very much." Bam went the left elbow; bam went both feet and shins.

The man was barely able to speak now, but stammered, "You said you would get help."

"Yeah, well I lied, but don't worry, I'll be right back. I'm not going to kill you. I am going to drag you into the hotel before I burn it to the ground. I mean, you don't have to stay in there, you could just walk out. Oh wait, that would be hard now, wouldn't it? Oh well, just relax, your pain will end right after your skin catches fire, and begins to bubble, just before turning a crispy brown."

"Fire? No, wait, you promised not to kill me. Please, I'm begging, please, please don't let me burn."

"I leave you with this thought, back in my father's day a common phrase was *burn baby burn.* I just wish I could be here to watch your pain as your skin begins to blister just before it catches fire. I pray you don't die too quickly.You took my wife from me. There is nothing I can think of, nothing that would be too horrible to do to you," sobbed Levi. "I just wish I could kill you over and over again. Sarah, please forgive me for what I do here, but lawless and violence are now the laws of this land."

Levi went through the man's pockets and found the .22 caliber pistol he had been reaching for. He then left the man sobbing without saying another word.

Returning to Sarah, he gently lifted her into his arms and carried her to the hotel lobby. In the lobby, several people, in a near panic were battling for the attention of the hotel manager. A woman screamed as Levi walked in with the bloody, lifeless body of his wife.

"My wife has been murdered, Levi proclaimed. I need you to call the police." Those still in the lobby turned to Levi, women began screaming, and men rushed their families out into the morning sunlight.

Now alone with the Hotel Manager, Levi said, "Please call the police, my wife has been murdered."

The manager's nametag read, Mr. Holt. He backed up against the wall and said, "Please don't hurt me. Take what you want, but please don't kill me."

This actually helped Levi regain a bit of his composure, and he said, "I didn't kill anyone, and I don't want to hurt you. Now, please call the police."

Relaxing just a bit, Holt stuttered out in a voice nearing panic, "N…Nothing is working, no phones, no cars, nothing. I don't know what to do!"

Levi's military training forced itself above his sorrow as he said, "Okay, then I will tell you what you are going to do. Get a sheet, and then you and I are going to the 2nd-floor landing. Once there we will wrap her in the sheet and take her back to our room. Then I'll go find the police."

"But, but, I, I can't just leave the desk. I have to stay right here. If I see a policeman, I will send him up to you."

Now Levi was becoming angry as he said, "Listen, Holt, I didn't ask you to come up to help. I gave you a direct order. Now, either you come and help me, or you will be covered in your own blood. Am I clear here?"

"But, but…"

Screaming now, "But nothin', get your ass moving!"

Seeing the blood on Levi and wanting to keep his own blood secured, he jumped to it, got the sheet and together they gently, and with great care wrapped Sarah in the sheet.

Holt then asked Levi to lead the way.

"Listen, moron, if I lead, you'll split, so get your candy ass moving. Holt led Levi to their room. Levi's door failed to unlock, and he realized that with no power the electronic lock mechanism would not disengage from the outside.

"Holt, is there another way to open this door?"

"No, no, I don't know, no, I don't think so; at least; I don't have any idea how to open it."

"Levi leaned on what he had learned from his deployments to Berzerkistan. He stepped back from the door and kicked it directly adjacent to the locking mechanism. On the third attempt, the door lock snapped, and Levi pushed Holt into the room before lifting his Sarah into his arms. Light from the window filtered into the hallway as he gently, and with great reverence, placed the body of his beloved Sarah on the unmade bed. Levi covered her, kissed her on the forehead and turned to Holt.

"Get out!"

Holt fled.

Upon seeing himself in the mirror, and seeing the image of a blood-soaked mad man, Levi stripped down to his underwear and washed off Sarah's blood.

He then lay down on the bed, took his beloved Sarah in his arms, and while holding her, Levi Levins cried for a long, long time before falling into a troubled slumber.

Finally, some time later he felt the early stages of rigor begin to take hold of Sarah's body.

Levi steeled himself to the fact that some other great tragedy must have befallen the area. He again showered, dressed in clean clothes, and made his way back to the lobby.

Holt had not stopped running until he was well away from the maniac in room 269.

Now, Levi's face displayed a renewed terrible resolve to finish his mission with Sarah's murderer.

He returned to the parking lot where he found her killer unconscious upon the ground. Without ceremony, and with great prejudice, Levi dragged the man into the hotel and up to the third-floor landing. In his anger, Levi's plan was to burn the hotel down and he did not want this monster to die too quickly. He wanted him to have some time to contemplate his fate.

29 March
What happened
Kill Devil Hills, NC

Returning to his car, Levi pressed the unlock button on his clicker but got no response. Ignoring the man still limp on the ground, he used the key, opened the door, seated himself behind the wheel, and attempted to start the car…nothing.

Upon exiting the car, Levi looked around and saw that there were no vehicles running anywhere that he could see, but he did see many people walking away from their stranded autos. He also saw several billowing clouds of smoke rising high into the air. Plane crashes…

Just moments before Levi had been nearly suicidal, but the realization that suicide would not put him in heaven with his beloved Sarah, nor that it would not help him bring justice to the man who had done this to Sarah, *justice, yes, Old Testament justice!*

Levi Levins rapidly evolved, though many might argue that he had mutated, or perhaps even devolved. His heart was shattered, but his mind became clear, abruptly halting his plunge into shock or madness.

Levi began walking up the street searching for the police, but none were to be found. He did see two abandoned police cars, but no uniformed officers. Checking the cars, he had hoped to find a shotgun, but this was not his lucky day.

Levi now knew for sure exactly what had happened. There was only one thing that could take out the electricity, cell phones, and autos at the same time, Electro Magnetic Pulse (EMP), and only two things were known to be able to create an EMP capable of destroying the national electric grid; high altitude nuclear detonations at approximately 225 miles above Kansas would completely destroy the grid from southern Canada to northern Mexico, or a Coronal Mass Ejection (CME) from our sun which would likely fry the electrical grid of the entire world.

A direct hit by a large enough CME to destroy the worldwide grid systems would likely fry the entire earth. This is called an Extinction Level Event (ELE). A near miss, however, could well fry the entire worldwide electric grids, but an EMP near miss would be completely harmless to life, yet would destroy all unshielded electronics.

He also remembered reading something about a CME strike called the Carrington event of 1859. An amateur astronomer, Richard Carrington, made a note of a large CME being ejected from the sun.

Seventeen and a half hours later that same CME made a direct hit on the Earth. Fortunately, it did not have sufficient strength to cause an ELE, but it did set fires in many telegraph offices and destroyed telegraph lines and equipment in both Europe and The United States. It is estimated that if another Carrington-like CME struck the Earth today, the bill would rise beyond two trillion 2013 dollars, and take many years to recover.

It would take years because the largest regional transformer stations are no longer made in America. They took years to manufacture in Japan, Korea, and China, in addition to replacing the tens of millions of miles of wire and replacing the millions of local neighborhood transformers. These components were just the beginning, so, no old-style electricity for decades, at least in the hinterlands.

Shaking the trivia from his befogged brain Levi realized that at this exact moment, it made absolutely no difference what had caused this EMP event, it was done, and now he had to deal with it.

No safe spaces, therapists, or coloring books would help now. Either buck up or die.

The farther he walked, the more he thought about what he, must do in the here and now. Number one on his list was to find a real weapon. He didn't consider the .22 pistol reliable, and there was no way he was going to keep the tire iron that killed had his wife. Two, he had to find food, and three, decide what to do about Sarah's body.

There was so much more, but he would think about them when the time came. Right then his survival instincts were kicking in and saving his sanity…he would think about that later, too.

People everywhere were wandering up and down the streets, much like Levi, but with no goal, just wandering around waiting for the government to turn the lights back on, or AAA to get their car running.

He thought these people are truly the first of the walking dead.

29 March
Defense 101
Kill Devil Hills, NC

A block from Virginia Dare Trail, Levi found a sporting goods store and thought, *well, well, well, my personal little weapons depot.*

Of course, a Walmart Superstore would have been ideal, but none were available close by.

He entered the store and found the owner standing guard over his merchandise. "We're closed until the power comes back on, please come back then."

In his most polite and soothing voice Levi said, "Sir, the lights will not be coming back on for years. The entire grid is fried, as are cars, and cell phones. Didn't you see the smoke trails from crashed planes? No one is coming to help you.

"My best advice to you is to leave, don't lock the door and you might save the windows, as if that should ever become important.

"Go home, gather the family, hug them to you, and get out of town. I suggest bicycles, even though others will try to take them from you unless *you* are willing to shoot first."

"Nonsense, this is just a power outage, and the power company will have it fixed soon."

Levi looked down at the floor and said, "Sir, ok, you have been warned. Now, I have a problem that you can fix."

The owner looked warily at Levi as he responded, "…and that would be?"

"Wonderful, now we can get down to business. I need a gun, but since you do not sell those, I would like to purchase an aluminum baseball bat. Do you have any for sale?"

"Well, yes, of course but my registers are locked."

"Sir, I assure you that is of no concern. I will take one bat and pay you $25 cash. Is that a fair offer?"

"Well, yes, but they don't cost that much, and I don't have any change."

Smiling now, Levi said, "Sir, I will pay you $25 in cash, right now," and he reached into his back pocket retrieving his wallet and took out $30. Well, dang, I don't have any fives, so I guess the price is now $30. Is that all right?"

"No, that's too much, how about $20?" and with that Levi had his first weapon. He did feel sorry for the owner. Not for the price but because the man had, as yet, no inkling of the wrecking ball about to fall on his head. Oh, well.

Ah, now this feels so much better, thought Levi as he walked away from the store and back to the hotel, where he knew he would still find food. Levi decided to eat dinner from whatever he could find in the hotel kitchen, and then he planned to burn the hotel to the ground after putting the scumbag that had murdered his wife inside it. It seemed appropriate for his Sarah.

Some like it hot

29 March
Old Testament Justice

Kill Devil Hills, NC

There were still a couple of rooms occupied on the first floor, and Levi suggested that they would definitely want to go to another hotel. Just as he was finishing his cold meal, he thought he heard a woman scream.

"I am so sorry, Sarah that I was unable to protect you. I love you, and I now know what my new path must be.

Goodbye my love, May God rest your soul and forgive what I must do. The salty taste of his tears ran into the corners of his mouth as he left to find an appropriate accelerant."

With no way to put the fire out, it raged out of control, leaving only ashes and a blackened steel shell. No human remains were ever found, then again, there was no one left who even cared to look.

CHAPTER TWO

Transportation

```
30 March 0600 hours
Holiday Inn, Virginia Dare Trail
Kill Devil Hills, NC
```

Levi awoke, as usual, with the sun. He'd left the curtains open to provide light.

After showering in total darkness, and in very cold water, he dressed in the same clothes as yesterday, fussing at himself for not having brought clean clothes.

Levi thought, *oh well, no matter, there is a clothing store just across the street. So, what do I need to do next? Okay, first I must find transportation. This pair of Leather Personnel Carriers (shoes) will not get me out of the riot zone which I'm sure will start in earnest by tomorrow, possibly even tonight.*

There are thousands of pre-electronic ignition pre-fuel injected vehicles out there. They should run fine having no electronic circuit boards to have been fried.

I need to find at least one Firearm today. By tomorrow, the looting will start, and I do not want to be toting a .22 in a serious encounter; crap shit, I might as well have a bb gun.

Walmart will still have much of what I need, if, that is, I can get there today.

So, armed with his pop gun and a plan, Levi made his way down the hall to the snack machine. He broke the glass, filled his pockets with the high-calorie junk food, and left the hotel to begin his search for transportation. On the next block Levi came to a bicycle shop and went in.

"Sir, we're closed today. Please come back tomorrow," shouted someone in the rear of the store.

Levi looked over the stock and chose a sturdy 3-speed touring bike.

A man came out from the back and said, "Sorry, sir, I guess you didn't hear me. We're closed until this power thing is sorted out."

Levi gave the man a crooked half smile and said, "No, I can't come back, so I'll just take this bike here. How much is it?"

"All right, sir that is a top-end touring bike and sells for $900. I can't take cards right now, but if you have the $900 in cash on you, we're good to go."

"Really? $900 for a bicycle? Seems a bit steep to me. Really, what's the bottom line, here?

"Sir, the bottom line is $900."

Sighing heavily, Levi reached into hefted his pocket containing his vacation cash and the funds he had liberated from both hotels. He said, "Okay, here ya' go," and he fished $900 from his wad and paid the man.

Stunned, the man said, "What, oh, well okay, but we have to add the tax."

Something in Levi's eyes sent a chill down the man's spine causing him to say, "Oh, what the hell, enjoy your bike."

As an afterthought, Levi asked, "Oh, may I use your telephone book? I'm planning on some hunting, and my rifle is in the hotel that is still burning. I need to get the address of the nearest Gun store?"

"Sure, but you won't need the phone book, it's only a few blocks away, you just go down…"

As Levi turned to leave the bike store, the owner asked, "Do you have a helmet?"

Wheeling the bike outside Levi looked over his shoulder and said, "Pleeze," and rode away.

The Deal

30 March 0930 hours
Patriot Firearms
Kill Devil Hills, NC

It took only five minutes to arrive at Patriot Firearms. The store was open but had two armed guards at the entrance. *Smart man, this owner,* thought Levi.

As he approached, one of the guards insisted on patting Levi down before allowing him inside. When he found the .22 caliber pistol, he smiled and said, "Sir, I think you are at the right place. Things will get bad by tomorrow, and this pea shooter just won't cut it."

"Ya' think? That's why I'm here," chuckled Levi as the guard opened the door. "Thank you."

Upon entering the store, Levi noticed that the staff was loading everything up and preparing to move the merchandise it to a safer location.

A salesman sighed as he looked at Levi, and said, "Sorry, sir, cash only today, and we can't deliver until the internet comes back up to do the background check."

Levi smiled and stuck out his hand saying, "Hi, my name is Levi Levins, and it appears to me that you are obviously aware that the net is not coming back up, at least, in our lifetime, so let's get down to brass tacks.

I have cash…I need three weapons, a carbine and two pistols with a minimum of eighteen magazines. I would prefer twenty-four, and of course, I need ammo, too, say a thousand rounds, all in 9 mil hollow point, and since I don't have transportation yet, other than a $900 bike that fortunately has saddle bags. Can we make a cash deal? I really do need some help here."

"Eighteen mag minimum, but prefer twenty-four, hmm, you military?"

Levi smiled and asked, "It shows, huh?"

"Well, eighteen mags *is* pretty specific, as opposed to, say, lots of magazines. Eighteen magazines is exactly the Infantryman's basic load for the three weapons you seek, and I never knew a grunt who didn't want eight mags per weapon plus one locked. So, yeah, that degree of specificity means you're ex-military."

"Yeah, and the shit of it is that I retired three days ago… twenty-one years."

"Can you prove it?"

Levi laughed and said, "Will my retirement ID card or DD-214 work?"

The salesman laughed back and said, "My name's Ralph, Ralph Bassett, and I own the joint.

Now, Levi, if you don't mind, tell me what you think happened?"

"Easy enough, we were either attacked with nukes in the upper atmosphere around 225 miles over Kansas, or we had a near brush with a CME.

Either way, the result is the same since they both produce an Electro Magnetic Pulse. In another three days, the rioters will burn cities everywhere, people will die right away from dead pacemakers, no meds, murder, disease, hell, lots of reasons, and I'll bet you knew all this before asking, right?"

"Yeah, I just wanted to know who I was talking to. So whadaya need?"

"Okay, right to it, I like that. What do I need? Let's see, for starters, I need a lightweight carbine, two semi-auto pistols. I'd like one to be a Diamondback DB9. Incredibly small, lightweight and shoots well. It's a great little pocket rocket.

On the standard sidearm, well I'm not a Glock snob, so anything light and dependable is fine, oh, and as I said; about 1,000 rounds. Everything in 9 mil hollow point."

"9 mil? Why not a .45 in pistol and a .556 in a long gun?"

"As I said, right now the weight is important, and I like the nine mil hollow points. I mean, hell, if they are good enough for the FBI then they should certainly be good enough for me. Besides, one ammo caliber for everything simplifies things, a lot.

Hopefully, if someone wearing body armor wants to play rough, I plan to run, hide, then ambush him and take his body armor later that night."

Ralph now looked respectfully at Levi and said, "Well, damn, I can't find one single flaw in your plan. Keep it simple stupid; the kiss principal works every time."

"So, Ralph, can we make a deal? I have cash."

Ralph laughed again and said, "Cash, smash, you and I both know cash won't be worth spit in another 48 hours. You know, Levi, I like you, sure we can make a deal, and here it is; you get your weapons *if* you agree that if you ever come across me in the future, you must help me if I am in a jam; deal?"

"Ralph, I gotta' say your offer is tempting, and I will agree with only one exception. If you are the bad guy in a jam, then no, I will not only, not help you, but I will help whoever you are going after. If you need help and you are the good guy, then hell yes, I'll help every single time."

Ralph stared at Levi for several long seconds before saying, "Levi, you're one of the last of the good guys, aren't you? It will probably get you killed, but yeah, we have a deal."

"Thanks, Ralph, look, I hope we'll always be friends, and yeah if you are the good guy, I will be there for you.

Ralph asked, "Now, how far out do you want to shoot? I've got the D'back DB9, nice little hideaway piece; damned thing only weighs 11 ounces empty."

"Thanks, Ralph, look, I hope we'll always be friends, and yeah if you are the good guy, I will be there for you.

As far as distance, I'm thinkin' right now out to about 100 yards. The Keltec sub2000 fold up carbine in 9mm is light weight, but the front sight sucks. I found that taking the front sight from an M-16 series really improves the Kel."

"Damn, Levi, the Kel 2000 is hard to find these days, but yeah, what the hell, I've got seven of 'em, and you can have one, and Glock snob or not, that's what you get, 'cause that's what I like. Another upside to the Glock 17 is that the mags will also fit the Kel 2000. I'll have our gunsmith change out that front sight thing, too. It's an easy fix; won't take 10 minutes.

Oh, wait, I almost forgot, there is one more condition to make this deal work."

Oh, crap, thought Levi, *here it comes*. "Yeah, what condition is that? I ain't robbin' no old ladies."

"Easy, Levi, let me finish, the last condition is that you never, ever tell anyone where you got these pieces. I mean it. I'll take your word because you've convinced me you are a good guy, deal?"

"Now *that* is a deal I am *happy* to make.

If you don't mind my asking, what's your plan?"

Ralph looked Levi up and down for several long seconds as if deciding exactly what to say. He finally said, "We got a place, been working it for years for just this kinda' fustercluck shit.

Look, Levi; I just might be able to get the boss man to bring you in, just you. Interested?"

"Ralph, I gotta' say that is the best offer I've had all day, but no thanks. I know what I must do, and as soon as I can find some motor transportation, I'm off."

"So, ya' need a truck, huh? Not many available these days, but I may have an idea where you might be able to get a nice one."

"Okay, Ralph, what's the deal, how much is it gonna' cost me?"

"Hey, buddy, that's up to you. I got no dog in that fight. Did you know that there is an antique car museum, not ten miles from here? Bet ya' can find a nice ride there, if you hurry.

But cost? I'm pretty sure that mean old fart he won't sell. I reached a point where I refuse to sell anymore weapons. Hell, he's always threatening people. You'll have to persuade the crazy old fool, hell, half the time he thinks he's still in Nam."

"Okay, thanks for the heads up. All I can do is try. Now, how do I get there?"

"Levi, I mean it, that crazy old coot might start shooting.

Man, I sure wish you'd change your mind; having a place to ride out the coming craziness is a very good thing. C'mon, we both know what's going to happen."

"Yeah, I guess that's so, and that's why I have got to say again, thanks, but no thanks. You have your path, and I have mine. Good luck, Ralph, I sure wish you well."

"Okay, Levi, I think I understand, but I ain't real sure, anyway, same to you. Take care, friend. Now let me get Ben to get your stuff.

Ben, drop what you were doin' and help my friend Levi…whatever he needs. New Glock 17 with a laser, and whatever else he wants. Clear?"

Ben nodded his head and looked at Levi with respect saying, "Now sir, what can I get for you?"

It was nice of Ralph to give Levi carte blanche, so he scored a backpack, too.

He thought, *I don't think I'll ever see Ralph again, but I owe him more than I can ever repay.*

Hands up

30 March
East Coast Auto Museum

Outside the antique car museum, Levi dismounted his trusty bike and, not being willing to leave his carbine unattended, he carried it as he approached the front door.

"STOP RIGHT THERE! I ain't sellin', and you ain't stealin'. So, drop yer piece and walk real quiet like back to your bike and ride away, NOW!"

Levi immediately dropped behind the engine block of a stranded Lincoln and yelled back, "Hold on Mister, I only want to talk…"

Bang, a round simultaneously made a *spranging* sound as it hit the engine block.

Holy crap, thought Levi. "Okay, dude, you wanna' play rough, let's play, but for true, I just want to talk." Now Levi wished he had a bit more powerful long gun with a scope, but he knew that he had to evaluate, adapt, overcome and defeat this threat… but damn shit…it didn't look all that good.

He yelled to the shooter, "Come on Mister, stop shooting and I'll move on."

"Fine idea sonny boy, now leave your piece on the ground, and I might let you go all peaceable like."

Levi thought, Oh crap, so much for the diplomacy route. Damn, what makes this old guy want to shoot it out so badly?

"Come on, man, you know I can't leave my carbine behind. Why do you want it anyway?"

"I want it, ya' danged fool 'cause I need to build up my arsenal afore the rest of you Viet Cong come tryin' to take my cars. That damned Ralph at Patriot Firearms wouldn't sell me no more. So, I'll just take yours. Now drop it and git!"

Levi thought; That crazy old bastard is having a flash back to Viet Nam. Well, crazy or not, the old shit is trying to kill me…not gonna' happen.

As Levi lay behind the tire, he slowly peered around the edge and could see nothing when…"

Bang! Blood spurted from Levi's face as the shooter's round was so close it kicked sand and pea gravel into his face. *Okay asshole, now I am pissed. Since I can't run, I'll play possum; maybe you'll make the big mistake and come to me.*

"Ooh Rah, boy, did I git cha?"

Levi didn't respond, he just lay there and waited. It was nearly twenty minutes before he heard the door open, but Levi did not move, or make a sound. The blood from his face quickly dried up, and Levi was really happy that he was wearing sunglasses.

"Ha, ha, ha, I got that VC peckerwood," and then the crazy old rat bastard actually stood straight up and walked toward Levi.

Levi pulled out his little pocket rocket; the DB9 Ralph had given him and waited. The old man then came around the car and saw him lying there.

The dumbass didn't even look to see if there was a blood pool or even to check to make sure that Levi was dead. He just started dancing around like a loon. He took a few seconds before reaching down for the Kel, and that's when Levi shot him right in the head. Considering that the old fool had tried to kill him, Levi did not feel the least bit sad for shooting that crazy old bastard."

Levi's Ride
Inside the East Coast Auto Museum

"Holy crap, I can't believe this. There must be fifty perfectly restored cars and trucks in this place."

As Levi walked around the museum to choose his ride, he came upon a section containing 1960's era military trucks. One, in particular, caught his eye. A perfectly restored Viet Nam era Jeep and trailer, complete with a gudgeon mounting for an M-60 squad machine gun.

Levi knew his search for transportation was over. This jeep was just too perfect. It would go just about anywhere.

Levi opened the hood, and then checked the wiring and all of the fluids. Thinking out loud, he said, "Damn, this thing is cherry."

"Yes, it certainly is," said a voice from the front door. "I suppose you'll be wanting to take that one on your travels, eh, Levi?"

...Oh crap.

CHAPTER THREE

30 March
East Coast Auto Museum

"Ralph, what are you doing here? Oh crap, right, now I get it. I've been set up, and now I guess I get arrested, and hung, while you take all the rides?

Ralph's face took on both a hurt and surprised look as he said, "What? No Levi, none of that is right. Oh, well, I guess I did have an idea that it might come to this, but there is nothing sinister here. Honestly Levi, I did just give you a heads up. Our plan was to come out here after we had our trucks loaded up and try to reason with the crazy old swamp rat one more time.

From the looks of things, it sure looks like self-defense to us. The old man's rifle is still beside the body, and there is no question that he fired it at you. No, you're clear."

Levi's face turned from anger at being successfully set up to sheepish embarrassment. "I'm sorry Ralph; I guess I owe you an apology…I apologize, but you have got to see where I might get that impression."

"Of course, I do, in fact, that's why I came in here alone with no weapon. Now, having said all that, I must add that most of my group is waiting outside for me to call them in to start moving these vehicles out to our little town."

"Town? How many people do you have in your group?"

Smiling, Ralph said, "Well, not too many right now, but we intend to grow beyond the fifty-two we have.

Levi, please rethink your mission, whatever it is. We need you. I hate to admit it, but what we do have is fifty-two individuals that need to be united into a viable, self-sustaining group. Are you willing to even talk about helping me gel this group into a community?"

Levi looked thoughtfully at Ralph before saying, "Yeah, we can talk. I was just thinking that with three hundred million Americans condemned to death over the next twelve months there will be no one to bury the dead. The bodies will just lie where they fall. Disease is going to run rampant, typhoid, dysentery, hell; even the common cold could kill millions of starving, freezing Americans.

So, yeah, maybe my personal quest can wait for maybe up to a year, but then I leave."

"Wonderful, Levi, let's get out to Defiance, and figure out where you'll best fit."

"Defiance, huh? I like it.

Ralph, have you secured the local Walmart Superstore, and Home Depot, yet?"

"No, but you're right, that is a great idea. We can get to it later this week."

Now Levi's face turned cloudy as he responded, "Ralph, by noon tomorrow both will be fortified by some group with a bit more foresight than you apparently have, because if we wait, some of these people will die. Not, may die…will die. We have to secure them today. The sooner we act, the fewer casualties we'll take.

I don't know Ralph; I'm not sure you see the big picture here. The migration will begin as soon as the rioting and murders become the law of the land. You cannot afford to wait a day, not even an hour.

If you don't have a secure location, capable of 360°security, and that means sentries, wire, traps, mines, then forget it. You are destined to fail."

"Levi, I knew you were meant to join us from the first few moments of our conversation at my store.

In answer to your question, the answer is that some of it is done. We have one hundred and twenty-five acres, with fifty acres dedicated to farm production, and another fifty acres for grazing. The northern and eastern flanks of the property border the river…"

"Ralph, that's fine, but we need to act now, you can tell me all about the finer points Defiance later. Right now, we gotta' lay claim to both the local Walmart and Home Depot. Therefore, the question of the hour is, do we have twenty veterans ready for the job? Taking these objectives is the easy part. Holding them is entirely something else.

Each objective will require ten men with four squad machine guns (SAWs) and lots of ammo. Do you have that capability?"

Looking more stressed by the moment, Ralph said, "Levi, you do realize that moving before things fall completely apart will make us criminals, right?"

"Ralph, things have already fallen completely apart, it's just that we are the only ones around who know it. Haven't you seen the huge smoking ruins from the plane crashes?

Look, I've given you the tip of the iceberg that you need to make Defiance work…and believe me there is so much more, but there just isn't time to discuss those issues now. So, you do what you think is best and I'll just mosey on down the road. Ralph, I truly do wish you well, but…"

Ralph interrupted Levi saying, "Levi, I am in a jam, and I am the good guy. Just tell me what we need to do, and we'll do it."

Levi stopped in his tracks, turned back to Ralph, and said, "Already with the help me I'm in a jam thing? Dirty pool, Ralph, but I did promise, and a man's word has got to be the one thing people in this new world can count on.

Okay, but you must promise to take Walmart and Home Depot now, and I mean right now, because…"

Ralph interrupted and shouted, "Ben, get in here, and bring everyone."

While Ben left to get the troops, Levi said, "Ralph, now listen to me because this is important. You are the Mayor. I do not want anyone to think I have taken over…and I won't, not ever. I do know what needs to be done, but the folks must know that you are in charge and the approving authority. We good?"

"Yes, real good. You really don't want to take over?"

Levi slapped Ralph on the back and said, "Oh hell no. I told you I'm here for no more than a year and then I have my own path to take, so don't worry, you da man.

"I mean if I get too pissed, I can always leave, right?"

Ralph did not answer.

CHAPTER FOUR

The Defiance Militia
East Coast Auto Museum

The doors flew open, and thirty men and women rushed into the building. They milled around Ralph and Will Thurston said, "Okay, boss, we ready to move these velocipedes to Defiance?"

"Ben, everybody, I want you to meet our new Head of Security, Captain Levi Levins. You will follow his orders exactly as if they came from my mouth. None of us have his qualifications, so when it comes to security, we follow his lead. Anyone having a problem with that should turn around right now and move on down the road. Any questions?"

As though one, the group said, "No questions, sir."

Levi smiled and asked, "All right, how many of you are vets?"

All but two raised their hands, "Well, well," said Levi, "Things are looking up. Okay, NCO's and Officers move to my right."

Turning to face this group of six, Levi asked, "Officers?"

Levi was not happy that this bunch didn't have even one officer. "Okay, in ten seconds I want the senior NCO to report to me. The rest of you get this mob into a semblance of a formation."

The transformation was incredible. Within seconds former Sergeant First Class (SFC) Bradley Cobb, US Army retired reported to Levi in a fine military manner. "Sir, Sergeant First Class Bradley Cobb reporting a compliment of twenty-eight, with six NCO's from the rank of Corporal to Sergeant E-5."

"Very good, Sergeant, let's see what we have, here," and without being told Sergeant First Class Cobb moved three steps to Levi's left, and three steps behind. Levi was impressed.

To the members of the just formed Defiance Militia, Troop A, Levi said, "As of this moment you hold the military rank from your date of discharge. Over the next few weeks, most, if not all of you will be promoted to higher responsibility as our small force grows sufficiently to be able to secure and protect Defiance. You must understand that this is not a game. If you agree to go, then you are in the Army. Not a single man crossed that invisible line in the sand.

Today, we have the crucial task of securing two objectives; Walmart and Home Depot. We must have these assets not only to secure Defiance but also for us to grow into a community encompassing the surrounding area.

Please let this sink into your heads, civilization, as we knew it is gone. The only thing we can do is to try to prevent Defiance from falling into the New Dark Age which is about to wash over us.

To accomplish this task, Sergeant First Class Cobb will organize you into two assault groups. Group one will secure the Walmart, and Group two, the Home Depot.

Each group will then be broken down into four two-man teams plus one runner. The weapons requirements are side arms, individual rifle, and four squad machine guns. Each SAW will cover an unsecured entry point.

Mayor Bassett, is your gunsmith a veteran?"

"No, Captain, sadly he is not, though I am sure he will do us proud."

"Thank you, Mayor. Sergeant First Class Cobb, gather your teams, then proceed to the Arms Room to retrieve weapons and ammunition. Any questions Sergeant?"

"No questions, sir."

"Very well Sergeant Cobb, get to it," and with that Sergeant First Class Bradley Cobb did indeed get to it, as he immediately began organizing his working groups, selecting two large trucks from the museum. The museum had a 1,000-gallon gas tank and a 500-gallon diesel tank. Within 15 minutes, the Defiance Militia Troop A was on the move.

Ralph looked at Levi with an even greater level of respect as he said, "What the…Levi, how did you do that? That was amazing. If I hadn't seen it, I would never have believed it.

I was a Coastie for four years, but we could never have…well, I'm impressed. What next?"

"Thank you, Ralph, but it wasn't me, I just drew on the training and the desire of these fine men to be a part of something worthy of protecting Defiance and their families. These men, and that term, men, will be used across genders for those in our militia. How does the name Troop A, Defiance Militia sound?"

Ralph asked, "Well, it sounds good, but why Troop instead of Company?"

Smiling Levi answered, "Actually I spent almost ten years in the Cavalry before transitioning to Military Intelligence. Cavalry uses the word Troop for Company, and besides, our new Troop will have to be highly mobile and reflexive. Are you okay with that?"

Ralph laughed and said, "Oh hell yes, and the word Troop does sound a bit more dashing than Company, so Troop it is."

"Thank you, Mr. Mayor; it is, after all, your call. Come on, Ralph, let's get to Defiance and see how this thing unfolds.

CHAPTER FIVE

The Walmart Campaign

Defiance

About ten minutes before our forces cross their Line of Departure (LOD) you and I will recon the objectives. We need to arrive before our assault teams. You go to Home Depot, and I'll take the Walmart. We need to make sure they have not as yet been taken, and if they have, then we need a new plan to take them away."

Ralph said, "Oh man, all this military talk does get one's blood flowing. Levi, I think you must have been sent to us by God Himself."

"Not bloody likely Mr. Mayor. If you knew my history of the last 48 hours, you might rethink that remark."

"Yeah well, say what you want, but I know what I know, and Levi, if you ever want to share that piece of history, I'll be there to hear the story."

"At the Walmart, assuming success, we will allow the locals to take one cart each of frozen and perishable food, baby supplies, and the like, but nothing else. Once we have assessed the Defiance need, we can then proceed to distribute supplies which we, in Defiance, do not need.

"Each shopper will be searched for weapons before entering the store. Those weapons will be returned upon their departure. If the shopper has no weapon, one will be supplied from Walmart stores until they are gone. Each weapon will also be issued with one box of ammunition.

"Pregnant mothers or those with children get top priority and will be allowed a second cart for child type supplies and one toy or game. We can provide clothing for the children after things settle down a bit.

"Shoppers will be allowed to take produce, refrigerated items, and frozen foods.

"You okay with this, Mr. Mayor?"

Looking somewhat confused, Mayor Bassett asked, "Why are we giving so much away? If we take the store, why turn around and give stuff away?"

"Ralph, giving up some supplies now, will go a long way to winning the hearts and minds of the community. It will make it much easier for locals to trust us later when we want to bring them into the fold, increasing our area of influence, and trade with other communities. Please, Ralph, trust me on this."

"Okay, I get it now.

"Levi, maybe I'm not the guy to lead this group. You definitely know what you are about. Maybe I should just turn the reigns over to you?"

Levi backed up from Ralph and said, "Forget that shit, Ralph. I want to help you get things off to a good start. I have no desire to be El Presidente. Besides, I'm leaving next April. No, Mr. Mayor, you are the man for the job. The civilian government must have precedence over the military. Like the police force, we intend only to serve and protect…not rule. Disaster awaits us at the end of that path."

"Okay, brother, I'm in."

Smiling now, as they walked to the Mayor's truck, Levi said, "Really…Captain?"

"Yeah, well, I got carried away, and anyway, I think it was the right call."

30 March
Defiance Headquarters

Early on, when in the company of others, both Ralph and Levi used formal titles to cement their positions of leadership within the community of Defiance.

In private they quickly became true friends and respected each other's professional boundaries.

"Ralph, let's roll. Right now, we may still have an opportunity to get there firstest with the mostest. It's 1400 hrs, so let's meet at Walmart at 1730."

Smiling Ralph said, "Dang, all this military time and planning stuff makes me feel like Special Forces."

Also smiling Levi responded, "Well, we may have a way to go there, so right now I'd say we were more like Special Feces."

"Cute Levi real cute! I'll see ya' at 5:30 pm," and he left for the Home Depot cackling like a loon.

As Levi climbed into his Jeep, he smiled again, and thought, *oh boy, I've got my work cut out here*.

Levi watched as his force entered the Walmart, he saw his troopers secure the store, and after only ten minutes, the store was emptied, and the Managerial and Sales Staff were seated in the shade of the smoking area.

Dozens of shoppers stood around wanting to know what was going on, so Levi walked to the front of the store, raised his hand for silence and began speaking in a normal conversational tone. It didn't take long for those who continued talking to be shushed by those around them.

"Please, may I have your attention? This Walmart is now under new management of Troop A, Defiance Militia, and there will be some rule changes.

"Those changes are as follows:

"Single women with children, families with children go first.

"When one family exits, another will be allowed in.

"Please take food selections from the fresh produce, coolers, and the frozen section, only.

"No firearms are allowed inside. Please leave any weapons with our guard at the door. They will be returned as you leave.

"If you have no firearms, please let the man in sporting goods know this, and he will give you one rifle, one pistol, and one box of ammo for each until stores are depleted.

"Each family will be allowed one basket for each adult.

"Children need toys in this new reality of ours more than ever before, so please feel free to select one toy for each child accompanying you today.

"Nursing mothers and those with toddlers, please help yourself to Pampers, Similac, and anything else you may need for these youngsters. An additional cart for each child is acceptable.

"There will be no charge."

"When fall arrives, clothing will be issued to all who need them.

"I know you are all wondering what the hell is going on."

The group again began to murmur, and Levi waited until the crowd brought itself back under control before continuing,

"Only two things can cause the power, cell phones, autos to fail, and planes fall out of the sky everywhere at the same time.

"One, we have been attacked with nuclear weapons at an altitude of approximately 225 miles."

The crowd all looked up and began to speak among themselves.

"Please, please, everyone settle down. With this kind of attack, there is absolutely no danger from radiation, but these detonations do cause something called an Electro Magnetic Pulse.

"This pulse fries all electronics. That is why your cars won't start, unless, of course, the car or truck was made before 1978. You see those vehicles had no electronic devices that made them run. I see many of you have already found that out from the number of year appropriate vehicles in the parking lot.

"The second possible cause of this disaster is that our sun created, and expelled, a plasma storm called a Coronal Mass Ejection. This plasma ejection causes the same effect as a nuclear attack in the upper atmosphere. Personally, I think it is much more likely that we have received a CME, but there is no way for us to know for sure, as of yet."

Questions began to be shouted to Levi, who said, "All right folks, do you want to begin shopping or stand here and scream at me?"

That settled the crowd right down, and like most good country folk, they began lining up to wait their turn to begin gathering supplies.

A young black man walked up to Levi and said, "What 'bout us?"

Levi looked at the man and said, "What about you?"

"You gone let us black folk have the same as the white folk?"

"Oh, I see, first of all, I don't, nor do any of my people give a rat's ass what color you are. Of course, you get the same as anyone else. That black, white bullshit has got to stop. If it doesn't, we'll fail miserably and get nuthin' done but killin' each other. From where I stand, you are a man just like me."

"Yeah, I hear ya', but you givin' them white folks guns and ammo. We git 'em, too?"

"Yes, of course, you do. We have to work together and help each other. It's a new world, and we just can't afford the same ole racial nonsense. Can you put it behind you? I have. From now on if you want to be my equal, then act like it, and so will I. Deal?"

"Oh yeah, it sound good, but that ain't never mean shit befo. I spos'ta believe you now?"

"Yes, you work with me, and I'll work with you. I can't put it any other way."

"Ok, it juss that I don't see no black folks in yo group. You got any?"

"Nope, not yet, you got any white folks in your little group here? I don't see any. Look, what's your name?"

He became immediately defensive and asked, "Why you need my name?"

Levi smiled at him and said, "My name is Levi Levins, and I just want to make a new friend." Levi offered his hand.

"Hmmm, okay, I give you a try. My name Willie Washington," and he shook Levi's hand.

Levi held onto his hand for a few extra seconds as he said, "Willie Washington, if you get attacked, we will help, and we expect you to do the same for us.

"If you want to be left alone with your people then that's okay, too, maybe we can work trade deals. It's a new world now and the only ones who will be alive one year from now are those who are willing to work their asses off to survive. There just ain't no more rich or poor, black or white and this time next spring only one person in ten will still be alive.

You need to understand this; we want to be friends. We want to work together for a new life. But anyone who doesn't stand with us gets no help of any kind. Those who attack us will die. What do you say?"

"Ok, we give it a try," and again shook Levi's hand before turning to go on his shopping trip to Wally World.

One old man walked up to Levi and asked, "Genrul, what if you're wrong? It'll go bad for ya'."

"Yes, sir, it will go bad for all of us in the Defiance Militia, and actually I wish I was wrong…but I'm not. Did you see the smoke from all the burning planes?"

"Smoke hell, I seen a few go down, happened while I had ta' git up ta' pee." Then the old man shook his head and said, "God Bless you, son, even though I still hope you are wrong, but if you are, I'll ask to be on the jury at your trial," and turning; he walked away without another word.

Ben came running up and said, "Levi, that was brilliant, just brilliant, ya' done well, sir, but do you think he believed you?"

"Ben, I can only hope so, and for the record, I meant every word."

"Sounds good, but what do we do with the Walmart staff?"

"Ben, I love it when folks think. So, here's what we do, we shoot 'em…No, no, no, just kidding. After everyone has finished their shopping, we stand them up and let them have a cart. They ain't the enemy.

"You better help out at the front. I'll tend to 'em."

"Roger that, sir," said Ben, and smiling, saluted Levi. He received a salute in return.

"Oh Ben, one other thing, is there an Army/Navy store around here somewhere?

"Yeah, sure there are a couple of 'em back toward town, why?"

"Why? Because I want to visit them and see if we can get them to join up, that's why. Do you know a better way to get uniforms, and all that sexy army stuff?

Look, things are goin' well here, find the sergeant in charge and tell him I want you to go with me. If he can spare you then let's pay those stores a visit."

"On the way, sir," said Ben as he turned and ran to see his boss.

Levi walked up to the Walmart employees and said, "Hello, I am truly sorry if you've suffered any discomfort since our arrival. But please don't worry, we mean you no harm. Just as…"

"You're going to prison for this; you know that, right? Just as soon as the power comes back on the police will hunt you down," shouted a female cashier.

Levi smiled and said, "Ma'am, in normal times you would be absolutely correct, then again, in normal times this would not be happening. Look to the horizon, do you see the smoke trails?"

"Yes, what are they?"

"Those are the burning wrecks of planes. If you look, you will also notice that there are no planes flying overhead.

"Please, let me explain exactly what has happened, and what will happen.

"First, the power will not be coming back for many years. The entire grid is fried…

"…so, having heard why the power is off and cars don't run we get to the current conundrum. What do we do with you? Easy answer, using our bus, which does run, we will allow each of you to take one cart full of food and give you a ride home if you need one.

"If you have children, you may also take whatever supplies you will need for them in an additional cart. You will, of course, have to bag your own groceries to take on the bus; any questions?"

One of the ladies raised her hand like she was in school and asked, "Why are you doing this? If what you say is true, won't you need all of the supplies for yourselves?"

"Ma'am, even though it doesn't look like it right now, we are not thieves. We will make every attempt to assist the local population where, and when we can. I guess you could say we are paying that part forward."

"Thank you, sir, we appreciate the help, but I sure hope you are wrong."

Another employee shouted out, "What about the money inside? I bet you are nothing but thieves."

"Whoa, oh my, no, we will not take a dime from the store or anyone in it. Besides, in another 48 hours, money will only be worth using for wallpaper, or very uncomfortable toilet paper. So, in answer to your question, no, we are not after any money."

The store manager stood and asked, "Sir, may I speak with you privately. I'll go in last. My name is Scott, Scott Eldridge."

Levi smiled and replied, "Of course Scott, please stand by."

After everyone had gone, Scott offered his hand and said to Levi, "Sir, I spent four years in the 75th Ranger Battalion. I believe you are right, and if you can find a spot for me, I would like to join up. I know I don't have much to offer, except my military skill set, but you will need men with military skills."

"Did you make any deployments?"

"Yes sir, two deployments to Afghanistan. I was a Buck Sergeant in an Explosive Ordnance Demolition (EOD) Detachment. I am married and have one son, aged 8."

Levi looked Scott Eldridge directly in the eye and was impressed when Scott did not flinch or look away. "Yeah, Scott, report to Sergeant Mike Guyardo. You'll work for him tonight, and we'll talk again in the morning.

"Now about your family, I'll loan my jeep to you with the trailer so you can go home and get the wife started packing. Leave the trailer and tell her to be ready to leave no later than 0600.

"Can I trust you with my jeep, son?"

"Sir, where would we go? We'll be dead if we stay where we are, or if we run off. She'll be ready, and thank you, sir. I'm committed to you all the way."

"Well, all right then. Ben, get with Sergeant Guyardo and make it happen. Go with him, Scott."

"Roger sir, on the way."

"Oh, are we still going on our shopping trip?" asked Ben.

"Just as soon as you get us some transportation. I seem to have lost mine somewhere."

Levi and Ben were able to get to both stores and convince the owners that it would be smart to join up before the looting started. The interesting thing is that both owners knew exactly what had happened and didn't like the idea of the destruction about to befall them.

He then went back to the Walmart where Ralph, with a huge smile, was waiting.

"Ben take the truck and hustle back to Defiance. Grab a crew and some trucks to get started on retrieving the goods from the Army/Navy stores. You up to the task?"

"Up to the task? Sir, I was born for this…I just hope we stay out of prison."

"Yeah," said Levi, "well, there is that…"

Ralph ran over and shook Levi's hand saying, "Oh, man, oh, man, I can't believe how well this operation is going. The Depot went well, and it's a good thing because we need all that lumber. Oh, man, oh, man!

"Hey, where you been?"

Levi said, "Well, since things were going so well here, I took Ben on a recruiting trip to the Army/Navy stores and convinced them to join up."

"You did what? Did you offer a place to outsiders without conferring with me? What were you thinking Levi?"

"Ralph, remember what I said about things being in a state of flux right now, and making the most of what time we have before people start shooting and burning?"

"Yeah, I remember, okay, were they worth it?"

Levi smiled again and said, "Oh, yeah, you'll be very happy.

The foodstuff's here will keep us going until the crops come in. However, if we can swing it, I'd sure like to snag a couple of grocery stores. I know we can't do it until tomorrow, even though we may be cutting it a bit close, and if it can be done without getting all of us killed, I believe it will be worth the effort.

"Grocery store, why, the food here will keep us going for quite a while."

Levi turned on his serious face and said, "Ralph, we have no chance to hold on to even a semblance of our humanity and culture with only fifty people."

"Yeah, I see what you mean, but how many are you thinking about? Another ten or so?" asked Ralph.

Levi laughed and avoiding the question, for now, saying, "Things are sorting themselves out well here, just let me speak with the troops. Then we need to go back to your quarters and figure out exactly what, and how many we do need."

"Yeah, good idea, I'll go with you and maybe I can get an idea of what in the hell you are up to," but he was smiling…a little.

"Okay, let's get the lead out, we've got a lot of work to do, you know, places to go, people to see, and things to do."

Sergeant Juan Miguel Dominique Mesa Garcia Guyardo…or just Sergeant Guy. Anyway, Sergeant Guy had a good handle on things and was already preparing positions for the night. He expected trouble, and being a six-year Force Recon Marine, Mike knew what he was about when it came to preparing positions.

As Levi and Ralph approached, Sergeant Guy snapped to attention, saluted and said, "Sir, may I brief the Captain on our preparations for night operations?"

Levi looked him up and down and knew this man was a great choice for this job. He said, "Yes Sergeant, but the short version please."

"Yes, sir, we have squad machine guns at each entrance manned by two men. As we speak, they are moving heavy boxes to fortify the entrances. Tomorrow we will replace the boxes with sandbags from the Home Depot, but for tonight, this was our best solution.

I gotta' tell you, sir, I used to think Army stood for, **A**in't **R**eally **M**arines **Y**et, but not anymore 'cause every single one of these guys would make good Marines. So, sir, all in all, we have it covered at least for tonight."

"Ain't Really Marines Yet, huh? Well, I always heard USMC stood for **U**ncle **S**am's **M**isguided **C**hildren. You know, Sergeant. Guy, I think we are going to get along just fine. Good brief, stay alert, I want everyone alive in the morning."

Saluting, the sergeant said, "Count on it, sir."

Levi returned the salute, shook his sergeant's hand and said, "I'll see you at around 0800. Roger?"

"Ooh Rah, we ain't got no place else to go. Don't worry, sir, we won't let you down."

As we walked away, Ralph said, "Did you notice how both Ben and Guyardo both said that they wouldn't let you down? Not Defiance, but you, Levi.

"Should I be worried? Because, if that sergeant cleaves to you, the others will follow. I will not allow Defiance to turn into a military dictatorship. I mean it, Levi."

"Mr. Mayor, I know you mean it, and I give you my oath that you have nothing to worry about. Our sole mission will be to serve and protect Defiance. Will you accept that, or are you asking me to leave?"

"Leave? Are you out of your mind? Of course, I'm not asking that. You have already proven that you are even more of an asset to Defiance than I had, at first thought.

Bottom line, Levi, is that I want to build a place where people can live in safety and prosperity instead of like cavemen."

"Oh, I see, you want Shangri-La, a Utopia, well, Ralph; there will always be storms, and struggles...and trusts. We just have to strive to find some kind of happy middle ground."

"Say, do you remember a song called *Whiskey For My Men and Beer For My Horses*?"

"Yeah, I love that song, why?"

"Because, Mr. Mayor, I am absolutely positive that we will have to live up to that song. We gotta' draw a hard line to protect our own, and perhaps a hard line even within our ranks."

On the way back to Defiance, Levi wouldn't talk about his vision for Defiance saying that they needed to be seated with a cold beer before looking into the crystal ball.

CHAPTER SIX

Buckle up Buttercup

30 March 1830 hours
Levi's tent
Defiance, NC

Sitting down with a cold Bud, Ralph said, "Ok, Captain Levins, share your thoughts and plans."

"Wow, jumping right in, okay. First, we need to discuss the survivability of Defiance, and without a lot of work and dedicated activity, it will not happen. Ralph, the bottom line is, you ain't ready. With six former military combat guys, I could take this entire place in ten minutes.

Therefore, my job, as I see it will be to secure Defiance against a Battalion of Infantry, and that should have been done a year ago. No matter now, I have the skill set to get it done, and Ralph...we will git 'er dun. Okay?"

"You are a rascal, you know that? But seriously, why do you say we are in such desperate shape? Don't you think this is a pretty nice place? We have good fresh water; we're secluded enough to be off the beaten track, I mean there's just a dirt road to the county road. I've stockpiled hundreds of weapons and over two-hundred thousand rounds of ammo over the years, a crap load of dynamite and blasting caps. We have enough food for around 60 people for a couple of years with the Walmart stuff. Come on, Levi, we're in good shape here."

Portraying a wry smile, Levi said, "There are a number of reasons why you only have a start, but the two most glaring reasons are *numbers* and *intelligence*.

Ralph looked indignant and started to say, "Now just hold on a min..."

"Easy Ralph, not individual intelligence, I meant knowing what is happening around us, and what may be coming at us."

"Oh, well... okay," said a mollified Mayor.

"Starting tomorrow at the latest, food is going to be gone from the stores, and not in just the big cities, which, incidentally places this area very near an inevitable migration route for those going south to find a place to start again, and those moving north to find relatives who they believe can offer them shelter."

Ralph, looked doubtful and asked, "Okay, I get that but how many can there possibly be? We can handle it."

"How many you ask? Okay, I'll give you the low number first, and the high if you want to hear it…ten to twelve million on the move over the next two weeks, and that's just along the Eastern Seaboard, hungry and desperate people. They and their families will be starving, dirty, exhausted and desperate to take what we have if they can.

I'm talking about good, church going people. They will steal, murder and do anything else to feed their starving children. Shit, 99% of them were good honest people when civilization controlled the food distribution. Now, there simply will be no food. The old rules are gone. From this day forward, we must be prepared to fight for what we have or what we must have if we can't trade for it."

"Levi, how do you know this? I mean, you could be wrong, couldn't you? Oh, crap… no; that just cannot be right! No, you are wrong, you just have to be. Ten million starving refugees… No, wait, we are so far east of the main routes. Won't they just keep going north and south, bypassing us?"

"*Most* certainly will, but we could still face a hundred thousand refugees coming our way, just foraging, and that is at a minimum. Ultimately, does it matter whether the number is one hundred thousand, one million, or ten million, with those numbers; does it really matter how many?"

Ralph stared at the map Levi had placed on the table, "Yes, of course, you're right. A million or a hundred thousand is still an army searching for food. Sorry, Levi, it's just so much to absorb all at once, I mean, honestly, we had no idea it would get that bad."

"Ralph, remember, I was in Military Intelligence, and I participated in many exercises for just this exact emergency…we were never successful in controlling them."

Our people in training exercises pretended to shoot tens of thousands of Americans. I mean, come on, we can only kill so many people before we are overrun by sheer numbers.

"Ultimately, the commanders would just wave their magic logistics wand and declare victory. Realism was non-existent. Moreover, those in the Head Shed realized that in a true disaster, no organized movement was possible, because, well, how do you stop ten million people, coming from all directions, who have nothing but the hope that they will find salvation over the next hill."

Ralph hung his head, and in a whisper uttered, "Oh, dear God, if what you say is true, we *are* doomed. All of the work we've done has been wasted…"

"No, Ralph, I believe that it can be done, if we hurry and get the necessary things done, and I do mean quickly."

Ralph was almost in shock but raised his head at this single ray of hope from Levi. "What? If what you've said is true, what can we possibly do?"

"Okay, now listen up. We need to take this thing in stages. Since we know we cannot fight our way out of this mess, we have to think our way out. Oh yeah, there will be lots of fighting, but if we rely on that we will just be overwhelmed, and we will die.

First, you need to understand that the refugees will not be thinking, they will be following whoever is in front of them. It's called herd mentality; where those in front go, the rest will follow.

Tomorrow we must crater Route 34 leading to us…"

Ralph started to interrupt, but Levi silenced him with a hand-up, palm out motion, before continuing.

"Yes, we both know that will not stop the walkers, but it will divert those in trucks. Those guys will tend to be in better health and thus far more dangerous; they'll also be armed.

We then place signs along their path announcing that our no-go area is mined. Signs alone will not deter them for long, so we must get mines and punji pits into the ground, ASAP."

Again, Ralph started to interrupt.

"Ralph wait, please let me finish.

Sadly, we'll have to kill perhaps thousands at these points to redirect them around us. You see, the minefields will guide them around us, and we will only fire on those who do not take the path we want. As the days pass, the dead will become an additional deterrent to the moving mass of people.

Those in front will, hopefully, not want to go through a killing field when a clear, far easier path lies before them. Put yourself in the shoes of the walkers; where those in front of you go, go you."

Ralph was near to tears and knew that he could not help those in this mass migration, but asked in a pleading voice, "Levi isn't there anything we can do to help, rather than murder thousands of fellow Americans?"

"Ralph, there is no way this is murder, it is quite simply kill or be killed…Self-defense. If we do not try to protect ourselves, we will die and the millions remaining will just keep walking.

"Consider one hundred thousand rolling over us, taking our food. How many could actually eat? The number would be less than one or two hundred out of one hundred thousand, and they'll be killing each other left and right for what's here. You see, again the end result is the same, they die, only in this scenario, we also die, and that is not acceptable to me. Those people are doomed, but I do not intend to join them, do you?

"Ralph, I need to know, and right now; are you up to this? If not, I won't stay to be killed by starving zombies. I'll just head for my home in Paradise, West Virginia.

"Look at me, my friend… *DAMN IT! LOOK AT ME!* … Thank you, now listen up because what I have to say now is also going to be very tough for you. It must be you, and you alone, who presents this plan to the residents of Defiance."

"Me? Why me? You are the one who understands what we are facing. Don't you think you could convince them better than I?"

Realizing that Ralph was losing it, Levi's tone again became even less like a Priest, and more like a Drill Sergeant, "Ralph, you are the face of the government in Defiance, so put on your big boy boxers and buckle up, buttercup. If it comes from me, no one will ever again look to you for leadership, and I will be expected to take the reins, and Ralph, that I will not do. I know that you've been through a lot today but stop the crybaby bullshit. You have got to snap out of it and be the leader these people need. So, what's it going to be?"

"Levi, I just don't know if I can do it…kill thousands of people just because they are hungry and need help."

Levi stood and looked down at Ralph as he continued to wallow in his own self-pity before saying, "Ralph, I guess I was wrong about you. I thought you were a man who had the guts to lead these people, but I was obviously wrong. So, go ahead and wallow in your little pity party. You're acting like a piss ant wuss who would let his friends die, rather than save them and maintain a bit of humanity and civilization. Go screw yourself, Ralph; I'm just glad I won't be around to see your dead body being cannibalized by the starving walking dead."

Levi turned to leave when Ralph calmly said, "You're right Levi, and I guess have been wallowing in a first-class pity party. Look, I know you're right, I know it, but that pep talk you just gave me made me realize that I must *not* be that wussie guy.

"The turning point was when you said that I was willing to let my friends die. Well, no, I'm not that guy, so yeah; I'll put on my big boy boxers and buckle up. If we can stop them from overrunning us, then I'll do whatever it takes. How long do you think the migration will last?"

Levi laughed out loud and said, "Now *that's* the man I feared was gone. Let's get to it, and I don't think the migration will last more than a couple of weeks at the most because starvation and preying on each other will kill them off fairly quickly. It's that initial push we have to blunt."

"Only a couple of weeks, hey we can do that, and our troubles will be over, right?"

"Ralph, you are the eternal optimist, you know that? But no, our troubles will just be beginning. How do we clean up all the dead bodies? We don't, because we just don't have the manpower, or the ability to bury just the fifty to one hundred thousand dead in our area. At that point, we hunker down, and maybe, just maybe we can avoid most of the myriad of diseases about to overtake the country. It only takes one person to become infected to kill us all, and though that is a real concern. Sadly, we can't just hunker down and wait until the danger passes. There is just too much to be done in far too short a time. That is not even my biggest fear. Rats carrying disease is my worst fear."

"Rats, why…Oh…My…God…they'll be feeding off the dead! We're in for a Biblical explosion in the rat population. What can we do?"

"Not much in reality", Levi said, "but we still have to try. If we had the time, I'd build a moat around the settlement area, but it's too late for that. Let's bring in every rat trap from our stores and set them everywhere, especially around the perimeter of the housing area. We'll use copious amounts of rat poison. See a rat, kill a rat.

Ralph, that's only one aspect of the coming plagues. Starting from the bottom of the food chain, ants; they, along with other critters will consume the rotting bodies out there, but ants become prey for other critters, like spiders. Because of the sudden and immense increase in available food, the devourers of those rotting carcasses will have a population explosion right up the food chain. This summer we'll be overrun by ants, spiders, rats, snakes and God knows what else.

The entire cycle will be short lived; hopefully, it will begin slowing by late June and end when winter sets in. Once the bodies are cleaned to the skeletons, the over populated food chain will collapse and fall back to current levels fairly quickly."

Stunned by this forecast, Ralph slumped back in his seat and stammered, "My God, I had no idea…ew…I hate spiders."

"Which brings me to the next point; we need to find at least twenty carpenters, a dentist, two doctors, a pharmacist and some nurses…yesterday. Then, after we find them, we must convince them to join us. Our Walmart has a large pharmacy. That should entice some medicos to join us. Those who turn us down will probably die when desperate druggies attack and ransack their infirmaries and hospitals. So, if we identify a clinic or infirmary, we recruit. If the Doctors say no, well that's just hard cheese. We take it because if we don't, the druggies will.

"I'll send Sergeant Eldridge out to the local clinic with a security squad tomorrow to start our recruiting drive.

"Sergeant Cobb will be running my Orderly Room. If he works out, I'd like to promote him to First Sergeant (1SG), okay?"

"Yes, of course, I guess I need a clerk too. How about screening the walkers for a couple of clerks for us? Levi, you find what we need, and we'll pretend they were my ideas. Seriously, teach me, I have so much to learn."

"All right Ralph we'll find some clerks and a tub full of carpenters. We have a huge building project to be completed before winter.

"My friend, the Huns are at the city gates and like Rome, our civilization will fall if we don't get busy. Hopefully small enclaves like ours will survive and begin the long climb out of the New Dark Age that will be impossible for the world to avoid."

"Damn, Levi, you paint one helluva dark picture of the future. Will it really be that bad? I mean, my head won't accept it, but I feel like you may have been sent to us to save at least a semblance of America."

"Yeah, sure I have, and yes, it will be at least that bad, hell, disease alone will kill a greater percentage of the world than the Black Plague as it raced through Europe and created a Dark Age that lasted for eight hundred years. But, not here, not for those inside of Defiance; at least if you and I have anything to say about it."

"Okay, my friend, and as depressed as I already am, I have to ask; what is the very next thing we have to do?"

"Good, let's get right to it. How many blasting caps, dynamite, and pressure switches do we have?"

"We have over a thousand sticks of dynamite, and the same for blasting caps, but no one thought to get pressure switches. What can we do?"

Levi smiled and said, "God willing and the crick don't rise that will be no problem. Since the switches have no electronics in them, they should be fine."

"But, Levi, we don't have any."

"Easy Ralph, we have millions of them. Every car in America has at least two, right under the seats. Think about it, when you sit in a car the fasten seat belt light comes on. That's because of the pressure switch under your arse. Sit in the seat, and the pressure switch is pushed down completing a circuit. Fastening your seat belt opens the circuit again. Add a battery and when someone steps on it we get a charge igniting the blasting cap and the circuit is complete; boom.

"Let's see, it's 2100, that's 9:00 pm to you. What say we grab Ben and have him get a crew to start removing those switches from the dead autos out on the road? Let us not forget, time is of the essence, and we have much to do and miles to go before we sleep.

"Since most of the heavy lifting is done by the men, I recommend that we put some of the ladies to work cutting the dynamite sticks into quarters and send four guys out to start retrieving the switches."

"Good idea, let's go to his tent and get started. You like Ben, don't you?"

"Yes, I do. He accepts his place in the hierarchy, knows he has the opportunity to advance, knows what he is about, and doesn't bellyache. Yeah, I like him. Unfortunately, for him, and Sergeant Guy, we're going to ride them both like rented mules."

Ralph said, "Well okay, come on, let's go."

Levi asked Ralph to go alone and bring Ben back, so he could begin making a list for the next few days.

Levi looked down at the blank sheet of paper and began writing:

- Soldiers
- Farmers
- Heritage seeds
- Mechanics
- Supply personnel
- Doctors
- Nurses
- Veterinarian
- Carpenters
- Plumbers
- Masons
- Clerks and bean counters

"Oh crap, this list will never end. Oh well, at least we'll be able to save some of the refugees, and even one is better than none. I hope that they will all be Veterans.

I better make sure that both Ralph and I both do the vetting of newcomers. I don't want him thinking I'm trying to take over."

When Ralph returned with Ben, Levi asked if he knew how to disconnect the seat pressure switches?

"Captain, I'm pretty darned sure I can figure it out. Yes, sir I know what to look for. How many do we need?"

Levi smiled and said, "Five thousand. Do you think you can get them tonight?"

"No sir, but I bet we can get a hundred if you give me three to help out."

"Fine, get ten; put Sgt. Eldridge in charge, then get right back here."

"Roger sir, I'm on it," Ben saluted and left the room."

Levi looked to Ralph and said, "Mr. Mayor, with your permission I really could use an XO. I would like that XO to be Ben. Do you have any objection to my promoting him to First Lieutenant?"

"I think he would be a wise choice even though I did have him slated to be my Deputy Mayor. I've noticed how well you two work together and being your XO is, I think, a good option. He has worked for me for five years, and went from receiving to Manager, but you don't need me to approve these promotions."

"Actually Ralph, I think it would be best, at least for now, if you did approve any Officer Promotions, and I'll take care of the enlisted folks. It will increase your status in the community, hopefully easing the minds of anyone who might think I'm in command, instead of you…and Mr. Mayor, you are in charge and I serve at your will and pleasure.

"I know I'm being kinda' bossy and pushy right now and that's because I know what we need to get us through the hardest times ahead.

"Remember when you said that I was a good guy?"

"Yeah, sure, why?"

"I asked that to remind you that I am still that same guy. Before God, I tell you that I am not suited to be the Mayor, Ralph, you are. Together we will make a great team, but ultimately you and you alone are the boss. We good here?"

Ralph gave Levi a sincere smile and said, "Yeah Buddy, we good."

Little did the two men realize it, but it was at this exact moment in time that a true bond of trust was cemented between the two men who would try to persevere and save Defiance.

"All right, my friend, let's get to work, we have a hell of a lot to do."

Levi rose from his chair and retrieved Ben, who followed them back into Ralph's office.

"Ben, the Mayor has decided, and I certainly concur, that I need an XO, and that man is you. By order of the Mayor, and the Captain of the Defiance Militia, you are hereby promoted to the rank of First Lieutenant.

"I want you to know that I have the utmost faith in your ability to carry out your duties in accordance with your new pay grade, which for the time being is the same as mine…zero…lots of responsibilities…no pay, of course there is that room and board thing."

Lieutenant Ben Smith smiled and said, "Oh man, I wanted to buy a new car. Seriously, sir, I will not let either of you down, and I can't think of a thing to spend money on, anyway.

"Though you will take on the responsibilities and wear the grade insignia, your promotion will become official in a couple of days when we also promote several others.

"Congratulations, my friend. I'm gonna' wear you out.

"Oh, LT, with the addition of the Army Stores I expect you to have uniforms issued yesterday. Ah, the life of the Executive Officer."

"Yes sir, will do," chuckled the new XO.

Ralph said, "Well, that's a job well done. Now what?"

"Levi your list is, well, I don't know, are we building a city? Don't you think it may be just a bit early to add this many people?"

"Ralph, it we don't grab them now from the refugees, they will be dead. I think it is highly unlikely that we will ever again, at least in our lifetime, have the chance to corral so many critical people…especially if we are eventually going to build that shining city on the hill," smiled Levi, "besides, they can serve in other capacities until their specific skills are needed.

"XO, in the morning, would you please take a couple of Troop A's finest as security and go to the propane dealer? Find a way to convince him to join us. We'll figure out how to get the propane here later. This winter we will most definitely need that fuel.

"Ben, put together a couple of four-man teams to begin inspecting the abandoned Semis along the roads. I got a feelin' they will prove to be very useful with all kinds of supplies.

"One other important thing for consideration about the people we ask to join us; I'm sorry, but we must insure that each one is a Conservative Constitutionalist. We don't have time for bleeding hearts or socialist ideals. We must close ranks on this issue. Agreed?"

"Oh, hell yes! Agreed," said Ralph and Ben in unison.

The meeting went on until midnight making lists of who was needed from the refugees and the myriad of things Defiance still needed, before Ralph hit the wall and said, "I'm sorry, but I have got to get some sleep. Good night my friends."

As the two men left Levi's tent, he said, "Night Ralph, night Ben."

Levi was also dead tired and decided that he too must quit for the night. As he lay on his cot, and the darkness rolled over him, his thoughts involuntarily turned to Sarah. Those thoughts left him softly crying until he fell into a deep, but troubled sleep.

In a dream, Sarah came to him, sat beside him on their hotel bed, and said, "Levi, I will always love you, but right now you need to focus on the job at hand. Don't worry, about me. I will always be with you until you need someone else. I understand, and nothing can change the wonderful years we had together."

Levi awoke and reached out for Sarah, but his hands found only empty space. He knew she was right, but that did not help the loneliness, or the tears…he slept, but fitfully.

One day I will avenge you, Sarah my love, I will avenge them all…whiskey for my men and beer for my horses.

CHAPTER SEVEN

The March Begins

8 May 2300 hours
Defiance, North Carolina

Levi woke from his slumbers at 0200 hours and stepped outside to get a breath of the fresh spring air before going back to bed.

As he looked around, he saw the light from many fires. The looting and death of America had begun in earnest.

His attention was drawn to the horizon by flashes of lightening, followed much later by distant thunder.

Defiance was in blackout condition as the refugee march was steadily growing.

He turned to go back into his tent then decided to take a turn around the encampment to check on the guard posts.

"Halt, who goes there?" whispered a guard at the main entrance.

"Captain Levins," whispered Levi.

"Double dog," came the challenge.

"Dare," answered Levi.

"Advance and be recognized."

Levi stepped forward until the guard, in concealment could see his Captain.

"Good morning sir, couldn't sleep?"

"No, I just thought I'd take one last look at our listening posts. Anything going on between here and the road?"

"No sir, not so far. The forward Listening Post reported back at 2200 that the refugees seem to have stopped for the night."

Levi said, "Good report, soldier. Stay alert, some of 'em may well be foraging. It'll get worse if this weather holds. We could sure use a tropical storm."

"Yes sir, but it is a little early in the year for that."

"Yes, I suppose it is, stay sharp, we don't want anyone hurt."

"Roger that, sir, don't worry, we're on it."

Levi smiled in the darkness and said, "I know you are, well, good night."

"Good night sir and I hope you get some rest; you've been going pretty hard these last few days."

"Yep, haven't we all," said Levi as he returned to his tent.

Sleep did come…after many more lonely tears, and as he slept Sarah returned with the same message, but this time with a kiss on his cheek. His sleep improved…but not his yearning for Sarah.

Yes, Virginia There Is A Santa Claus

29 May 0400
Defiance

The entire camp was brought fully awake by the loud rumble of thunder as black skies, heavy with rain closed rapidly with the shoreline. Lightning flashed nearly overhead lighting up Defiance in flashes of a brilliant, but cold, frightening light.

Gunfire erupted near the gate, and the four-man designated Reaction Force (RF) grabbed their weapons and advanced to the sound of the action. Others made their way to defensive positions around the camp to prevent a flanking attack.

By the light of the flashing lightning, the RF could see bodies lying in the road. "Hold positions, everyone stay put. We can wait for sunrise to find out if there are anymore."

Captain Levins arrived and received a Situation Report (Sitrep) from the sergeant in charge of the RF.

"Sir, it appears that some people came up the road and were engaged by our LP. I've ordered everyone to hold position until first light before we check them out. Since I don't hear any moaning, my guess is that our LPs are good shots."

"Yes, so it would seem," replied Levi, "Good Sitrep sergeant, I'm pleased.

"Since you obviously have things so well in hand, I think I'll head on back to my tent and get dressed. Oh, what's your name?"

"Sergeant Scott Eldridge, sir. My last active duty posting was the 75th Ranger Battalion."

Just as Levi entered his tent, the skies opened up in sheets of rain nearing the horizontal.

Levi looked out at the deluge, knowing that it would reduce the number of foragers, as well as help to put out some of the non-gas fires. He thought, *Not that it will make any difference in the long run, but it may give him another day or possibly two, to secure additional materiel. Yeah, looters seem to be fair weather shoppers.*

The refugees would, for the most part, just trudge along in the rain, becoming more desensitized by the mile.

CHAPTER EIGHT

"Sixty is a tragedy…sixty million is a statistic."
- Josef Stalin

Defiance Front Gate

Levi was up with the sun and at the gate. Sergeant Eldridge said, "Sir, please wait here until we have cleared the area. It will not do us much good if you get taken out by some fool with a gun."

"All right Sergeant, but let's get a move on, you and your men need to get some chow and into dry clothes."

"Roger that, sir, just give us a few," and with that, he led his RF out to the bodies, after spreading out his men to secure the area.

After about ten minutes, Sergeant Eldridge signaled 'all clear.' Levi was impressed and satisfied that the area was, in fact, secured.

Levi walked from the gate to the first of three bodies. He turned him over and found a middle-aged man in a filthy business suit. He still held a .38 caliber Smith & Wesson revolver in his right hand. His wallet contained $27, six credit cards, driver's license, and pictures of a woman and two children…damn.

He returned the wallet to the man's back pocket before going to the other two. They seemed mirror images of each other; perhaps they had been friends or coworkers before the lights went out. Now, they would become a warning to those entering the minefields where the bodies would be dumped this morning.

These bodies would be the first to be placed at the edge of the minefield going in today. No funerals, no words.

"They Shall Not Pass" -Battle cry at Verdun, 1916

Mess/Class Tent
Defiance

Levi gave the job of teaching how to properly prepare the mines to Ranger Sergeant Eldridge.

"People, it is best if you pay close attention because we need each of you.

Okay, first we connect the wiring to the pressure switch on these two pins. Pay attention to the negative and positive terminals before inserting the blasting cap into the dynamite. Finally, we connect the battery and cover it with leaves. Any questions?"

"Sergeant, won't the battery send a charge when it gets connected to the pressure switch?"

"The simple answer is yes, but only to the switch. Until sufficient pressure is applied, the circuit is not complete."

Since there were no further questions, Eldridge began supervising the connections and emplacement of the new minefield. One hundred were laid that morning and warning signs were posted along the road. Danger, this is a minefield. DO NOT ENTER.

At the road, four armed guards kept the pleading refugees lined up three deep and into a plywood chute. They were gently prodded along, while being asked about their occupation, and if they were veterans. Using this method, Defiance was able to add critical personnel.

It was as clinical as possible, but in fact, it resembled a chute used to count cattle after a long drive to a railhead. At first, it depressed those working the chutes, but by noon it had become just another job. The pleading families with small children were heart-rending, though several families with needed skills were saved.

Statements such as "Now, you just wait a minute. You have to help us; we have rights. I'll sue you. I'm an attorney. I work for the Mayor," were heard from so many, while others pleaded, "Please help us, we'll do anything. Here, please, at least take my baby. We need help."

There were the rich, celebrities, lawyers, union bosses, and bureaucrats to name but a few who just refused to believe they could no longer demand preferential treatment.

The lifelong welfare recipients also demanded to be taken care of. They just could not comprehend how the government teat had suddenly dried up. Without that lifeline, they had no possible way to support themselves, no life skills to offer a struggling community.

Liberal policies, well-intended or not, had created a lifeboat cradle to grave society that in but a millisecond sank beneath the tsunami of a new and terrible reality.

What this new world needed mostly were those who worked with their hands; carpenters, mechanics, ditch diggers, soldiers, and every former occupation that actually required that something be created.

Oh sure, there was a need for specific skills other than the dirty hands jobs, but the ratios took on a new balance in year Zero.

The Killing Fields

By 1400 the roads had been cratered, stopping all, even four wheeled drive, vehicles. One-half sticks of dynamite mines were laid out on both left and right sides of the craters.

Today, these walkers were just refugees. In two days, they would resemble zombies, staggering along, ill and desperately hungry. The very old and very young would be the first to fall out of the line. They would be left where they fell along the trek to some government encampment where they would find help; on this imaginary road to salvation.

On this day, twenty-three people with needed job qualifications were cut from the crowd, fed, cleaned up, rested and put to work as new citizens of Defiance.

One such refugee stood out from the others, Dale Dannen. He was a Solar Panel Engineer who not only could build solar panel kits but also knew where thousands were stored along with the inverters and wiring necessary to create lots of electricity.

CHAPTER NINE

Evil This Way Comes

9 May 10:00 a.m.
Abandoned Police Station
Eastside of Raleigh, NC

"Pablo, Raleigh ees burning, and food ees becoming difficult to find. I have decided that we move east to the coast. Put out the word that a meeting for all Rican Rogues to meet here at 4:00 this afternoon. We got to pack up and get on the road," announced Gang leader Romeo Cruz to his lieutenant, Pablo "Gunner" Rivas.

Rivas looked dumbfounded. He had not been outside of Raleigh since he arrived from Ponce, Puerto Rico, ten years ago when he was only fourteen years old. "El Jefe, other than our weapons, what would ju have us pack up?"

"Ah Pablo, we must find things like food, pots, and pans, tents; things to make life easier for us on the road," said a smiling gold-toothed Romeo Cruz."

Like his friend Pablo Rivas, Cruz also had not been out of Raleigh since he had arrived, with Pablo from Ponce, ten years ago. Cruz was thirty-three and wore his jet-black hair in dreadlocks. At 5'7", he weighed 175 lbs.

Cruz was El Jefe of the Rican Rogues, a gang steeped in drugs, prostitution, porn, gambling, and murder. Both he and Rivas were born killers.

Rivas blurted out, "Romeo, are ju crazy? How can we fight if we carry all of that stuff without trokas?"

"Pablo, Pablo, Pablo, are there not still many remaining gringos and gringas? Slaves Pablo, slaves to carry the load, do the work, and provide certain comforts. For me, ju must find two beautiful blonde teenage gringas, for those certain comforts.

I theenk we get fifty Whities at first, so we can keel maybe ten of them for the slightest mistake, and we weel do it publicly, with great pain. That should keep the others in line. Make chure ju also get cooks and a doctor. Comprende, Amigo?"

Now Rivas also displayed his golden "grill" as he smiled and said, "Si Jefe, I weel see to it at once. Ju are so smart, Jefe."

9 May 1600.
Abandoned Police Station
Eastside of Raleigh, NC

Forty-two members of the Rican Rogue Gang made their way into the abandoned Police Station for the meeting with their Jefe, Romeo Cruz. All were heavily tatted and wore their long sleeve shirts with only the top button fastened. Their pants were baggy, and all were heavily armed.

Romeo told them to shut up, so he could tell them of his plan. When Romeo would tell someone to shut up, it was always best to oblige. The room quieted in an instant, and Romeo Cruz said, in his native Spanish, "My bros, no longer can we stay here. The city is burning, and the food is becoming scarce. Disease will soon follow from all the dead bodies rotting in the street, so I have decided that we will move eastward to the coast.

Here is what each of you must do; you must find four gringo or gringa slaves to carry our belongings. We must get tents and camping supplies that our slaves will carry and do not forget to find chains to keep the slaves from wandering off. We will scrounge for food along the way. We will live off the land, and the walking will keep us in good shape, so we can take what we need as we go.

The slaves will be forced to eat human meat. We will kill three or four gringos per day. If anyone refuses to eat, then they become part of the next meal.

We will pick up new slaves and recruits as we go. Perhaps the smell in the countryside will be better than here in the city.

I have given Pablo the mission of finding cooks and a Doctor in case any of us get sick or injured.

We will leave tomorrow at 1:00 p.m. Does anyone object to my plan?"

There were no objections because those who questioned Romeo's decisions only did it once, and besides the idea sounded exciting. Getting away from the smell would also be a blessing.

What Romeo didn't know was that they would be walking right into the refugee migration, easy pickings.

CHAPTER TEN

The Migration Falters

9 May
America's Roads

Levi walked over to see Mayor Ralph to share this conundrum of the refugees.

"Levi, hi, come on in. What new disaster do we have to deal with now?"

He poured himself a cup of coffee and sat across from Ralph before saying, "Ralph, I've been obsessing over the walkers and thought I'd run my thoughts by you to see what you think."

"Okay, I'm listening, go ahead."

"Thanks, old buddy, maybe if I can verbally express my thought, I might stop brooding about it. Consider the tens of millions of Americans on the road when at the instant the lights went out, and their vehicles failed them. Millions were far from home and had no choice but to begin the trek to return to their families. Add to this the untold millions who live in the big cities and find that no food is being delivered which means their only options are starvation, thirst, murderers, burning cities, or the road in the hope of finding somewhere, anywhere they can find food and safety for themselves and their families… and the criminals, what do they do when their cities burn, and there is no food and no one for them to prey upon? There is only the road to anywhere better than where they are.

"By preying on the unfortunates migrating to somewhere these criminal bosses will become Warlords growing rich upon the misery of others who are either unable or unwilling to fight to survive. So, there you have it. All across America, and most of these walking dead are east of the Mississippi. Almost all have destinations they will never reach, but most are just trying to find…somewhere."

Levi looked around the desk to his new friend and said that he began thinking about where these walkers came from. New York City alone holds nearly 9,000,000 people. What would they do if there was suddenly nothing to eat?

When those from the big cities hit the road, they become locusts, devouring every resource they come across. Baltimore, Boston, Washington, Cleveland, Chicago, the list seems to be unending. Hell, in the first year, 90% of the population of this country will be dead.

It was then I came to realize that the predominance of that 90% number would die in the first thirteen days because of the lack of food…and *the road*."

"Why thirteen days?"

"Easy, it will take a couple of days for most to realize that the power isn't coming back on, and another day to be out of food. That leaves the road for the next ten days, and the road leads to so very many ways to die, but mostly to starvation and toxic water, leading to disease that will spread like wildfire through the walkers.

"In addition, that doesn't even begin to consider those in nursing homes, hospitals, those with medical devices…aw crap Ralph, again the list never ends.

"The death toll in the first thirteen days along the roads of America will be littered with more than 200,000,000 dead and probably more.

"I just can't wrap my head around the simple fact that there was no longer any way to distribute what food is available. If food cannot be distributed, then it doesn't really exist.

"The reality is beyond distressing, and it's eating at me to realize that for a reset of civilization these people have to die. They have to die because the resources no longer exist to maintain the population at anything even near current levels.

"I guess I mean that before the world can even begin to recover, the sheer numbers of people have to be reduced to a sustainable agrarian balance, able to feed themselves. Then, and only then will mankind begin to revive civilization."

Ralph spoke as Levi paused, "I think you have to realize that these mass die-offs have occurred throughout the history of man. This scenario is just the most recent such population reducing disasters in our history.

The Dark Age following the collapse of the Roman Empire lasted for nearly 1,000 years. That Age was further retarded by a pandemic disease called the Black Plague and carried by a flea…a freakin' flea!"

"Yes, and I know mankind is now facing another insidious fate of our own making; overpopulation and reliance upon technology, which brought on more population. When disaster struck in the form of a near miss by a Coronal Mass Ejection or whatever it was, humankind was irretrievably locked into technologies that in less than a Nano-second ceased to exist as the cornerstone supporting the population Ponzi scheme which crumbled like the temple of King Solomon.

"At first, I thought we might just be able to lay low until the worst of the disease was over, but we can't do that. There are resources out there that we have to get now, not later."

"Levi, it is what it is, and there is nothing we can do to prevent the pain that is out there.

"We just have to accept that the result will be nature's reset to manageable levels before once again climbing the ladder of civilization."

"Ralph, I know you are right, but the enormity of it is off the charts, and until their end comes, well, I'm just gonna be miserable about it."

"Well, well, well, now it's my turn to say Buckle up Buttercup. You brought me out of my pity party, and now I get to do the same for you. Here are the facts; there is nothing we can do to help them, which I recall being your words. We can only try to help our little Tribe. Stop fretting about what you have no control over.

"You said it yourself; those people are already dead. They just haven't fallen down, yet.

"Please, my friend, don't fall into the same rabbit hole that you pulled me back from. Defiance needs for us to be strong and, yes, defiant.

There, did I do a good imitation of you?"

Levi managed a weak smile and said; "Yeah Mr. Mayor, not bad," then Levi placed a hand on each side of his head and pretended to get his shit together.

Ralph chuckled at his effort and said, "Good plan, and I am reminded of the words of Jesus at the Last Supper; *'There will be poor always, pathetically struggling, look at the good things you've got,'* or words to that effect. Levi that is exactly what we have to do right now.

Yeah, it's miserable out there, but here you will not be as miserable as those who are just walking along while waiting to die.

11

CHAPTER ELEVEN

The Doctors Monroe:

"You Put the Lime in the Coconut, Then You Feel better." - Harry Nilsson

9 May 1030 hours
Monroe Clinic
Miller's Creek, NC

Sergeant Scott Eldridge led a patrol of six men to the Monroe Free Clinic in Miller's Creek. His objective was to convince the Doctors Monroe, both General Practitioners, to relocate themselves and their clinic to Defiance.

For security, Sergeant Eldridge ordered the vehicle stopped about ¼ of a mile from the clinic and left two patrol members to guard and camouflage the truck while the remainder of the team cautiously made their way forward.

To date, the immediate area around Defiance had been relatively calm, but nightly gunfire could be heard as distant farms and suburban areas were attacked, and the fires from looters drew closer each night. Eldridge knew that this horror might just fall on them like a sledgehammer on a railroad spike.

The patrol arrived only seconds after a group of druggies had burst into the clinic. Staff Sergeant Eldridge could hear the screaming from both the attackers and Dr. Faith Monroe.

One older truck sat outside the clinic, but no guard had been posted. These were simply drug users with no idea of covering their asses.

"Well boys, this should be pretty easy. Still, I don't want either of the Doctors hurt so let's do a bit of a recon. Corporal Carter, you and Simms work your way to the west side of the building. Maintain cover from the wooded area that runs right up to that side of the building. Carter, if there are only a couple of raiders and you can handle it yourself, go ahead and take them out. We don't need any prisoners. Any questions?"

Corporal Carter shook his head and whispered, "No, we got this Sarge. C'mon Simms let's go have a look see. Lock and load."

Simms acknowledged with a head nod and checked his weapon to ensure he was cocked and locked, then followed Carter.

Eldridge and PFC O'Brien provided over watch as Carter and Simms made their way to the west side and managed to get a vantage point where they could see into the clinic.

Inside, two young men and a teenage girl had tied the Doctors back to back and were just shooting up some drug; Carter guessed it was probably an opiate.

Dropping to the ground, Carter whispered to Simms, "Okay, here's the plan. In about one minute, all three will be unconscious. I'll peek in the window to make sure they have gone to sleepy town, then we just walk in, disarm and drag 'em outside and put a bullet in their brains. You good?"

Simms whispered, "Good plan Corp, let's do it."

"Roger that," said Corporal Carter as he eased himself back to the window and saw that all three were passed out.

"Okay Simms, let's go, these three stooges are down for the count. Let's get this done."

As they walked to the front of the building, Corporal Carter waved Eldridge and O'Brien over.

Carter carefully, and quietly opened the door and gave the shush sign of finger to lips to the hogtied couple. He cut them free and sent them to join Sergeant Eldridge coming across the street.

As he started for the door, Simms said, "Hey, Corp, look at this. This creep passed out before she was even able to remove the needle. Yeah, this kinda' crap makes me think that what's left of the world will definitely be better off without these wackos."

Corporal Carter looked at the sleeping druggies and said, with disgust, "Come on let's take out the trash," and began dragging them out to the west side of the clinic.

Sergeant Eldridge came to Carter and said, "Okay, let's take care of these silly shits and get this place secured while the guys at the truck take it back to camp and bring a detail here to get this stuff loaded up."

Sergeant Eldridge began to pull out his sidearm when Carter placed a hand on his forearm and said, "No worries, Sarge, Pfc already handled it. Simms has potential; we should keep adding responsibilities to him."

"Roger that and thanks for the tip. I'll keep watch on both of you."

"O'Brien," shouted Sergeant Eldridge, "double time back to the truck and tell them to send a detail to clean out the clinic."

"Roger Sarge, on the way. Should I take their truck?"

"No, we'll go ahead and get a start loading it up."

Back in the Monroe Clinic Staff Sergeant Eldridge introduced himself and asked, "Hello, my name is Sergeant Scott Eldridge. Do you mind if I take a seat?"

"Oh, yes, please do," said Dr. Faith Monroe. "Thank you, thank you, and thank you. I can only imagine bad things happening for us if you had not come along.

Are you help from the Government?"

"No ma'am, sorry. We are a squad from Troop A, Defiance Militia, and we're probably the closest thing to help you are going to see for years."

"Well, poop, are you saying that we are completely on our own?"

Scott thought, *poop?* But said, "Yes, ma'am, there is no more USA, so it's up to us to pick ourselves up, dust ourselves off, and start all over again, and we will, too."

Mr. Monroe said, "Sergeant, I like your attitude, so what can we do to help?"

Before Scott could answer, Faith asked, "Would you like some coffee? I just made a fresh pot."

"Why thank you, ma'am, that would be very nice, that is if you also have enough for my men."

"Of course, I'll be right back."

Dr. Tom Monroe then asked, "Scott, is it? May I call you that?"

Smiling, Sergeant Eldridge said, "Yes, I would like that. I guess you must be wondering why we happened to come by this morning."

"Well, yes, that is exactly my question. What does bring you here? Oh, my name is Tom, and my wife is Faith."

Scott had noticed that the Doctors had nametags that said Dr. Tom and Dr. Faith, "Tom, the reason we are here is to ask you to join our little town of Defiance. I had planned to spend considerable time convincing you that you are no longer safe here. I guess those nut jobs out back saved you from my pitch.

Anyway, having said that, I must say that we do want you to join us. We offer a safe place to relocate your clinic, good people, around one-hundred and ninety so far, and a new start with a Conservative Constitutionalist environment.

We have a Mayor, two barbers, and…well…aw just about everything you could need. It's kinda' like Mayberry. We are building a strong militia that answers to the civilian government headed up by our Mayor.

So, the bottom line is, you must realize that you can't stay here. By tomorrow there will be more druggies coming through and following them will be the gangs. Tom, if you decide to stay here, you will be dead by tomorrow, and your wife will not have a happy ending."

Faith was bringing in the coffee urn and said, "I heard everything you just said. Let me understand one thing. You are saying that if we do not agree to come to; Defiance was it, then you will not protect us?"

"Ma'am, I guess that pretty much sums it up. We don't have sufficient resources to protect anyone outside of our immediate area. Our position is, if you do not wish to join us, then you are strictly on your own."

"Hmmm, well, if we decide not to go with you, are you planning on taking our medical supplies and equipment?"

Scott looked down at the floor and after a few seconds of thought said, "Dr. Monroe, I cannot believe that you do not understand that your clinic will be looted, and anything the bad guys don't want they will destroy."

"Oh, no, we certainly do not want that," said Tom.

"Well, then what would you have us do? Secure this clinic back at Defiance where it can do lots of good, or leave it for the gangs to loot and destroy? I guess what I am saying is, yes, we will take everything here even if you decide not to come with us. A working clinic is of more use to the overall community even if we have to just take it and find other Doctors.

I'm sorry, but there it is. We really would like for you to join us. The community needs you, and this clinic.

"I see. Tom, I agree with Scott that we are no longer safe at this location, I personally have no death wish, so my vote is to go to Defiance where we can continue to be doctors, rather than lying dead on the floor in the middle of a destroyed clinic."

Tom began to beam and said, "Then let's get to packing, 'cause I'm with you, too, Scott."

Smiling now Scott said, "Go ahead and start packing your personal belongings. We have a truck coming with a detail to make short work of the movement. You just tell 'em what, and how. They will do the heavy lifting."

"Oh, Scott, will we be taking the x-ray and other electronic equipment?"

"Yes, hopefully, we will soon be able to produce our own electricity. We do have a plan to regain power, and our philosophy is; if it can be done, it must be done."

"Scott, have you found any Nurses yet, because if not, I'm pretty sure we can find four, but only one is married. The other three are in their twenties, and single. Is that a good incentive to recruit them?"

Scott gave a bit of a nervous laugh and stammered, "Well, uh, yeah, oh I think, uh, yes, ma'am, that is a wonderful incentive. Hot damn, this day is shaping right up…wait, are they fat and ugly?"

"Scott, shame on you for being so judgmental," laughed Faith, "and no, they are not. Are your young men fat and ugly, or more like you?"

CHAPTER TWELVE

What to do? What to do?

9 May 1100 hours
Barracks building site
Defiance, NC

Ralph came roaring up to Levi saying, "Levi, oh crap we got problems."

"Of course, we do, what else is new, Ralph.

"Shut up a minute, and I'll tell you what's new. There is a state prison about ten miles from here, and one of the newbies told me that the Warden is planning to release the prisoners."

"WHAT? No way! We have to stop this nonsense."

Ralph was very excited when he said, "But, Levi, what can he do? Most of the guards have not shown up for work since the lights went out, and they are running out of food."

"First, calm down, damn it. I will tell you what that Warden can do; he can walk away and let them starve or go in and end their suffering with 9 mils. They must not be turned loose to prey on these people. Come on, let's go visit this Warden."

They took Levi's jeep, Sergeants Guy and Eldridge accompanying them as they drove straight to the prison gates where Levi introduced himself and the Mayor. After they were disarmed, Levi and Ralph were escorted to the Wardens Office and introduced.

"Let's see; Captain Levins is it, and Mayor Bassett? Yes, how may I help you?" Two armed guards stood by the door.

"Sir," said Levi, "we have heard a rumor that you plan to open the gates to free the prisoners. Surely, this cannot be true."

The Warden looked at Levi and Ralph with disgust as he said, "Gentlemen, that is exactly what I plan to do. We can no longer secure or feed them. With no electricity, conditions are rapidly deteriorating. What other option do I have? There are only five of us remaining to run this entire facility."

Levi turned to the guards and asked them, "Do you think this is a good idea?"

Before they could answer, the Warden quickly stood up and declared, "These morons don't make the decisions around here, I do. Do not even think of asking them anything."

"Sergeant Eldridge, please ask to borrow a pistol from the guards."

The Warden now screamed, "You must be crazy, Williams, arrest these men."

Williams drew his service pistol and shot the Warden in the chest, then handed his pistol to Sergeant Eldridge.

Taking both men's weapons, Levi ordered them to go with Sergeant Guy and bring the remaining two guards to the Warden's Office.

Williams said, "Sir that is not necessary. They are just down the hall waiting to be called in. May I do that now, Captain?"

"Please do."

The two guards came in, saw the body of the Warden, and smiled. "Well, that dumb bastard won't be letting murderers run amuck in this community.

Sir, we are at your orders, well, as long as you do not order us to free these assholes."

Levi said, "Men, as I see it, we have two choices. One, we just leave them in their cells and walk away, or we shoot them to ease their misery. Which do you suggest?"

"Captain," said Williams, we have all been attacked, insulted, and spit on. I say let 'em rot." All four guards agreed, and with that, all eight men walked out of the prison and locked the gate behind them.

The guards' weapons were returned, and they began walking back to their homes. They were not offered a place in Defiance.

On the way home, Levi said to Ralph, "See Mayor, nothing to get your panties in a wad about. Let's face it, those criminals made their beds, and now they must sleep in them. No way do they go free."

"Well done, Captain, even though I do feel sad for what is coming to them, but I would pull the trigger myself rather than set them free.

You know, Captain Levins, if you will pick it up a bit, we might get home in time for supper."

"Oh shit, I am so glad you said that. Sergeant Guy, I want you to pick a detail from those we saved today and go to the Wagon Wheel Restaurant and move it to Defiance. Can do?"

"Well, yes sir, but it'll be quite a job, but sure, can do, sir."

"Good, let them get a shower, a good night's sleep, and a couple of meals under their belt, then get on it at 0700, Roger that?"

"Yes sir, Roger that, Captain." Sergeant Guy immediately began planning the mission, and who to add to the detail to take care of the gas pipes and well, everything.

"Wait, Mike, you can leave the stoves. Pick up new propane models at our Home Depot and go first class."

"Roger that sir, it will sure make the job easier."

Ralph turned to Levi and said, "Great idea. If we consolidate the food preparation, we save on food, and everyone gets better acquainted. I like it…yep, glad I thought of it."

Levi said nothing; he just smiled like a Cheshire Cat.

CHAPTER THIRTEEN

All Work and No Play…

9 May 1130
Captain Levins' tent
Defiance

"Levi, things are going pretty well even though too many people decided our minefield was a bluff. Now, though, they do seem to be avoiding the area.

We've annexed a Walmart, Home Depot, two Army/Navy stores, two more gun-shops, and a Food Lion.

Oh, yeah, the idea to hire some walkers for a day's labor for food and water was brilliant. Ben, ya' done good. It's a danged shame that in a couple more days they'll be too weak to hire on.

I want to thank each of you for the effort you have provided; sadly, it's not going to be enough. The next ten or so days will be not only difficult and dangerous but also incredibly heartrending as we will be forced to watch the death of so many fellow Americans.

We are entering a new era of unimaginable tragedy and danger. We cannot afford to let our guard down for even one second. To avoid this calamity, we must stand firm in our resolve to preserve Defiance.

We have all seen the increasing number of fires in the area, and they are getting closer. Those we have saved from the road say gangs of murderers are everywhere. Is there anything we can do to smack and stack a few of them?"

"Ben," said Levi, "I wish we could, but we just don't have the manpower yet to take on that mission…Wait a minute, what if we find a few vets that we can't use, you know, the older guys, feed and arm them. Maybe they can begin to police themselves.

I hate to turn vets away, but we need the strength of youth. I was thinking that if we arm them, we, at least, give them a chance. Yeah, I like it."

Ralph piped in, "But what if they decide to hit us instead of the bad guys?"

Levi said, "Ralph if we handle it right by moving them, say 10 miles up the road I don't think they will walk the 10 miles back. Not when they think they might be able to take some bad guy stuff. You know, payback is a bitch."

"Yep sure is," added Ben, "Though I can't help being reminded that every time the U.S. tried to arm one faction against another, it always blew up in our faces. Our good people often became bad guys. Still, I think it is the right thing to do, so yeah, let's do it. I can get started on it now."

Levi said, "Mr. Mayor?"

"I must admit that Ben has a good point, but yeah, sure, I'm on board, let's roll. Get to it, Ben, see ya' later."

Rising from his chair, Ben said, "Roger that, sir, I'm on the way."

Levi then turned to Ralph and asked, "How are things going on the civilian side of this circus?"

"Pretty danged well. We've got supply organized, and the team is sorting and cataloging. Yesterday in a meeting with the team leader, Mary Collins suggested that we make a quick grab of a Goodwill store. They have lots of every size of clothing.

She also said the same thing you did about passing out winter clothing this fall to put the locals solidly behind us."

"Ralph, I'm embarrassed, you or I should have thought of that exact thing on day one. What is Mary's background?"

"You're gonna' love this; she was a Regional Manager for…wait for it…Goodwill Industries. Don't you love it?"

Both men laughed heartily before moving on to other business.

"Day before yesterday we found two seamstresses, and a couple of barbers, both are already very busy. I should add that they are so busy because they are getting your militia boys groomed and uniforms altered to fit."

Levi said, "Ralph, I would not have thought of that until it was too late to get them, very good acquisitions."

Levi then called out, "Top!"

First Sergeant Bradley Cobb shouted back, "On the way, sir. Two seconds later his head popped through the tent flap and said, "Yes sir, what'cha need?"

"Come on in Top. Is Guyardo still in charge of the Walmart crew?"

"Yes sir, he is, and he needs resupply of men and bullets. So far, he's been able to hold his own against the walkers, but we need to reinforce him and the grocery stores. We just got a report from him this morning saying that shots were fired at him from an attempt by some gang bangers to take the Walmart. They left ten dead gangsters behind them and over a hundred walkers who were just walking behind the gang."

"Top, when did this information come in?"

"I just finished reading the report when you called me in here, sir, but the action occurred at 0600 this morning."

"Well, hell shit, guys we have to find a quicker way to communicate. Okay, let's get all three food stores resupplied and add four men to each. That's gonna' put us in a tight spot if we have to fight here, but we need to hold on to those supplies.

"Mr. Mayor?"

"Oh yes, let's get on it right now."

"Fine, Top, make it happen, then make a recommendation of an NCO for a four-man shopping trip."

The First Sgt. thought for a second before saying, "Cap'n we're a bit short on E-5's, but I do have a really good young corporal who I'm sure will do you a good job. It's Corporal Todd Carter, you remember, the one on the Clinic mission."

"Okay Top, your call. Send him with a fire team out to some antique shops and find some old working treadle sewing machines. We're gonna' need 'em until we get some power back.

Hold on, have Carter take one of the tailors so they can see if what he finds is gonna' work."

"Roger sir, I'll have him on the way this morning. Anything else sir?"

"No Top, not just now, but I'm sure that will change momentarily."

"Yes sir, I figger it will," said Troop A's Top Sergeant. as he went back to his duties."

"Levi," said Ralph, "we can't lose those supplies."

"Yeah, I know…"

9 May
Evening meeting
Levi's Tent

"The carpenters we saved from the walkers plan to start construction of a clinic first thing tomorrow. Personally, I think it will be a good thing to get the pharmacy, and clinic supplies moved to our building. They also have battery powered hand tools running, well, until the batteries die."

"Why is that a problem? Home Depot has solar panels and inverters. We can let the sun charge batteries.

Solar…Powered…Batteries, oh crap, Home Depot has miles of solar powered fencing. We can set them up not only as deterrents to cattle and horses but also as an alarm system. Shit, we might even be able to get some rudimentary communications up and running, that is if we have an Electrical Engineer…Ralph, do we have one?"

Ralph chuckled and said, "Funny thing you should ask, why yes, yes, we do, one of the original group."

"Well, dang, get him on it…I mean if you think it's a good idea, of course. Oh yeah, let's see if we can find some telegrapher types, you know Morse Code and all that?" said a smiling Levi.

"Smartass."

"Think about it, Ralph; we should go ahead and put in wiring for all new building projects for when we do get power. I mean, there's solar, and this near the coast there's always wind.

What say we start a think tank with our Engineer in charge to figure out how to do it?"

"Yeah," said Ralph, "great idea, and don't forget we found that Solar Engineer guy, dang, I can't recall his name right now, but he'd be a great addition to that team. He says he knows where there are thousands of panels and everything we need to put them to good use. The downside is that they are in a warehouse in Raleigh. I'll get with him right after we're through here. What else is on your agenda?"

Levi looked thoughtful and finally said, "I'll send out a fire team to secure American Propane, today, and start transporting it here. We can also take propane tanks from deserted houses if we can figure a way to load them on our trucks."

"Levi, it's already done. We began this effort a few days ago. Have you forgotten?'

"Oh, yeah, sorry I remember now. That does it; I'm sending Top out to get some poster board and acetate, so I can keep better track of what's going on around here.

Okay, what was I saying, oh, yeah right, we'll also send out details to find solar and wind equipment. We need to grab some solar and wind guys from the walkers, that is unless we already have them."

"Levi, we just spoke of that not two minutes ago. Are you okay, old buddy?"

"Oh yeah, so we did, and yes, I'm fine just a little tired I guess."

Quickly changing the subject, Levi said, "I also noticed you had the tractors out tilling the soil. When do you plan on the first planting?"

"We figure around the 5th of May. This fall we'll build some greenhouses for fresh winter veggies."

Levi was tired and immediately jumped to another subject, "Now open your mind to this idea. I would like to send out a small volunteer force of say a four-man fire team, led by Eldridge, to start clearing out the bad guys in the area. If we do it right, the word will get around not to come and play in our sandbox."

Ralph looked at Levi, and said, "I would not have considered it, but I must admit I can see the merits of the plan. If you think it's worth doing, then you have my blessing."

"Thanks, you know, another plus is that the locals that are in jeopardy will be very pleased with us, and down the road a few months we should consider making treaties to help each other in a fight and to begin to develop trade. Treaties, of course, fall under the purveyance of the Mayor's Office.

Also, since we are thinking long term, do you think it might be a good idea to begin planning for a new currency? If we move quickly, we could bring a jeweler on board and let him guide us to the most valuable jewelry to confiscate, you know, diamonds and stuff. We might also bring a banker on board if his bank has any precious metals, and if he can get the safe open. What do you think?" asked Levi in a voice that seemed to get faster with each sentence.

"Well, let's see, if it is abandoned I guess it's okay, and if a banker is brought along…yeah, I think it's a good idea. We can put him in charge of developing a new currency. Yep, glad I thought of it."

"Funny man, you're a funny man, but okay."

"Levi, getting back to the law enforcement thing, are you also the police?"

"Ralph, as the legally elected Mayor of Defiance you can certainly authorize, at the least, Regulators, though I prefer the terms *Marshall* and *Deputies*. I'll check around to see if any of the local Sheriff's Deputies are still around that might make good additions to Defiance."

"All right, I wonder if we can find a lawman named Dillon."

"Dang Ralph, you are in rare form today. Did you find a new girlfriend to look after your raggedy butt?"

"Why yes, I have, her name is Eileen, and we'll just have to see where it goes from here."

Levi smiled a rather sad smile, and said, "I'm happy for you Ralph, ya' old reprobate."

Ralph blurted out, "Levi, you should be open to finding someone. Nights are long all by yourself."

Looking down to the floor Levi said, "Ralph, I haven't spoken of my wife Sarah before because it has been just way too painful, but I guess you have the need to know. My wife Sarah murdered the morning of the blackout, so please let that dog stay under the porch…I need time; I think I just need lots of time. We understand each other, old buddy?"

Now Ralph knew he had stepped over a line that he could not re-cross. "Levi, I am so sorry. Take all the time you need, but if you ever want to talk about it, I hope you will let me help by listening. I'll be there for you buddy. No more discussion on that until you feel the need."

Levi stood and said, "Wait, one last thing for today, we need to find some cowboys and start rounding up loose cattle and horses."

"Okay, find me some cowboys and let's do it."

"Old buddy, we certainly have a lot on our plate today, and not enough time or personnel to clean that plate, but we can at least get started. You done?" asked Levi.

"Oh, hell yes, see ya' later."

After leaving Levi's tent, Ralph made a beeline to Dr. Tom's office.

"Tom, I think Levi is in trouble. During our daily meeting, his voice kept getting faster and faster, jumping subjects and going over things we already have in motion. Something's wrong. Can you help?"

"Easy Ralph, Levi is just super tired and wound tighter than a $2 hooker on meth from lack of sleep and too much coffee. Ultimately, he's suffering from lack of rem-sleep and way too much caffeine. If we can get him to take a sedative and get him to sleep for about eighteen hours, he'll be fine."

Turning in his chair, he called out, "Nurse Fields?"

"Yes Doctor, what do you need?"

"Please get two tabs of Valium, max strength."

"Yes Doctor, I'll be right back."

After receiving the Valium, both Ralph and Dr. Tom Monroe walked back to Levi's tent to find him highly agitated and speaking rapidly to himself.

"Hey guys," said Levi "come on in."

Ralph asked, "Levi, who is in charge of this settlement?"

Levi looked questioningly at the Mayor and replied, "You, why, did you forget?" laughed Levi.

"No, my friend, I just wanted to hear you say it because I don't want any guff from you."

"Okay, what is it? Would you two like some cold coffee?"

"Levi," interrupted Dr. Monroe, "please sit down. The Mayor and I are concerned about your health. Now, with no nonsense, I want you to take these two sleeping pills. They will knock you out until tomorrow morning."

Ralph cut in, "You are acting nuts, so I am ordering you to take these pills and go to sleep."

"What, is this a joke? I don't have time to sleep. I can do that when I'm dead," laughed Levi.

"Levi please; no excuses, as the Mayor and your friend I'm telling you to take these pills."

"Okay, okay, actually I have been feeling a little on edge, but so is everyone else in the Troop."

"No Captain Levins, while it is true that everyone is tired, the added responsibility for Defiance Security only makes it worse. Come on, no more nonsense, Doctor's orders."

Yeah Levi, don't make me come over there."

"Okay, you're the boss, there's just so much to do."

"I know, Levi, but Ben knows what needs to be done today. Now please," and Ralph nodded to Dr. Monroe who handed over the pills to his friend.

Without another word Levi picked up a bottle of water and washed down the Valium, "Nighty night guys," said Levi as he removed his boots and stretched out on his cot. Sleep came within minutes, and Captain Levi Levins slept for nearly twenty hours.

This was the first really restful sleep for Levi since he lost Sarah. In his dreams, he spent those hours walking and talking with her, and she gave him the strength to carry on.

CHAPTER FOURTEEN

Snake

12 May 1025
Abandoned Semi

Sergeant Todd Fowler led a scrounging team to locate semis with usable cargoes. Bolt cutters in hand a young private cut the lock on the rear trailer door.

Jackpot! Inside the 54' trailer was a treasure trove of canned meats.

"Tillerson," ordered Sergeant Fowler, "take the truck and go back for a detail to unload this lip smackin' bunch of goodies."

"Roger Sarge, on the way."

While Tillerson was on his quest for help to offload, Jacobson, the diesel mechanic looked at the engine to see if he could get it running. "Sorry Sarge, this baby is currently unfixable."

"Yeah, okay."

A new voice spoke from the rear of the trailer, "Well, well, well, what'cha' got boys?"

Turning to face this stranger, Sergeant Tillerson found himself staring down the barrel of a sawed off 12-gauge Mossberg shotgun.

Though Tillerson's eyes saw the flame from the barrel, his brain had no time to register it as the blast hit him full in the chest. He was dead in a millisecond.

The two remaining troopers reached for their weapons, but before they could react two new faces appeared and hit both.

"Hey Snake, wad'ja find?"

"Jake, jump up in there and see what's what."

"Yeah, sure Snake," said Jake as he climbed into the trailer. "Looks like nuthin' but canned meats, Snake. You want some?"

"Yeah, throw down a case of sumthin', and we'll split it for lunch."

Jake grabbed the first case he managed to cut free from the pallet and handed it down. The case was broken open and distributed to the three men.

Once the cans were stored in the motorcycle saddle bags the fat assed beer bellied bikers kick started their ancient bikes to life and sped off down the highway.

An hour later three 1965 M-85 five-ton cargo trucks arrived with a detail of ten men to load the cases of canned goods onto the trucks.

Seeing no sign of activity around the trailer, Sergeant Carter ordered his two Corporals to assume a defensive posture while he investigated.

He called out to Sergeant Fowler but got no response. He ordered one of the Privates to climb into the trailer to check it out.

"Sergeant Carter," yelled the Private, they've been shot." He began to inspect the bodies as Carter, and two others climbed onto the trailer.

"Come here Sarge; it looks like Keller is alive."

Sergeant Carter rushed to Billy Keller and quickly assessed that his time was indeed short, but he still applied the limited first aid available.

"Private, can you tell me what happened?" asked Carter.

Billy opened his eyes, and with difficulty said, "Three bikers just started shooting. They left heading for Miller's Creek. Get Snake."

"Okay, now you just take it easy, Billy and we'll see about getting you back to Doc Faith. You hang in there now, you hear?"

Billy didn't answer as Death had claimed his first three A Troopers.

Sergeant Carter looked to Corporal Simms and asked, "Bikers, where in the hell did they get working bikes?"

"I don't rightly know Sarge, but I'd guess they were able to get some older bikes running. They must have one hell of a mechanic."

"Yeah, that must be it."

Calling to one of his Corporals, Sergeant Carter said, "Okay, establish OP's up and down the road a hundred yards or so. The rest of your party will start loading the trucks after you secure our guys. We leave no one behind. You with me?"

"Damned straight, Sergeant, we got this." The three dead troopers were wrapped in plastic sheeting and with great care were laid in the back of one of the M-85s. Sergeant Carter was most impressed and pleased with the respect his men displayed in securing the bodies of their brother's in arms.

"All right then, Simms and I will go back to Defiance to report and pick up two more men to track those animals down. Carry on Corporal."

He thought, 'Damn what I wouldn't give for some working radios.'

Man down

Troop A Orderly Room
Defiance

"Top, is the Old Man around? We got trouble at one of the semis."

The First Sergeant sent a runner to get Captain Levins.

When Levi arrived, he asked, "What kind of trouble Sergeant?"

"Sir, we left a Sergeant and two Privates at a semi on Miller's Creek Road. When we returned, we found the Sergeant and one Private dead. One of the new recruits was found alive but with a sucking chest wound. Before he died, he was able to tell us that three bikers had shot them, before riding off toward Miller's Creek.

Sir, I request two additional men and a Jeep to track down those rat bastards and kill them."

Levi looked hard at the newly promoted Sergeant Carter and said, "Yes, that is exactly what we will do, but I've got to ask. Sergeant Carter, are you ready for this mission, or would you prefer some help from one of the more combat seasoned NCOs?"

"Sir, I can handle this. Corporal Simms and I took out the druggies at the Monroe Clinic. I know my experience is limited, but I can lead this team. I can do it, sir."

Levi smiled and said, "Yeah, Sergeant Carter I know you can. Go get 'em son, and if possible, I'd like one prisoner to have a chat with before we hang him. Can do?"

"Can do sir," and with that Carter and Simms left the tent and set off to find the two men needed to flesh out his fire team.

He drew a 1973 Jeep Wrangler with no top from the motor pool and departed for Miller's Creek, which is a small community that held around one hundred people before the collapse, but now probably held no more than forty.

Arriving back at the semi, Carter checked to see how the load out was going and to ask about any new information.

The load out was going well, but no new information was available.

At two miles from Miller's Creek Sergeant Carter came across a family of four people…all dead. There was one man and three females ranging in age from around twelve to perhaps thirty-five. The man had been shot, and the women abused before they too were murdered.

Sergeant Carter hid the truck in a stand of trees, and in ambush patrol formation proceeded to the village.

At the forest's edge leading into the village, Carter ordered a reconnoiter of the area. Thirty minutes later the scouts reported that there were ten motorcycles in front of the small tavern, the Dew Drop Inn. All of the biker gang was in the bar and seemed to be having a wonderful time.

Sergeant Carter and his fire team withdrew one hundred yards to a secure location where Carter gave his plan for the attack. "Okay, with ten bikes there are obviously ten men and probably six to eight women.

I think Occam's razor is the best plan for this mess. Keep it simple. With luck, they will all come out together, but of course, they won't; so, when anyone comes out and walks over to the bikes, we watch to see where he goes. If he stays close by, we'll take him out with our silenced M-4s then slip in and hide the body.

If they all come out at once, we take them just as they are on their rides. Carter assigned positions for each man fronting the tavern.

Let's try to take the last one out as a prisoner. We ready?"

Damn straight was the attitude of this fire team, eager for revenge.

"All right, let's move out."

Once in position, the waiting began and shortly before 1700 hours a shot rang out from inside the Inn just before all of the partiers exited the tavern at one time.

The bikers and six females were fairly drunk as they made their way to the bikes and just as they began to straddle their rides, Sergeant Carter opened fire followed by the entire fire team. The SAW raked the bikers, sending them flying off their bikes and face first into the dirt.

The last man to exit the bar threw his hands high into the air and began screaming, "Don't shoot."

The fire team advanced to the bodies to check for signs of life. Those few left alive were quickly sent to Hell.

The biker known as Snake was taken alive.

Once the danger of being shot was over, Snake became tough again saying, "You dumb asses, you ain't got no idea what you just done. Our brothers will go through you like shit through a goose, so you best just let me ride on out of here."

One round from Sergeant Carter's 22 cal Ruger pocket pistol into the fatty portion of Snake's left calf ended the conversation as this tough guy began screaming and crying like a ten-year-old little girl, "You shot me, you actually shot me, oh shit get a doctor."

"Mays," said Sergeant Carter put a plug in the hole in his fat ass then gag his pie hole.

Simms, go to the bar and see what happened in there."

"Roger Sarge, on the way."

A few moments later Corporal Simms opened the door and shouted to Sergeant Carter, "Sergeant, you better come in here and see this."

Upon entering the Dew Drop Inn Sergeant Carter's eyes slowly adjusted to the dim light of its interior and quickly wished they hadn't. The bar was trashed, and five naked women lay dead on the floor. The Bartender had a bloody third eye in his forehead.

"Simms, get the others and bring all the bodies inside. Place the women and Bartender in chairs and put the dead bikers laid out at the feet of the civilians."

"Then what Sarge?"

"Then what? We burn it to the ground."

As the tavern burned the team checked to see if any of the bikes were serviceable. They found two that had been shielded by the beer bellies of the bikers.

Corporal Carter asked, "Any of you guys know how to ride these things?"

Corporal Simms and one Private affirmed they knew how, and Sergeant Carter ordered them to take the bikes back to Defiance. A couple of working engines could always be of use. Later the mechanics would come back out to see if any of the others were salvageable.

Snake continued to fuss through the dirty rag shoved into his mouth, along with crying about his pain, "Poor baby," said Carter.

Orderly Room
Defiance

Back at Defiance, Doctor Tom was called to look at Snake's wound. He said, "It's not too bad, but I'll have to dig that bullet out before I sew it up."

Levi looked at the Doctor and said, "Bones, just stop the bleeding for now. We'll see about the rest later, okay?"

Dr. Tom looked closely at the wound and said, "Yeah, sure, the bullet is in the meaty part of this lard ass's leg. Just let me know when I can dig it out."

"Thanks, Bones," said Levi that's all for now. Oh, Top, is the Mayor in town today?"

The First Sergeant said, "No sir, he's at a meeting with a couple of other mayors today to talk about trade."

Levi said, "Pity, say Top, do we have a chair that will take the weight of this lard ass?"

"Oh, yes sir," said the First Sergeant as he directed the Runner to move the chair behind Snake."

The Runner removed the gag and pushed Snake into the chair by three burly guards who strapped him to his chair.

Levi said, "Snake, you screwed the pooch this time. You killed three Troopers today, and I want to know why."

Snake winced in pain, but defiantly spit on the shipping pallet floor and said, "That was just for starters. You are all dead; you just don't know it yet. We are gonna' make you pay for this."

Having read the motorcycle club patch on Snake's leathers, Levi asked, "Who are The Death Dealers, Snake?"

Snake laughed, which caused him some pain, but he still said, "We are the future, you dumbass. We will control all of Eastern North Carolina from LeJeune to the South Carolina border. Give us a year, and it's a done deal."

"But Snake," said Levi, "We don't plan to do that."

"Do what?"

"Give you that year. Where is the rest of the gang?"

Snake laughed again and said, "Gang? We ain't no gang; we are a group of motorcycle enthusiasts."

"Snake, I don't like asking twice." Top hand me one of the rubber gloves Doc left for us."

"Yes sir, and sir, may I do the honors. He murdered my guys too."

"Sure Top, go ahead."

Snake shouted, "Whatever you're thinkin' of doin' just forget it. I want a lawyer. This conversation is over. I got my rights."

"Rights, yeah, okay, we agree you do have the following rights: the right to answer my questions, the right to remain silent, but that's gonna' hurt. Say Top, can you think of any other rights Snake has?"

"No sir, can't say I do. May I continue sir?"

Levi looked into Snake's eyes and said, "Snake this is going to hurt you a hell of a lot more than any of us. Go ahead, Top."

"Wait!" screamed Snake, "You can't do this 'cause I said I wanted a lawyer."

"First Sergeant, have you seen any lawyers lately?"

"No sir, nary a one and with that he ripped the patch off Death Dealer's leg and quickly stuffed it into Snake's mouth. He then inserted his finger into the wound and began probing for the bullet."

Snake screamed through his gag.

"Any luck?"

"No sir, but I'll find it…eventually."

Snake folded up like the proverbial cheap suit as he mumbled through his gag, "Okay, okay, what do you want to know?"

"Snake I told you that I don't like repeating myself…First Sergeant, try again to find that bullet."

"No, please no. The boys are meeting at one of the hotels on Virginia Dare in Kill Devil Hills."

"Come on Snake, when?"

"Please," begged Snake, "if I tell you they'll kill me."

Levi smiled an evil grin and said, "Snake, you really don't need to worry about them. They will never be allowed to kill you. You have my word.

First Sergeant, the bullet?"

"No! Wait, it'll take another two or three days to get everyone there."

"Which is it Snake, two or three days?"

"I don't know; the first ones should get there in a couple of days."

"How many Snake?"

"I don't know, fifty or sixty. It depends on how many bikes they could get running."

"Now, that wasn't so hard was it?

First Sergeant arrange for a twenty-five-man force prepared to move out this evening for the beach and take Snake along."

Snake's leg was now truly paining him, and he said, "Now will you go get that damned doctor? I need pain meds."

"Now Snake, you know we don't have extra pain meds for murderous bastards like you, right?"

"The best-laid schemes of mice and men, oft do go awry." -Robert Burns

12 May 0730
Advance Scouts
Virginia Dare Dr,
Kill Devil Hills

Voices calling out through makeshift megaphones warned civilians in the area to remain in their homes.

"Residents of Kill Devil Hills, Virginia Dare Drive is temporarily under Martial Law by order of the Defiance Militia Commander, Captain Levi Levins.

You are ordered to remain in your homes until further notice. A murderous motorcycle gang is heading this way. We will not let them harm you.

As soon as this action is complete, we will depart, and you may return to your normal routine."

This message was repeated up and down Virginia Dare Drive. The Troopers had no way of knowing that there was no one along Virginia Dare to hear them, as the food was gone, so were the people.

Snake's body hung limply from a lamp post and was riddled with bullets. His body had been used to zero the A Trooper rifles.

Around his neck hung a large sign which read:

I WAS CAPTURED, AND I SPILLED MY GUTS ABOUT THE PLANS OF MY RAT
BASTARD BROTHERHOOD KNOWN AS THE DEATH DEALERS.
-Snake

NOTICE:
ATTACKING MILITIA FORCES OF DEFIANCE
WILL **NEVER** GO UNPUNISHED.
THE ONLY POSSIBLE SENTENCE IS **DEATH**.
ANYONE SEEN WEARING LEATHERS WITH THE DEATH DEALERS LOGO WILL
BE SHOT ON SIGHT.

L. LEVINS
LEVI L. LEVINS
CAPTAIN, COMMANDING

In the buildings surrounding Snake's body, twenty-one Troopers of Troop A lay in concealed positions patiently awaiting the arrival of The Death Dealers. Two four-man ambush positions were established on Virginia Dare Dr. at five-hundred yards on opposing ends of the kill zone to ensure that no Death Dealer could escape Troop A's ambush.

At 1030 hours on 13 May the first motorcycles could be heard approaching. Troopers assumed their positions in upper floor windows and rooftops. Members of this gang of rogue bikers had murdered their friends, and the Troopers wanted blood.

This grouping consisted of ten bikes and the body hanging from the lamp post enticed the bikers to approach. One dismounted to read the sign. As he finished, he flashed the signal to fire by turning around.

Withering fire erupted from all around Snake's lifeless body, within five seconds; sixteen bodies lay dead at his feet.

Throughout the day groups of bikers rode onto Virginia Dare Drive. They all thought a battle had been fought there and the survivors had left…until one of them read the sign and turned around.

By dark, there were sixty-three dead men and women laid out before Snake's ever stretching neck. None had escaped, and no more arrived.

The bodies were placed in an arc around Snake's hanging body and left in the street to rot.

CHAPTER FIFTEEN

Sheepdogs Protect the Flock. It's what they do

LEVI'S TENT
16 MAY

Sergeant Eldridge, I need a volunteer for a risky job. Are you interested?"

"Captain, you saved my family's lives, so yeah, I'm in for whatever you will ever need."

Levi smiled, "Scott you might want to hear what I have to say before you say yes. So, I'll not hold you to it until after you hear me out.

We are hearing more and more about raids at some of the outlying farms and villages. I want a volunteer to take a four-man strike team out, at night and start killing bad guys. Let's start with one prisoner for questioning. Now, are you in?"

"Well, sir, I have to assume that you ask this of me because I am an Army Ranger, and once a Ranger, always a Ranger. It seems to me that I am the perfect candidate, and I already know who to ask to join me.

"So, when can I start?"

"Tonight, Staff Sergeant Eldridge, but you may not take Sergeant Palmer. He's locked into moving a restaurant from there, to here."

"Yes sir, oh, sorry sir, it's Buck Sergeant, not Staff Sergeant, but thanks."

"Eldridge, are you saying that I don't know my own mind? What, you think I'm getting senile?" smiling now, Levi said, "You and Mike Guyardo are both getting promoted at our 1800 daily brief. You are doin' good son, I'm proud of you, and it doubles your pay, too. Two times zero is a lot of money so don't spend it foolishly."

Laughing now, Scott said, I'll make a point of good money management Captain."

"Yeah, you do that. See ya' at 1800, and have a short brief prepared for your concept of the operation, weapon requirements, and who you hope to take.

Dismissed."

Promotions on the Village Green

18 MAY 1800
VILLAGE GREEN,
DEFIANCE

Standing before the dais Ralph opened the meeting with, "I have directed that another dais be erected on our village green, and have invited the entire population, all one-hundred and ninety-four of them to join us for a portion of this meeting.

"Captain Levins please join me."

Standing atop a stack of shipping pallets so all could see, Ralph said, "Ladies and Gentlemen, I have given much consideration to a decision regarding our Captain Levins.

Captain, our small community is growing, and fast. I guess time will tell if this pace is too fast. At any rate, since you are the Commander of our Defiance Militia, and as we reach out to other community leaders, I feel those leaders may look down on a mere Captain.

So, as the Commander in Chief of our little Militia, I hereby promote Captain Levi Levins to the grade of Colonel.

While I am concerned about other community leader's attitudes, this promotion is based upon merit, for none here can say that Levi has not, even in such a short time, earned this honor. I truly shudder to think of the peril we would be in had not Levi Levins graciously agreed to join our efforts here in Defiance."

In unison, Sergeants Guyardo, and Eldridge both shouted, "Uh-ten-shun!" causing everyone to stand just a little straighter.

"Seriously, Levi, we need to project an image of both strength and authority. Thus, promoting you to the grade of Colonel is appropriate, as well as being deserved.

"I admit I did consider making you a General, but after mulling it over, I felt that other communities might assume you were nothing but a self-appointed tin pot Warlord, but Colonel denotes a lack of pretension while intimating authority without any delusions of grandeur.

"Colonel, you have proven yourself to be more than capable of leading our Militia and Security Forces.

"Paul's Army/Navy store contributed these Eagle collar pins. Congratulations Colonel Levins.

"Sergeants Guyardo and Eldridge please join us and do the honors of pinning the Colonels Eagles to the collar of his brand-new uniform. Lieutenant Smith if you would please do the honor of pinning an Eagle to the Colonel's hat.

"As Mayor of Defiance, and with the Colonel's approval I have also taken the liberty of promoting his XO, 1st Lieutenant Smith to the grade of Captain.

"Additionally, the following Militia members will also be promoted, Sergeant First Class Cobb to First Sergeant, Sergeant Guyardo to Staff Sergeant, Sergeant Eldridge to Staff Sergeant, Corporal Carter to Sergeant, Private Simms to Corporal and PFC Jones to Corporal. That ceremony will take place immediately following some words from Colonel Levi Levins.

Following the pinning ceremony Colonel Levins, looking most ill at ease made his way to the dais. "Wow, I really did not know that I would be speaking to anyone, but the Mayor and my XO tonight, but here goes.

"We, the founders and initial settlers of the small settlement of Defiance have little to look forward to but hard work, fear of invasion, combat, hunger, failed crops, lack of medical resupply, struggle, and building President Ronald Reagan's shining city on the hill.

"Our labors will make life easier for our progeny and help to return the light of civilization to our neighbors and in some far distant future lift the country out of the New Dark Age in which they are about to find themselves.

"We will suffer plagues, marauders, weather, obstructions to industry, and so many other things that we cannot yet even imagine. But we will persevere and you, my friends will be the ones to do it.

"In closing I would like to quote from one of my favorite old movies called Independence Day, *'We will not go quietly into the night.'* No, Defiance will live up to its name and we will not go quietly into a New Dark Age…we will not go quietly into the dark. WE WILL NOT! Thank you. Mr. Mayor?"

Riotous applause erupted from the founders of Defiance followed by handshakes, and raucous laughter immediately spread throughout the settlement. This small respite from the rigors of the daily struggle just to survive lifted the spirits of all.

For just in this short span of time, the citizens, this happy cheerful band of human beings dedicated to the proposition that from this small gathering, not only would a new Dark Age fail to take hold here in Defiance, but the light of civilization would eventually spread around the world.

Following the completed promotion ceremony, the meeting evolved into a block party.

CHAPTER SIXTEEN

Army of the Double R

22 MAY 10:00 A.M.
ABANDONED MOTEL
EASTERN SUBURBS RALEIGH, NC

The going was slow, but the Rican's were growing both in recruits and slaves. After three days the gang had not yet gotten beyond the suburbs of Raleigh.

Many of the houses still held treasures of food and slaves. The gang now totaled eighty members and one hundred and twenty-five slaves.

Each day, five slaves were murdered and butchered as food for the other slaves. Any slave who refused to eat was brutally beaten to death and became food themselves. The gang called it "tenderizing the meat".

The "meat" was then boiled with no seasoning, just boiled.

Of course, all slaves were beaten to some degree each day. Their will to resist rarely lasted more than one of the savage beatings, and for some, it was simply witnessing others being murdered and butchered like cattle that kept them in line.

Of course, many female slaves received better treatment, but not those belonging to Pablo. In his warped mind, the disposable nature of his playthings gave him a god complex. He was constantly on the lookout for replacement slaves…Pablo did not have a long attention span.

The gang members, of course, ate whatever real food they found, although at times,when meat in the city had grown scarce, wild dogs and cats were often used to fill their larders.

Romeo Cruz, the gang leader, decided when they would stop and when they would start. He had once seen a pickup truck bed in someone's yard and so he took it and had it furnished with a recliner and shade. Four slaves pulled his 'Royal Coach.' Pablo and others had followed suit. Slaves walked or serviced those in the coaches. The others carried the possessions of the gang.

"Hey amigo," Romeo said to Pablo, "we need more slaves to carry our treasures; perhaps when we have sufficient coaches, we may find others to carry the excess."

"Si Jefe, we will take whoever we find."

"Bueno Pablo. How is our gun collection coming?"

"Everyone is armed with pistolas, but we have no more than twenty long guns and leettle ammunitions. We have been searching, but no mosh luck so far."

Cruz smiled at Pablo and said, "Do not worry my fren, tomorrow we will be out of Raleigh, and we shall find all things on the road. Our scouts report millions of people walking along the roads going in all directions. Our numbers will grow very quickly into an Army. Whatever these refugees have is ours, they just do not know it yet. Personally, I cannot wait..."

Romeo Cruz was absolutely correct, other banditos who were living off the miseries of the refugee death march were quick to join the Rogues, and if they did not want to join, they simply became food for the ever-growing slave population belonging to the Army of the Double R, the Rican Rogues.

Cruz had one of the slaves create an **RR** and a **C** brand. Everyone was branded on the forehead. Soldiers bore the **RR** brand while slaves wore the *C for cannibal*...objecting to the brand meant becoming lunch. Personal slaves received their *C* brand on their right shoulder and were rebranded on the forehead when they were used up. This cruel procedure was one more step in identifying and dehumanizing their captives.

CHAPTER SEVENTEEN

Camp Lejeune

23 MAY 0900 STAFF BRIEF
CONFERENCE ROOM OF THE COMMANDING GENERAL
USMC CAMP LEJEUNE, NC

In addition to the normal briefing staff, Major General Matthew Starks, Commanding General of the 2nd Marine Division sat in attendance, along with his G Staff.

General Chalmers looked tired and most unhappy. He had just received orders to pack up what they could, secure what they could not, and move the Cherry Point, NC facility to Camp Lejeune.

This was a monumental undertaking as budget cuts over several years had forced the U.S. Military to purchase many vehicles and equipment that were not sufficiently hardened against Electro Magnetic Pulse. The resulting fact was that the transportation arm had far too few functioning vehicles to make such a move.

The G4 (Base Supply Officer/BSO) was first to speak this day. "Sir, we can get the Marines here, but it will take time. We simply do not have sufficient prime movers to make this complete this task in any semblance of a timely manner. Even if all trans assets were available this move would take weeks to facilitate. Currently our functional transportation assets are less than 10% of TO&E (Table of Organization & Equipment).

I would like to offer a possible scenario for your consideration, sir. Since we just do not have the assets to move all of Cherry Point's mobile equipment, i.e., weapons, munitions, rations, and such, to LeJeune promptly, why not leave a battalion-sized unit, say, the 3-5 (3rd Battalion, 5th Marine Regiment) to secure those items we must leave behind, i.e., the significant number of aircraft which are currently unflyable due to the CME.

There are sufficient canned food stores, along with MREs currently on hand to maintain a sole battalion for several weeks, until resupply is worked out.

The stocks of munitions of every caliber along with missiles and explosives are beyond the ability of trans to facilitate the move.

"Colonel," said the General, "on the one hand what you have said about transiting Cherry Point to Lejeune is unacceptable. On the other hand, your position is unassailable. Since we cannot move Cherry Point, in total here, we must assume the mission of securing that facility.

General Starks," said General Chalmers, "do you see a better solution to this dilemma in which we find ourselves?"

"No General I do not. I am in agreement with the G4. We must secure the facility at Cherry Point, and the 3-5 is more than up to the task. The 2nd Division accepts your recommendation for securing Cherry Point with the 3-5."

"G1 (Personnel), your report."

"Yes, sir. We have received reports from across the military spectrum that desertion rates have now reached epic proportions with estimates as high as 60%. These numbers are expected to increase should this crisis continue to escalate.

However, USMC reports show our own desertion rate to be in the 10% to 15% range, and here at Lejeune this number seems to verify these estimates."

Without further comment, Lieutenant General Chalmers motioned for the G1 to be seated and said, "G2 (Intelligence), your turn in the barrel."

"Yes sir, we have now confirmed that the entire worldwide grid has crashed. There is no longer any doubt that the Earth had a very close encounter with a massive plasma eruption from our sun in the early morning hours of 29 March. Had this CME hit us we would not be here right now as the entire Earth would have been scoured clean.

Worldwide reports demonstrate that everyone; everywhere, is in the same boat. It is our considered opinion that the U.S. Military cannot sustain its existence for more than another few days at current levels. As we are no longer receiving resupply of food stores, we find ourselves critically short, and we have insufficient stocks of MREs to continue operations for any appreciable time. Ultimately, sir, we simply will be unable to feed our Marines for more than another three days.

Current stocks of MREs stand at around 240,000 meals. Currently, Camp Lejeune is home to active duty, dependent, retiree and civilian employee population of approximately 170,000 people, counting those moving in from Cherry Point.

The current stocks of canned foods consist of a three-day supply. Any food items requiring refrigeration were eaten days ago. As you can see, sir, we will be out of all foodstuffs in no more than three days, maximum."

A nervous murmur ran through the staff attendees.

General Chalmers interrupted and asked, "G4, do you concur with this assessment?"

The G4 stood and said, "Sir, without the two hundred and fifty tons of food consumed daily just here at Lejeune we will not be able to feed our Marines for more than a couple of days, and that is living off MREs at the end. General, I am in complete agreement with the G2. We simply do not have enough, nor can we obtain, any further stocks of food to support continued operations of the United States Marine Corps at Camp Lejeune.

"I believe it is inevitable that all supplies of food will be totally depleted in as little as three days, at current consumption rates. The food is simply not available, nor will it be available for many years if the G2 projections are accurate, and I am sure they are. I'm sorry sir, but those are the facts."

"G4, how long could Lejeune remain viable if we reduced staffing to say two Battalions?"

"Sir," said the G4, "I do believe that we could maintain two companies for perhaps five months if they have steady rations of MREs, and if the remainder of this base is reduced to that number within the next forty-eight hours."

"Thank you. G5 what have you to add?"

"General, I believe that we simply cannot survive in this environment. Ultimately it all comes down to food. Even if we had the food, we have no way of training with so much of our equipment in a nonfunctioning capacity."

"Ammo, you, I presume, have plans to preclude ammunition from falling into the hands of potentially criminal elements."

Standing, the G4 said, sir, the only security we have at the Ammunition Supply Points (ASP) are the razor-wired fencing and the high-density locks on the doors of the munitions bunkers.

"I would suggest that we either destroy the stocks or place a mine field around the ASP to deter looters. Sadly, those same criminal elements will just force civilians to walk through the mines to clear a path. I recommend destruction, sir."

"Oh, dear God," said General Chalmers. Those of us in this room have spent our lives as Sheep Dogs protecting our people and our nation from the wolves of this world. Now it appears that we are apparently out of a job, and right when the wolves are at the door."

General Chalmers asked for a direct secure line to the Commandant and directed that everyone except for General Starks wait outside while the two General's discussed this development.

"Matt, my investigation of this matter has sadly forced me to agree with the findings of my staff. I see no option but to belay that order to secure Cherry Point. Do you concur?"

"Paul," said General Starks, "at this point in time I am completely at a loss. If what is reported here, and I am comfortable that this information is factual, does mean that we have nothing to eat, I see no choice to but to request that the Commandant authorize us to disband.

"Dear God, how has the world come to this?"

A knock on the door interrupted their commiseration.

General, I have the Commandant on a secure line. If you would please take the call in the tactical communications center?"

Both men rose and followed the Captain to the TOC.

Everyone in the room was directed to wait outside while the two Generals discussed the fate of Camp Lejeune with the Commandant of the Marine Corps.

"Matt, Paul, I was just about to call you. May I assume that you have been apprised of the food shortage throughout the country, hell, the world?"

Both men replied in unison, "Yes, sir we have just been discussing that exact thing. Commandant, we will be out of food in no more than seventy-two hours. General Starks, and I request that you authorize us to secure what we can, destroy what we cannot, and disband."

The Commandant said, "I cannot believe that I would ever have to issue such an order, but there it is. Just moments ago, the President directed the disbanding of all U.S. Military.

The President has issued orders that the Continuation of Government protocols be put into action," said a tired sounding Commandant of the Marine Corps.

"The entire Military Forces of the United States of America, following the disbanding will be two battalions of Army Rangers, and one Armored Cavalry Squadron, who will provide security for the government which has already initiated movement into selected safe facilities.

"The official end of the U.S.M.C. will occur No Later Than 1200 hours on 23 April.

"My friends, do what you can for our Marines and their families. Out-here," said the Commandant, who abruptly severed the connection.

General Chalmers muttered, "Dust in the wind; that is ultimately what we are about to become."

At this point everyone returned to the Conference Room.

"Supply, I do not want any Marines leaving this camp in uniform so arrange to recover all uniforms and equipment, less bivouac essentials before locking the gate.

General Starks, when do you plan to start releasing your Marines?"

"I think we'll try to get started in the morning, say around 0700. If we wait for noon on the 12th we will have a total fuster cluck that could quickly devolve into a mob scene. How about you?"

"I think we should do the same. I suggest we use separate gates to minimize opportunities for trouble or gridlock.

"Staff, coordinate with your 2nd Division counterparts to make this exercise in futility as painless as possible," said General Chalmers.

"Now, gentlemen, is there anyone here not willing to wait for the official disbandment?"

No one in the room said, "Yes."

"Thank you, Marines, I knew that none of you would, or could, abandon your post.

We have a very short fuse to accomplish this goal.

Upon their departure, I want one sidearm with two magazines issued to each U.S. military refugee as they exit the Camp, plus two MREs for each family member. May God have Mercy upon their Souls."

The G-1 asked, "Sir, are there any plans for the retirees currently on the base?"

General Chalmers sighed, and said, "Very good question, Colonel. Do you have a round number for me?"

"Yes, sir, that number is near eight-hundred.

"Excuse me sir, but what about the Hospital, and the Brig?"

"One thing at a time, Colonel. Okay, the retirees, inform them of our plan at 0700 hours on 26 May. They all have undeclared weapons, ammo, and hopefully sufficient foodstuffs to reach their new destinations.

"The Hospital losses since lights out have been tragic. I spoke with the Hospital Commander this morning and she told me that there are only a very few patients that are still recovering from pre-CME surgeries. She also informs me that she has sufficient volunteers to assist those patients, presuming, of course, that they have food, water, and band aids.

"G-4, make sure she has those things before we close up shop.

"Now, the Brig; fortunately, we have no long termers. I'm going to order their release since none of those in the Brig are there for serious crimes. They will, however not be issued a weapon. Thank God, we don't have the same situation as places like the prison at Newport News.

"Ammo, prepare to destroy all weapons and munitions stocks at 1200 hours on 26 May."

"What I am about to say is anathema to everything I have ever believed in my thirty-three years as a Marine. Our position is untenable; it's over gentlemen, it is simply over.

"Now I must ask for you to remain at your posts for another seventy-two hours, and when you hear the ammo dump go up, well I guess we go in search of a new home."

"Sir," said the G2, "I have been informed of an active militia just outside of Roper. I've heard good things about them. They are assisting the local community by providing food from local grocery stores they were able to prevent being looted, toys for the local children and security from bandits. To date, they have utterly destroyed several gangs of murderers pillaging the countryside.

"May I suggest sir, that I make contact and arrange for them to be supplied from our stocks of weapons, ammo, uniforms, whatever they need to continue to keep even that small community safe and at least somewhat civilized?

"I fully realize that three weeks ago this would be unthinkable, but the times they are a changin'. This random act of kindness to assist in their survival may be the last operation conducted by the United States Marine Corps."

"Damned interesting idea, I like it. Can you do it in seventy-four hours?"

"Yes sir, if I leave immediately, I think it can be done."

The General smiled for the first and last time that day and said, "Make it happen, you are dismissed."

General Paul Chalmers looked at his old friend, General Starks and said, "Matt, let's have a last cup of coffee together and speak of better times."

The two aging warriors sat discussing the past of their concerns for the future.

"Paul, something I fear is the possibility of rogue units forming around some senior officer that may set himself up as a Warlord."

"Yes," responded General Chalmers, "I have also considered that possibility and I am absolutely sure it will happen somewhere. Since we have no control over other areas, I just hope we can prevent such a thing happening in our own little sphere of influence."

"Agreed," said a sad General Matt Starks, "I must say that I approve of your directive to turn in all uniforms and most equipment. Still, I don't see how such a thing is preventable."

20 APRIL 1600
DEFIANCE ROADBLOCK

A Marine Corps, M-85, five-ton truck, complete with a dozer blade made its way to within one hundred feet of the Defiance Road Block. An unarmed Marine Lieutenant Colonel exited the vehicle and approached with hands raised until he was ordered to halt. A guard then warned the stranger that he was in the sights of a sniper who was more than willing to shoot if he made any aggressive movements.

"Continue to advance with your hands raised."

Marine Lieutenant Colonel Gus Murtaugh carefully followed the directions.

"Stop right there and state your business."

One of the other guards noticed the stranger was a Marine Officer and took off to find Colonel Levins.

Murtaugh said, "I am on General Chalmers Staff at Camp Lejeune. I have come to see Colonel Levins concerning a supply issue."

"Wait," he's on his way said the guard. "Stand real still, and you can lower your hands."

"Thanks," said Murtaugh as he slowly lowered his hands, "my arms were getting kind of tired."

The wait was no more than four minutes before Colonel Levins made his way to the gate. "So, Colonel, what can Troop A of the Defiance Militia do for the Marine Corps today?"

"Sir, I have come from General Chalmers, Commander of Camp Lejeune. He would like me to speak to you concerning both supplying and equipping your militia.

May I reach into my wallet to retrieve my ID Card?"

"You may."

After Levi had looked over the ID Card, he ordered the guard to open the gate, pat down the visitor and guide him to Levi's office. The truck, security team, and driver were brought into Defiance. They were fed and questioned about conditions across the country.

Levi was seated behind a new wooden desk. It was a gift from Mayor Ralph who had it brought in from a local furniture store. His First Sergeant and XO were also in attendance.

Levi rose and offered his hand to Lieutenant Colonel Murtaugh. "Colonel Murtaugh I am Levi Levins, commander of this merry band of miscreants."

As they shook hands, Murtaugh said, "I am Gus Murtaugh, G-2 for Camp Lejeune. Sir, it is a real pleasure to meet you."

Levi directed him to a chair and said, "Please, have a seat and tell me why you have made this dangerous trip all the way from Camp Lejeune."

"Yes sir, it may well be dangerous, but the traffic is murder, hence the dozer blade on my ride. I decided early on that it would be best to take the back roads. We found them, at least, a bit less blocked.

We, at Lejeune, have heard good things about your militia, serving and protecting the community. Sharing resources and the like. Because of this General Chalmers would like to assist you in upgrading your equipment and general supplies..."

A knock, on Levi's office door interrupted Murtaugh.

Levi had sent a runner to get Ralph to attend the meeting. "Come in Mr. Mayor, may I introduce Lieutenant Colonel Gus Murtaugh of the United States Marine Corps?"

Ralph shook hands and asked, "Are you bringing government help, or taking over?"

Murtaugh smiled and said, "Mr. Mayor I have come to offer assistance in the form of supply items which may help you and the community at large.

Sadly, this is a one-time offer as no further assistance will be available after 1000 hours the day after tomorrow. At that time, we will be destroying weapons and munitions."

Without thinking Ralph blurted out, "But why, why would you do that?"

Murtaugh looked at both men and asked, "How long could you hold your Troop together if you had no food? Sorry, that was a rhetorical question. Anyway, we will be unable to maintain a viable force beyond the next few days. As a result, we will be dissolving the Marine Corps in North Carolina, and soon, everywhere else. Gentlemen, America no longer exists as a nation. Therefore, we cannot maintain or resupply even the basic foodstuffs to support an active military.

We intend to lock everything up two days hence, and yes, we know that our facilities will soon be looted. Therefore, in an effort to assist those worth saving I am offering a supply of Marine issue weapons, uniforms, ammunition of all calibers suitable for your use, and we may even have a very small number of vehicles for you.

Are you interested?"

Levi looked past Murtaugh and said, "How do we know this is not a ruse to attack and destroy Defiance and its militia?"

"Sir, I can only ask that you trust me. Ultimately it comes down to wanting what the General offers or going on as you are. But please keep in mind that time is of the essence. If you want it, we have to get going, right now, tonight. So, what's it to be?"

Ralph started to speak, but Levi raised a finger to let him speak first. Levi looked to Ralph who was nodding his head and said, "All right, we accept, First Sergeant, please get a thirty-man contingent ready to move out in twenty minutes."

"Yes sir," said First Sergeant Cobb who rose and left the room to get the detail.

Murtaugh looked at Levi and said, "Nice…are all your people that motivated?"

"Who? Top? That slacker?" laughed Levi and Ralph.

FRONT GATE
CAMP LEJEUNE, NC

Levi and Lieutenant Col. Murtaugh arrived at the Camp Lejeune Marine Base front gate at 0130 hrs.

"Sir, I'm sorry, but the Base is closed. Is there some other way I can assist you?" asked the Marine Guard at the gate.

Lieutenant Col. Murtaugh leaned over Levi and handed his ID card to the guard, "Marine, I am the Camp G2. We're here to see the Commanding General. Please call his office and tell him Colonel Levins and Lieutenant Colonel Murtaugh are here and would like a moment of his time.

Please call his office. I'm sure he will make an exception and open the Base to us," replied Murtaugh.

The Guard saluted and then turned to another MP who entered the gatehouse to call the General's office.

The guard returned the ID Card, saluted again, and opened the barricade.

As they drove to the HQ Building, Levi noted that he was impressed to see that the Gate Guard was as professional as ever. He found this to be notable.

Gus told him that General Chalmers put out the word that any Marine wishing to leave could go ahead, but those who remained until the end would receive a sidearm, ammo, two MREs, and camping gear.

"Of course, the most likely reason is because they are Marines," chuckled Gus.

"My friend," added Levi, "I think that may be the most probable reason"

Gus was a bit surprised and said, "Sir, weren't you Army?"

"Yep, twenty-two years, but I had two brothers that were Marines and I respect the fact that The Corps has always been America's 9-1-1 since our first Muslim war in Tripoli. So, thank you my friend."

21 April 0200
Commanding Officer's Conference Room
Camp Lejeune, NC

Upon entering the Headquarters Building, they were met by a Marine Corporal who again asked for their ID Card.

"Yes, sir, one moment please." The Marine picked up a phone and called to verify their arrival.

After what seemed an eternity the Marine replaced the phone in its cradle and said, "I'm sorry, sir, for the delay. Please go right up these stairs and proceed down the hallway to your right. You'll be met there by the General's Aide."

They climbed the stairs to the second floor, which held the Commanding General's Office. Upon entering the hallway, Levi saw a young Captain exit an office and turn toward him with his hand extended in greeting.

"Colonel Levins? I'm Captain Wainwright, the General's Aide. The General said I was to be very nice to you. I will add this small caveat, however; please don't keep the General long. I have been trying to get him to his quarters since midnight last night."

"I understand Captain, and I sincerely hope that our meeting will not take long. In fact, I would be willing to wait until the morning to allow him to be rested."

"Sorry Colonel, but that would not leave sufficient time to accomplish your mission. We are on a very tight schedule."

"Roger that, Captain. I'll try to keep it short and sweet. Then I'll try to help push him to his rack."

"Thank you, sir. Right this way, please," said Captain Wainwright, who turned on his heel and led Colonel Levins into the Commanding General's Office.

Marine Lieutenant General Paul Chalmers was pouring his own coffee and looking very tired. He did, however; manage a warm and welcoming smile.

General Chalmers offered his hand to Levi saying, "Lieutenant Colonel Murtaugh, before we get fully engrossed here, I would like to be briefed on what you saw in Colonel Levins' community of Defiance."

"Certainly General, but to begin, I must relate that it is not Colonel Levins who is the Head Man. Overall command and control are provided through a Mayoral system of civilian government. The Mayor, Mr. Ralph Bassett has final say on most issues; both he and Colonel Levins collaborate when areas of policy overlap. It seemed plain to me that Colonel Levins is most definitely not the head of a Military Junta, nor is Mayor Bassett a King.

"Sir, I found their growing township to be full of relatively healthy and definitely happy citizens that were living in safety. Everyone has a job to do and, well, I guess if I did not have plans for myself and my family I'd apply for citizenship in Defiance. The building program itself is most impressive.

"My impression is that if civilization is to survive, then it is small communities like Defiance that can make it happen. I encourage you, sir, to approve assisting this community."

"Thank you, Colonel. Well, Colonel Levins, that was quite an impressive briefing on your little township, and since I have tremendous faith in Lieutenant Colonel Murtaugh's judgment, I do authorize this plan," smiled the General.

"Colonel Levins it is a great pleasure to meet a man who is willing to give the last full measure and to place the safety of his community above himself."

Levi looked a bit off balance, but replied, "Yes sir, thank you sir, but isn't that exactly what you have been doing your whole life in the Marines? I mean, even though I was Army I know full well that the Marine Corps is America's 9-1-1."

"Yes, and thank you, Levi; oh, may I call you Levi?"

"Of course, sir, I would be honored."

Sitting down and accepting a cup of coffee from the General's Aide, Levi began, "Sir, I am humbled that you find the Defiance Township and Militia worthy of so great a gift."

Continuing, Chalmers said, "Levi, the United States of America no longer exists, so by helping you to hold onto one small shaded corner of civilization the United States Marine Corps final action is one of honor. A pity that it will never be recorded in the Marine Corps history."

"Levi said, "But General it will be recorded in the history of Defiance. If we stand strong our, as you said, little shaded corner of the world will one day begin the expansion of civilization across America and the world. That simple task shouldn't take more than three or four hundred years.

General Chalmers interrupted, "Just a moment, please, Colonel.

Captain, please escort everyone but Colonel Levins out of the room. Send everyone but yourself home to get some rest. They all know what needs to be done tomorrow."

After the room was cleared, General Chalmers moved to the office sofa and leaned back onto the cushion, sighed deeply and said in a more relaxed and cordial tone, "Please go on Colonel. I'd like to hear more of your thoughts on this subject."

"Of course, sir, thank you," answered Colonel Levins, who did not fail to notice a not so subtle change in General Chalmers' demeanor. "The CME or EMP, whatever it was…"

General Chalmers interrupted and said, "Levi, we found out yesterday beyond a shadow of a doubt that the entire world's electronics infrastructure was fried by a monstrous CME that just missed a direct hit. Sorry for the interruption, please continue."

"Yes sir, thank you, I'm pleased to know that we were not attacked.

"As I was saying, the CME will throw the world into a New Dark Age. The year might as well be 1850. Within a few years, we'll all be riding horses again.

"The sole mission of Defiance is to hold onto a desire to progress with civility along with a modicum of our culture and civilization. In so doing the first objective is to secure our immediate border which we have established out to twenty miles from the center of Defiance."

"Interesting concept Levi, may I ask, how you came to decide on this particular sized perimeter?"

"General, twenty miles around Defiance is pretty much all we can expect to protect. Unfortunately, we are not quite there yet.

"In my career, the Army taught me to think, to extrapolate, and to postulate possible outcomes. The answers are there for anyone prepared to see the obvious, sir."

"Yes, I suppose that is true.

I also understand that you were able to rescue quite a few refugees in the early going."

Levi looked a bit embarrassed and said, "General we did save perhaps a hundred total. We have spent sleepless nights wishing we could have done more."

"Yes Levi, it is sad, but very few were saved anywhere along the line. We saved none.

Enough crying over that sadness, you must face the future, and your plan is solid. So…what do you need?"

"Sir, we need everything military. Weapons, ammo, explosives, rations, uniforms, transportation you name it."

"Wow, that's a tall order. Levi, if I weren't evacuating this Base, I would be staggered by your preposterous request. However, I am evacuating and will have to abandon hundreds of tons of gear," sighed the General.

"Does that mean that you can help, sir?"

"Yes, oh yes, we must, my friend, because small settlements like yours are the only hope we have, so yes, we'll help with everything except we cannot spare rations."

Jumping to his feet, the General called to his Aide, "Wainwright! Get in here!"

"Yes, sir," answered the Aide as he immediately stepped into the room.

"Captain, recall all the senior staff that just left. I need them all, and right now," snapped the General.

Smiling, Captain Wainwright said, "No problem, sir, the staff decided they weren't quite finished, yet. Frankly, I think that none of them wanted to leave before you."

"Well met. Please, bring them in here so we can change their direction. Damn, I feel just like Patton when he pulled out of a winter battle and moved the 3rd Army to Bastogne back in '44."

As the primary staff entered, the General made introductions all around.

"Gentlemen, I have a new task for you, and I want it to be your number *ONE* priority. Remember, I did say priority *ONE*!"

"Now pay attention. Colonel Levins here needs supplies from each of you to equip 500 personnel. Any questions?"

"Class V," asked the General, "Where do we stand on ammo?"

"Sir, we've got millions of rounds for whatever he needs, from an ammo perspective, we can give him all he needs as long as he can transport it. I have no more Trans assets. They're all up at Cherry Point," answered the Class V Lieutenant Colonel.

The General then turned to his Transportation Officer and asked, "John, do we have any assets left on the Base?"

"Actually, sir, we had planned to abandon the training vehicles in their motor pool. It's all stuff from the 60's and 70's, but they're in good condition. I'm sorry that I didn't think of them for our own use. They should run just fine. The paint scheme is Iraqi, though," smiled the Transportation Officer.

Turning to Levi, the smiling General asked, "Well, Levi, we'll find you some paint, but between now and then people are going to think Iraq has invaded us.

"I assume that you do want those assets?"

Levi, also smiling, said, "Oh, yes sir, and happy to have them, sir. But sadly, I'm not sure I have the human assets in place to drive everything. I have a detail of thirty with me."

"Levi, could you find a use for another fifty or so Marines in your little militia?"

Levi smiled and said, "No sir, but we could surely use some former Marines who want to be Troopers in the Defiance Militia. Seriously, sir, we could use some mechanics and grunts in the lower grades with only two or three corporals and maybe two E-5s. We just aren't ready for a larger influx of personnel to house and feed…"

General Chalmers broke out laughing and said, "Fair enough. Personnel?" snapped General Chalmers.

"Yes, sir, I will arrange the transfer of sufficient top-notch personnel to drive his trucks."

"Great, now, let's hear from the rest of you."

One by one, the Senior Staff laid out the available assets. Levi had his supplies, and fifty Marine mechanics and grunts to go along with them.

"Now gentlemen, comes the fly in the ointment. I want this convoy prepared to move out no later than 1000 hours. I know that's only a little over seven hours from now, so let's not waste our precious time bitching, and just git er done. I mean it, seven hours. Dismissed."

With that, his officers, still stunned, began to file out.

"John," said the Ammo Officer, "I'll have my trans requirements to you in about an hour and it's gonna' be big."

"General, how large an ammo issue, sir?"

"Say, two hundred thousand rounds each for the M4-A1s and M-249 SAWs. Use that as a guideline for the rest."

"Roger that, sir," replied Class V (Ammo).

"Sir, Class VI here. Do you wish an issue from liquor stores, also?"

Few men had ever seen the veins stand out on the General's neck. They saw it now, "Dammit, Claude, I said I wanted issuance from ALL Classes. Do I have to do it for you?" snapped the General.

"No sir, sorry sir. I understand."

"No, I'm sorry, Claude, we're all tired. Please, just find a way to get er done."

"Oh, Colonel Levins, do you have any preferences?" asked the Class VI Officer.

"Colonel, I am a traditionalist, so make the issue heavy on rum and a few cases of Rebel Yell Whiskey thrown in. I suspicion that a daily rum ration will go a long way for morale. I'd say half an ounce per day for 400 troops for a year. They'll be making their own by then, I reckon."

"Colonel Levins, that's a lot of rum, but we'll do our best."

"Damn, why can't I get through to you people," shouted the General, "I said give him what he wants. I don't care if you have to take an armed team and rob a liquor store. GET IT DONE! That's the phrase for this mission. Please do not make me say it again," growled General Chalmers.

"No, sir," answered his Staff Officers almost in unison as they scuttled out of the room.

"Now, for you, Colonel Levins, I want you to get at least six hours sleep. Captain Wainwright will wake you in time for a shower.

"Oh, Colonel Levins, do you have any of those fancy Dan Army gizmos, you know like jump wings, CIB, that sort of thing?"

"Why yes, sir I do. Jump wings, CIB and 25th Infantry combat patch."

"Captain Wainwright, find this man a uniform that fits, complete with jump wings, C.I.B., and the 25th Infantry Division patch."

"Of course, sir, I'll get it done," replied Cpt. Wainwright.

"One other thing, Colonel Levins, I would prefer not to issue regulation Marine BDUs (Battle Dress Uniforms), should some fall into the hands of a Warlord. I don't want people thinking the Marine's had turned into bad guys.

"Do you mind if we issue Iraqi uniforms to you? We have probably sixty-thousand of them in storage."

"Not at all sir, new beginnings, new uniforms, and I do agree with your logic."

As Levi slept Captain Wainwright was very busy, as were all of the senior staff officers who were dedicated to this mission.

"Initially, it appeared that the vehicle requirement could be limited to around six to ten, but with the addition of the Training Battalion Vehicles, the final tally came out to thirty-six serviceable deuce and a half and eighteen five tons. We've also got some old jeeps from the 60's if you want them."

As the staff officers screamed for volunteers that met the General's requirements, they were surprised to find that nearly everyone realized the importance of this mission. There was no shortage of volunteers, and some of the more senior NCOs were downright disappointed. Some even asked to be busted down to E-1.

Work proceeded through the night at a rapid pace. Each staff officer had his orders and conveyed these to his NCOs. The NCOs then proceeded to fulfill their portion of the General's direction, and within six hours only the rum ration and about ½ of the ammo remained unfilled. Munitions were certainly available; there just were not enough trucks or trailers.

Teams of Military Police were busy visiting liquor stores and cleaning out their supplies of rum. By 0830 hours all tasks were completed but for the remaining ammunition, and all vehicles were lined up in the proper order.

A new and bitter dark age was sweeping the world, and these new Defiance Militia volunteers were intent on not allowing that darkness to roll over them. They were prepared to do their duty, whatever that duty may be.

Generals Alexander A. Vandegrift, USMC and George S. Patton, US Army would have been proud.

21 APRIL 0850
MAIN GATE
CAMP LEJEUNE

Lieutenant Colonel Murtaugh walked with Levi to the convoy and said, "Levi, Lord have mercy, but you make that Iraqi gray uni look good."

Levi smiled and said, "Yeah, well I thank you for getting it all 'fancy Danned' up for me, yeah, I kinda' like it myself. I just hope our gate guards don't start shooting at the arrival of the Iraqi Army or for that matter a new Confederate Army what with us all so sartorially dressed in gray."

"Yeah well, you da man. Look, I am sorry that we simply did not have sufficient trans assets to totally fulfill your ammo request. We have however put a secondary plan into motion.

General Chalmers has asked me to give you this list of addresses and the combinations to every armory on this base, and here is a set of keys to the front gate and every armory door. Those armories are right now being stocked with ammunition and weapons resupply. Two of those armories showing a star beside the address hold medical supplies. Each armory door is secured by a combination series of locks. The keys will unlock the secure heavy-duty padlocks, which are bolt-cutter proof.

"Now, these doors are designed to be grenade proof. Of course, we have no idea if this will ultimately secure them for your use at some later date, but it was all we could think of to try to help you out. My guess is that others will quickly move onto the base, so sooner is better than later.

"The General has also asked me to give you this box. I have no idea what is inside, but he was misty-eyed when he had it loaded onto my vehicle, so it must be something close to his heart."

"Damn, Gus I don't know what to say other than thank you and that we will be, *always faithful* (Semper Fi) to the ideals of the Corps and with our mission.

"Listen, Gus, if you are ever over our way, I promise there will always be a place for you and your family."

Lieutenant Colonel Murtaugh was nearly overcome by the emotion of this offer, coupled with what he must do, today…the last day for the United States Marine Corps in North Carolina. Within another three days, the entire military structure of the USA would crumble, as Lieutenant General Chalmers said, into dust in the wind and cease to exist.

"Levi, I cannot thank you enough for your offer, but my family is in Western Kentucky in a little town called Philpot. I'll be heading out to the base stables and saddling up the horse I have there, and if there are any left, I'll take a couple as pack animals.

"It will be wise for someone traveling alone to stay off the highways for years to come, so I'll just sidle across country on my old horse, Tugboat.

"Oh, I almost forgot, I slipped in enough MREs to take care of the fifty Marin…er, I mean new Troopers in Defiance for a month should they create an initial food concern.

"Goodbye Levi, I am glad I met you, and may God Bless you and Defiance."

Levi almost choked up but managed to say, "Gus, I can never thank you enough. What you have done may mean the difference between the success or failure of Defiance.

"The written history of Defiance will include a large chapter on the generosity of the USMC. We will never forget.

"Good bye my friend and remember the offer will always be open to you."

Then, not knowing what else to do, they shook hands, hugged and turned to walk toward their independent destinies.

The explosions at the ammo dump rattled the windows and marked the final demise as the United States Marine Corps, dressed in civilian clothes, along with their families began departing Camp Lejeune, North Carolina for the last time…well, for most of them…

That morning, 23 April, at 1155 hours Lieutenant General Paul Chalmers, in his Dress Blue Uniform rose from his desk. He looked out the window and saw the last of his command pass through the gate, armed with a sidearm, two magazines, and three MREs. He watched as Lieutenant Colonel Gus Murtaugh tied his horses to the gate, turned toward the Headquarters Building, and presented one final salute to his General and his United States Marine Corps.

General Chalmers returned the salute, and now was alone on Camp Lejeune. He neatly squared away his hat on the corner of the desk covering a hand-written note, then pulled the coat rack behind his chair. He hung his winter coat in such a manner that it was partially open. He then drew his sidearm and sat behind his desk. He checked the coat to ensure that it was directly behind him. His final act was to place the barrel of his sidearm into his mouth and pull the trigger.

No one was there to hear the single pistol shot.

All glory is fleeting…

CHAPTER EIGHTEEN

Locusts

23 April
Best Western Motel
Drivers Store, NC

The Double R stopped for several days in the small bedroom community of Drivers Store. There were fewer refugees on the road through this small village, and from here Cruz could send out raiding parties to the other towns in Wilson County. They had picked up several old cars and trucks that would run. These vehicles were reserved for scouting and raiding; besides, Romeo liked his carriage.

Scouting parties were to find and recruit other gangs to increase his army, which had now swelled to nearly two hundred fighters and three hundred slaves. Recruiting went well as the food supplies were drying up elsewhere.

Cruz had decided to annex a line of farms along his route to the coast to initiate a food supply line. Those families were reduced to slavery. They were not, however, forced to eat human flesh since he needed these slaves.

Several gangs from larger cities, both Black and Latino were potential threats to Cruz, so they became his shock troops whenever they faced armed resistance.

The weapons situation had improved, but there was still a huge shortage of military-style assault weapons. The only one who seemed to have them were those locals willing to fight rather than surrender. Casualties were high, but recruitment eased that burden.

A favorite tactic was to march women and children slaves in front of his soldiers when attacking a fortified position. The defenders often could not bring themselves to shoot. This began to change once word got out that the slaves were cannibals.

The Rican Rogues or The Double R as they came to be known were like locusts. They scoured the land for food, abused, murdered, and enslaved everyone they came across. Slaves were chained, and usually left in the open during the night, come rain or shine, but for some unknown reason he had them moved into the multiplex theater.

Romeo Cruz was a King; perhaps even a god…life was good.

They remained in Drivers Store for five days before, once again returning to their march to the sea.

Word of their approach began to reach those along their route. While the RR was a large and formidable force, they were very susceptible to sniping attacks. Locals would take a few shots then disappear back into the pines. This began to take a toll on the morale, and the number of fighters. Their resident doctor, also a cannibal slave, treated the wounded.

He would often allow a wound to fester into gangrene and announce that he would have to amputate the injured limb. Romeo, however, had no inclination to have soldiers with missing limbs, so he ordered them shot and then buried with gangsta honor.

Each soldier was buried with two of his slaves. Romeo had heard of something similar being done for the old Pharaohs of Egypt and he liked the idea. No soldier was left on the ground among the untold millions of stinking dead all around them. The burials helped morale to some small degree. As the rat population exploded, no one wanted to be left on the ground to the rats. It did not seem to occur to any of them that they were being left to the worms.

CHAPTER NINETEEN

The Horse Cavalry

Colonel Levins' Office
Defiance

First Sergeant Cobb tapped on Colonel Levins door and said, "Sir? I've got Mr. Leon Pickett here to see you.

"Oh, good, I'm glad he could make it so quickly. Please send him in. I want you in here too, First Sergeant.

"Roger, sir. Mr. Pickett would you, please come into Colonel Levins' Office?" asked the First Sergeant.

Leon Pickett, a 35-year-old man of average height, a face already showing lines from years in a saddle in the North Carolina sun, entered the Colonel's Office dressed in riding boots, jeans, plaid shirt, and cowboy hat in hand.

Levi's first impression was a strong-willed individual more comfortable in the saddle than on his feet. This image was heightened by the fact that Leon Pickett appeared to be so bowlegged that he couldn't stop a pig in the middle of the road. Both the Colonel and his First Sergeant liked him immediately.

Levi rose, walked around his desk, and approached this man with the extended hand of welcome.

"Mr. Pickett, I am truly glad to meet you." said a broad smiling Colonel Levins. "I presume you know why I've asked you here, so let's get to know each other before getting down to business.

First Sergeant, please ask the clerk to bring in a pot of coffee, and some of Cook's fresh muffins."

"Roger that, sir." First Sergeant Cobb went to the door, and called to his clerk, "Corporal Jones, please see about getting some coffee and muffins in here." Corporal Jones, a young man of 25, standing 5'9" with a disarming smile, grinned at his First Sergeant and replied, "Already on the way, Top. Be back in a couple of minutes."

"Thanks, pal, and grab one for yourself, too," smiled the First Sergeant.

"Thanks, Top; like I wouldn't anyway."

All three took their coffee black. Leon looked up after stuffing a bite of muffin in his mouth. He looked over at Levi and said, "Genrul, my puhsonal background is pretty simple. I grew up 'bout 10 miles from here ovuh in Miller's Ford. Got me a bachelor's degree from North Carolina in animal husbandry. Back then, I thought I might be a vet, but it didn't take me long before I realized I was better settin' on a horse than lookin' up its ass. So, I come back here, and here's where I stayed. 'Cept for three years in the Army over in Baumholder, Germany. Cavalry Officer, a course, to First Lieutenant.

"Genrul, as you know, I ramrod the Lykes Brothers Ranch. Now they hain't much been around for years, but ever' year, one of their accountants comes by and goes over the books with my bookkeeper. Now, from what I can glean from the lack of any TV or radio, I'd guess that since they're in New York. It would seem to me that it is unlikely we'll ever see 'em again.

"So, with that in mind, I figure you'll want access to that 400 head of cattle, and 40 quarter horses, plus, we got wild hogs we're feedin' out.

"To run the spread, I got me sixteen employees, one bookkeeper, one cook, one blacksmith, one mechanic with a state-of-the-art equipment-shed, two fence riders, and ten all-around cowboys, who do all the other ridin' work on the place.

So, the way I see it, Genrul Levins, is that the spread is probably going to end up as mine. However, since y'all called me down here, so I figger you plan on takin' it away from me. That so?"

Colonel Levins smiled and said, "Tell me, Leon, how often does that good old country boy, down home dialectic crap really work? I mean, hell, it surely does sound real homey, and you know damned well I'm a Colonel, not a General."

Leon Pickett smiled impishly at the Colonel and sneaked a peek over at the First Sergeant saying, "Actually sir, you'd be surprised how often that poor old dumb Southern country boy routine puts Yankees at ease. Moreover, it often gives me a bit of an advantage. I hope it didn't put you off?"

"Leon, I think we're going to get along fine.

"Here's the deal from my perspective. As far as I'm concerned the spread is yours, but I need you, your ranch hands, your expertise, and everything you've got on that spread.

"Times have changed dramatically, and I do not see it going back to what we used to consider normal in our lifetime, and probably not in our grandchildren's lifetime.

"I never thought I would say this, but I need horse cavalry, and I need it yesterday. It sounds to me like you've got a good start, with ten troopers. We need a hundred.

"I'm willing to reinstate your commission to First Lieutenant. When you have forty mounted cavalry, I will make you a Captain. Get five hundred, and you'll be a Lieutenant Colonel.

When his mess is over, if it ever is, and there's no legal claim by the Lykes Brothers themselves, then this spread is yours. Fair enough?"

"And if I say no? What happens then?" asked Leon.

"Levi leaned across the desk, his eyes becoming blue steel. "Then, Mr. Pickett we have a problem that I see no easy way to fix. Please do not misunderstand me. I do not want to take over your ranch. What we do want can be summed up as allies.

"We do *not* want to take your beef or horses. We *do* want to trade for them.

"What we want is for you and your cowboys to join the Defiance Militia and form Troop B, Mounted Cavalry.

"Leon, you must understand that if you turn us down, we are not going to attack you or steal what you have. What we will do is deny any support when, not if, but when your very tempting spread is attacked. Then we'll go in and take it away from those who killed you.

"The bottom line is you need us, and we need you. Together we are a strong force, separate…not so much."

"That's not what I figured you would say. In fact, it is a much better offer than I expected. I agree with every aspect of your rationale and proposal, but for the record, just how long are we signing up for?"

"Lieutenant, I figure you'll be old, dead and buried before you see the end of your enlistment. No, wait… I can be a bit more definitive, we'll retire when our Alzheimer's kicks in. So, whadaya say?"

Leon began to smile and said, "Sir, please tell me more of how you see our future playing out."

"Well, LT, we figure that a Coronal Mass Ejection from our sun just squeaked by without making a direct hit on the Earth… so, there you have it. We are calling this, year zero, but for your reference, I'd say our way of life could become historically similar to around 1850. You in?"

"OK, Colonel, I believe you. Do we get cavalry uniforms?"

Colonel Levins smiled, stuck out his hand to now First Lieutenant Pickett, and asked, "Gray or Blue?"

"Well, sir, I can sign up thirty or forty cowboys born to the saddle within, say, three days…"

Levi sat up in his chair and said, "Did you say, thirty or forty? This is North Carolina, not Texas. Are there that many cowboys in North Carolina?"

"Oh, yes sir, there are over five thousand cattle ranches in North Carolina, and probably half a million cattle are now up for grabs. You know, people think of cowboys as being from out west, but we're here, too. The thing is, you just can't see us from the road."

Levi sat back and said, "Sorry for interrupting, please continue."

"Yes, sir, as I was sayin' all of them were born to the saddle, right here in eastern North Carolina.

"My guess is that all of them would prefer the gray of their ancestors. Sir, please forgive me for askin', but what kind'a gray uniform are all y'all wearin'. You know, with just a tweak or two like addin' a yella stripe down the legs, suspenders and a yella kerchief. Truth is, I like the color of the uniform that you're wearing'."

Levi looked at his First Sergeant and smiled broadly, saying, "Top, looks like we've got a bunch of Rebels on our hands. Whadaya think?"

"Yes sir, but if you're asking me, I'd say we're all Rebels. I can't say these uni's make us look like the U.S. Army. I mean, hell, most of our vehicles are painted in Iraqi colors, our uniforms are already gray, and to top it off, now we're going to build horse cavalry. But, please, son, no Confederate Battle Flags, huh?"

Laughing now, Colonel Levins said, "LT, my First Sergeant is right, no Confederate flags. We want to look to the future, not the past. We'll also be renaming our nation, complete with a new flag. I guess both Old Glory and the Stars and Bars are relegated to history. They deserve respect and remembrance, but they will not be resurrected in Defiance. Other than that, I have no problem with your uniform design.

As to our gray uniforms, well, since there is no more USA, we didn't want to be seen as a rogue U.S. military force trying to set up our own little Kingdom. So, we decided, with help from the United States Marine Corps to start from scratch. Our uniforms were Iraqi, from the Saddam era. We have a lot of them. Personally, I like them a hell of a lot better than those ugly assed old camo BDU's."

"Yes sir, I agree, they do look pretty good. So, when do I get sworn in?"

The swearing in ceremony will take place once you have your thirty recruits. It will be done before the entire population of Defiance, but consider yourself in, and I welcome you to what the XO and I think of, as The Sheepdog Brigade."

"Fair enough, Colonel, shall we just come ridin' in about Thursday, or would you like some notice?"

"Do you think you'll make that number in only three days?"

"Yes sir, I've already had mor'un thirty ask to sign up if I thought you was offerin' us a square deal."

Levi told his newest Lieutenant that the village would hold the ceremony on the Village Green. Oh, and let's change the name of your ranch from Lykes Brothers to Fort Pickett."

Lieutenant Pickett liked the idea and agreed to join the Defiance Militia.

"Top, when we're finished here, take LT Pickett to the tailor and let's get this uniform thing sorted out. I want them all alike. No individuality where uniforms are concerned. I want complete unit integrity. Any questions about that?"

"Gotcha' sir, I see no problem with getting this sorted out. We'll git 'er done," said First Sergeant Cobb.

"Good, now Lieutenant Pickett, we need to discuss logistics and requirements. Families are okay. If you need housing for your Cavalry Platoon, we'll get some manufactured quarters in there, stat.

English is the required language, not suggested, required, with no exceptions. I do not care what their race or nationality was, repeat was. Everyone is a citizen of Defiance. No Mexicans, Irish, African Americans, just citizen of Defiance. I hope I am clear on this. While everyone is both respected and needed, I am going to discriminate against anyone who does not speak English, by discrimination I mean that they will not be eligible to be citizens, members of our military, or have a voice in how things are run, and I mean they will have no input. We are in survival mode and can't afford sub-cultures or division. None of these policies are negotiable, Roger that?"

"Sir, while some of the cowboys on my ranch, and others, are of Mexican and African origin, and damned near all the rest of us think we come from Irish stock; we all speak excellent Southern English. I also completely agree with your decision on this. So, yes sir, Roger that," said a very serious Lieutenant Pickett.

"Oh, Colonel, do you and the First Sergeant ride?" asked his newest Lieutenant.

"Well, now that you mention it, yes, I do, how about you, First Sergeant?"

The First Sergeant began squirming in his seat, and for the first time since the Colonel had met him. First Sergeant Bradley Cobb looked truly uncomfortable. He said, "Well sir, there was that pony ride as a kid. Beyond that, I can't really say that I do."

Lieutenant Pickett, smiled broadly and said, "Don't worry Top, we can fix that. In fact, Colonel, I've got a workin' horse that the First Sergeant will like just fine, so you better send him on over to our place to learn to ride."

"Roger that, Top get on his schedule."

"Yes, sir, saddle sore central, I can see it now," said a somewhat woeful First Sergeant.

Lieutenant Pickett laughed and told the First Sergeant that he might also want to have some soothing salve on hand for his chaffed thighs.

The Colonel leaned back in his chair and said, "On a more serious note, Leon, when do you think you can field twenty men? I want mounted patrols up and running ASAP."

"Friday, sir, ya' see ever one of us is a Civil War reenactor. We have spent many a long day practicing how to fight as both Cavalry and dismounted Infantry."

Levi started laughing and just could not contain his pleasure to know that his Cavalry was already trained.

"First Sergeant, what will it take to get the uniforms together, that these boys want?"

"Well sir, we'll get with the tailors. The suspenders we can probably get from our Wal-Mart.

Okay, let's get over to the Wal-Mart to get the suspenders these boys need. Now Leon, can I assume you all have the cavalry boots and hats you need?

First Sergeant, don't we have some gold hat braid we got from the military sales stores?"

The First Sergeant sat up and said, "Yes sir, come to think of it, we do, but no cavalry style uniform hats."

"Sir," interrupted Lieutenant Pickett, "like I said, we are reenactors. We've done got the uniforms, but I'd sure like to transition to your lightweight gray as quickly as possible.

Colonel, there are also a couple of indulgences that I would ask you to consider."

"Uh oh," said Levi, "go ahead Lieutenant Pickett and what would those indulgences be, exactly?"

"Well, sir, it's our belt buckles, the only ones we have that work have CSA on them. It's the same with our hats. Oh, and just one other little thing sir, all of our boys are partial to their lever action 30/30s, and their side arms. You've just gotta remember sir; these are old-fashioned cowboys. I mean, hell, sir. We still carry Colt 45 peacemakers. Do you have any objections to them?" asked Lieutenant Pickett.

"None whatsoever for the weapons Lieutenant, but with one caveat, those sidearm's will be worn on the left side in a covered holster, and you will keep a regulation 9 mil service pistol in web gear and holster along with a basic load of ammo in your saddlebags. You will also add an additional boot for an M4-A1 Carbine. Can you arrange that?"

"Yes sir, but what about the buckles and the hat pins?"

"For now, I'll allow the buckles, but the hat pins are to be changed to the Cross Sabers of Cavalry, and yes, we have a large number of them."

Lieutenant Pickett was so pleased that he was nearly squirming from pure joy, and said, "Sir, while it's true that we all have fun with QuickDraw rigs, all of us have covered holster's that we mostly wear on the left side except for the left-handed boys. We've also got Sam Browne belts.

"Agreed, but you just remember that we are not reorganizing the Confederate States of America or J. E. B. Stuart's Cavalry. However, just between us chickens, my great, great, great, great grandpa was a major in Stuart's cavalry. He was killed in the Wilderness Campaign after Gettysburg.

See what ch'all can find fo these Southun Genelmen, Fust Sarnt." laughed Colonel Levins.

"Roger that, sir," chuckled the First Sergeant".

"Good, now back to my question Lieutenant When can you really field twenty men?"

"Colonel, I really can have them mounted up by the time you get us all sworn in. First patrols and availability of force first thing Friday mornin'. Sir, I just hope you're able to understand and accept the fact that Southern Cowboys are just a little bit different. I'll have more men anxious to sign up than we can probably handle. There's also a bunch of Black Cowboys around, and with your permission, we'll be seein' if they would like to join up."

"I am very glad you brought this subject up. I certainly am glad to hear that you would ask your black peers to join your troop. I meant what I said about each and every one of us being citizens of Defiance. That racial bullshit is over, and if there is anyone who can't make the adjustment, then they will be escorted outside the twenty-mile perimeter of our new nation."

"And I am equally glad to hear that sir, 'cause the only problems we have ever had with blacks in our lifetime were outsiders causing trouble, you know like those fools out'a Raleigh.

We been raised with the predominantly black communities and honestly, white nor black don't mean shit to us. Yes, sir, you'll have no problems on that score, at least not from anyone raised round here."

To us, it's a new beginning. It's like we're being offered the chance to return to a time that we have only been able to dream about. No matter what the weather, we'll ride for the brand. And sir, Defiance is that brand. We'll make you proud sir," said a now somber Lieutenant Pickett.

"All right Lieutenant, as soon as you get them together and we get your new troopers in uniform we'll get the patrols started. You are going to have to give us a few days to teach them about the military, how to salute, rank structure, and our expectations of you.

"You're going to have to prove to me that you can ride in formation. That you can dismount, form a defensive perimeter, and fight as infantry. Can you do that?" asked an equally somber Colonel Levins.

"Should be no problem, sir, damn near everone of these men have at least three years of military service, and mostly combat arms."

"Well First Sergeant, it do appear we got us some cavalry."

"Yes, sir, I think we do." smiled the First Sergeant.

"All right, let me escort the two of you to the door. Get him to the tailors and the clothing store," said Colonel Levins as he stood up.

"Sir, yes sir," said both the First Sergeant and newly commissioned Lieutenant Pickett. Both also saluted in unison.

Levi looked at the First Sergeant and said, "He'll do Top, He'll do," and returned their salute sharply.

After Lieutenant Pickett and the First Sergeant had departed, Levi returned to his desk, put his head between his hands and prayed, "God, I think we can do this. These are good men and women gathering here, and with your continued help, I believe we can build a better world," and with that Levi rose from his chair and left the office.

As the Colonel entered the orderly room, Corporal Jones jumped to attention and was immediately signaled by the Colonel to sit back down.

"Jonesy, I'll be in my quarters, send a runner over in two hours.

"Oh, yeah, tell the First Sergeant and the XO that I want to have a luncheon meeting. We'll meet in the mess tent."

He assured the Colonel that he would send a runner in two hours and would get word to the First Sergeant and XO about the meeting. He also asked if there was anything that the Colonel needed.

As Levi walked out the door, he said over his shoulder, "I think I need a little rest, Jonesy. I guess I'm just feeling a bit tired today."

Like all the members of this new Defiance Militia, Corporal Jones felt honored to serve with his Colonel. However, he did not like the look of the stooped shoulders on this man who carried such a heavy weight.

"Sam," said Corporal Jones, to his runner. "Truck on over to supply and tell Doc Faith that the Colonel's going to his quarters. She might want to check on him." He then returned to his paperwork, saying, "Man, this army is growing so fast. By next week I'll need two new clerks just to keep up with the records and duty rosters."

As the First Sergeant walked Lieutenant Pickett over to the tailors, he said, "Coupla' quick things you should know LT; first of all, you're in debt to me for one dollar as it's customary to give one silver dollar to whoever gets your first salute, and that would be me." With that, he presented a crisp parade ground salute and held out his hand for a dollar.

Leon smiled and said, "Do you take credit cards, Top? 'Cause I don't have any cash with me today, or any silver dollars."

"Certainly, sir, we'll likely be issuing chits for things a bit down the road. You can pay me with that."

"Deal, Top; dang, I'm in the Army for five minutes and I'm already in debt. Wait! What's your interest rate?" laughed Leon.

The First Sergeant slapped First Lieutenant Pickett on the back and said, "Oh, we'll figure something out," and laughing, both continued on their mission.

Secondly, this new job you've got is not a game, or a joke, please don't forget that, sir. The Army's Uniform Code of Military Justice is alive and well. Please make sure your troopers know and understand this fact.

I also suggest that you might want to begin thinking in the long term. What we have right now is the new normal. You're in the Army now, sir, for the duration.

Oh, sir, please don't forget your haircut," smiled a much amused First Sergeant Cobb.

"First Sergeant, it is what it is, and all it takes is all we got with maybe just a little bit more. My men and I will be there for whatever the Colonel believes we need to do. And, my friend, you have my word on it. But do I really have to get a haircut?" laughed Lieutenant Pickett.

"Youuuu betcha," chuckled his guide, as they entered what had been two semi-truck containers, which had been pushed together side to side and the center walls removed.

CHAPTER TWENTY

Skirmish at Wally World

24 April 0500
Walmart occupied by Troop A
Tree line fronting Parking Lot

Ten men, thieves and con men from before the darkness who traveled from New York to Florida each year following the seasons, watched the front entrance to Wally World.

Red Farnum, the leader of this merry band, had been having a wonderful time since the lights went out. The world was now their oyster. They had amassed a huge fortune in paper money and jewels, along with all the other valuables that had paid for their traveling lifestyle for many years.

Now they set their eyes on what was, to them, the crown jewel of supplies…Walmart.

This was not the first of the big chain stores they had cased, but gangs that did not play nice had owned the others. Here the ownership was not to a gang that would take a hammer and gleefully break every bone in one's body, starting with the toes and working up.

"No, here were just some local yokels who liked to play army, and from everything that Red and his cronies could see, the Rubes were asleep at the wheel.

"Slim, it looks like we can take the whole thing if we just slip up quietly and take out the guards, then go in and eliminate the threat. We grab what we need, and it's back on the road again."

"Yeah, looks like a piece of cake, *fa gid a bout it*, let's get to it before they wake up."

"Good thinkin', get the boys started, we'll ease through the cars in the lot and be on 'em before they know what's happening."

-

"Shultz, go wake up Sergeant Guy, we got company trying to sneak in."

"Yeah? Hey, let me see through your night vision monocle."

"Sure, here ya' go. Can you see 'em trying to sneak around the cars? I count ten, Whadaya see?"

Shultz counted in a whisper and said, "Yeah, Moose, I agree with ten. Hold tight while I go get the Sarge."

Moose gently shook Sergeant Guyardo. He came instantly awake and asked, "What is it? That you, Moose?"

"Yeah Sarge, it's me. Listen, we spotted ten guys trying to sneak up on us right through the middle of the parking lot."

Sergeant Guy jumped to his feet and pulling on his boots said, "Thanks, Moose, now I want you to go to the other front entrance and make sure they are aware and ready. Then I want you to go to the other doors and do the same. You got me?"

"Roger that Sarge, warn the other front entrance, then the other positions. On the way," and with that Moose was gone.

Sergeant Guy then saw that the others had heard and were getting dressed. "All right ladies, let's saddle up. This place is ours, and we're going to keep it."

A chorus of, "Roger that," resounded in the darkness as these men prepared for combat."

When Sergeant Guy arrived at the reporting position, he said, "Sitrep."

Corporal Shultz said, "Ten men, civilian clothes, no long guns visible approaching with stealth from the direct front. They are now about twenty cars deep in the parking lot.

"I can't believe it, Sarge; they are moving right into the open kill zone, I mean, it's like they want to get shot or some shit like that."

Guy said, "Damn, what morons. It's pretty obvious they have no military training. I would like one prisoner, maybe a round in the foot, just so it ain't a fatal shot. Can you swing it, Shultz?"

"Yeah, 'course. You got it, Sarge. Where's Moose?"

"He's warning the other positions. He'll be right back. If he says there are more approaching the other positions, send him to find me. I'll be back in a couple of mikes. Roger?"

"Yeah, yeah, Roger, I got it here."

As Guy approached the other main entrance, he heard, "Sergeant Guy, that you?"

"Yeah, did Moose fill you in?"

"Oh yeah, but we got nothin' on our side. Maybe we'll get lucky and not have to fire a shot, we just cleaned our weapons before we came on, and it looks like the SAW was cleaned real good, too."

"Damn, Chuckles, you are such a wuss. I gotta' get back, so sharp eyes, Roger?"

"Gotcha Sarge, oh, are the sleepy heads up and joinin' us?"

"Ayup, they'll be here in a minute."

Red stopped short when he realized why they hadn't seen any walking guards. They were behind sandbagged walls. "Shit, Slim, I wonder if they really are asleep."

"A'course they are. You seen any movement anywhere? If they knew we was here they'da started shootin' or at least we'd see movement by bringin' other boys up. Hell, it's quiet as a tomb in there. We caught 'em nappin', Red. Come on, let's go."

"Yeah, you're probly right. I'm not happy about crossing the road right in front of them, but if there's no movement then I think we got 'em. Let's go."

When the attackers had made their way to the last car before the open road, Red whispered to his men, Slim and I will cover you. Go ahead and take 'em out."

-

"Moose, did I just hear someone whisper over there behind the first car?"

Moose said, "I can't believe it, but yeah, I'm ready, you?"

"Born ready."

The sandbagged position was built with a firing port for the SAW. Moose waited, finger along the trigger guard just waiting for the group to show themselves."

Within seconds the attackers began a slow crouched march across no man's land. When they were right in the middle of the street, Moose heard the word…fire. The eight men crossing the street immediately fell to the ground dead or horribly wounded.

Rounds from the SAW also struck the car Red and Slim were hiding behind. Red was luckily behind the engine block, but Slim was not so fortunate. The fire from the SAW tore through the car doors and killed him right away.

Red was racked by a terrible fear and immediately shouted, "I give up, don't shoot!"

Sergeant Guy said in a calm voice, "Ok, weapons to the ground, place your hands on your head, stand and turn your back to us, then sidle sideways until you get to the car lane and begin backing up to us. Do it now or die!"

Red followed these instructions readily; this wasn't his first arrest rodeo.

"Now stop and kneel on the ground."

Once Red was cuffed, Sergeant Guy said, "Moose, grab the jeep and get General Patton here out to Defiance, and take Sterling with you to guard this dumbass."

"Roger that, Sarge," and Moose was off the get the jeep.

Red was a bit confused when he heard four pistol shots; then the bodies were placed in the bed of a pickup and taken out to the main road where they were hanged with signs around their necks saying:

"THESE MEN WERE MURDERERS AND THIEVES.
WE WOULD ADVISE THAT YOU KEEP MOVING;
AND DO NOT MESS WITH TROOP A."

THIS IS A PUBLIC SERVICE ANNOUNCEMENT
BROUGHT TO YOU BY
TROOP A, DEFIANCE MILITIA

After Red had been ushered into the Troop A Interrogation room, Levi asked him, "Name?"

"Huh, aren't you going to read me my rights first? That's when I say drop dead, I want an attorney."

"Funny boy, huh Top?"

"Oh, yes sir, funny boy."

Levi asked him several questions, and after being convinced that the law played by a new set of rules these days, he answered everything fully.

Levi then said, Well Red, you are charged with attempted murder, a crime punishable by hanging by the neck until you are dead, how do you plead?"

"What, hanging? You can't do that. Don't I even get a trial?"

"Actually Red, what you do get is a Military Tribunal, and I'm the Judge, and my First Sergeant here is the jury. Your Defense Attorney is Sergeant Juan Miguel Dominique Mesa Garcia Guyardo. You remember, the Sergeant in charge of all the men you planned to kill. I asked him if he had a defense planned for you and he said, 'I got nuthin.' Therefore, I pronounce you guilty and sentence you to be hanged by the neck until you are dead, sentence to be carried out this day at the scene of your crime. May God have mercy upon your soul."

Red's last words were something about his having rights

That afternoon Red was taken to the main drag leading to Defiance at precisely twenty miles out from the Village Green where he was hung by the neck until he was dead.

CHAPTER TWENTY-ONE

The Gift

```
25 April 0730
Levi's Tent
Defiance
```

The dawn sky was streaked with magnificent bright red hues as the sun made a grand appearance. Levi was sure that meant rain by this afternoon or evening.

Levi returned to his tent following PT and a shower. He suddenly remembered the box given him by Lieutenant General Chalmers. It lay on the back seat of his jeep behind the driver.

Trotting out to the jeep he retrieved the box and took it inside his palatial GP Medium Tent. He thought, '*Dang, this box is really heavy.*'

Once back inside he took his K-bar and cut through the hundred mile per hour tape, which secured whatever was inside. Opening the flaps, he saw a note on the top of several layers of old newspaper.

The note read:

23 April xxxx

> *FROM THE DESK OF:*
> *LT GENERAL PAUL CHALMERS*
> *CAMP LEJEUNE, USMC, COMMANDING*

Levi, I want to thank you for promising to mention the United States Marine Corps fondly in the historical record of Defiance.

While you slept, I sat wondering how to further assist your efforts in securing Defiance, even though I think Liberty may have been a better name, then again, the name is none of my business, and it is true that you must remain defiant. Under the packing, you will find the following items, plus a few toys for big boys:

- *My Military ID card in a manila envelope along with a letter addressed To Whom It May Concern.*
- *10 lbs. of C-4*
- *200 blasting caps*
- *2 claymore mines*
- *A further listing of combinations for the locking mechanism securing the Armory doors at Cherry Point (also in the envelope)*
- *Additional keys to fit the high-density security locks for those armory doors*
- *Keys to the front gate for both Cherry Point and Sunny Point*

At Sunny Point, you may find a Philippine-flagged RORO (Roll On/ Roll Off) transport vessel containing, among other things, thousands of solar panels, invertors, and complete electrical hookup boxes. These were purchased from China, of course, to complete the solar installations at Camp Lejeune and Cherry Point.

The ship is named Cortana. I have no idea if Captain Aaron Reyes or any of his crew are still aboard so be careful.

If the Captain and crew are still aboard attempting to repair the CME damage, show him my ID card and the letter. He will turn this cargo over to you.

If he seeks a place to stay with you, I would advise you to welcome him, and his Chief Engineer Adan Ramos. Ramos is a true genius when it comes to machines; running, repairing or inventing.

Levi, it is imperative that you make connections with the Cortana prior to 29 April as the ship is under repair and plans to sail, on, or about, 30 May.

Do not delay; the reward is worth the risk.

The final two items in the box are the USMC flag and my General Officers three-star flag, which hung in my office. It is my hope that they will be saved, and one day placed in a museum. Both are vacuum-sealed, so unless the plastic covering becomes pierced, they should remain safe for many hundreds of years.

May God Bless you, my friend. With deepest respect and regards,

Paul

Paul Lewis Chalmers
Lieutenant General, United States Marine Corps
Camp Lejeune, North Carolina, USA,
Commanding

Levi stood staring at the letter from his newfound friend for several long seconds before laying out the booty from this treasure trove.

Once laid out Levi shouted, "First Sergeant!"

Within seconds the Troop A First Sergeant stuck his head inside Levi's tent and said, "What the f…, sir, where did you get all of these neat toys?"

"Get Jonesy to chase down the Mayor, XO and Staff Sergeant Eldridge then bring them in for planning a new mission."

"Roger sir, on the way…Corporal Jones…"

All three were in the "Dining Facility" having breakfast when Jones found them and informed them of the meeting with Colonel Levins.

"Please, come in gentlemen, oh, you too Top," causing a small chuckle among his guests.

Everyone stood around staring at the contents of the General's gift and wondering from where it had come.

"What you see on the floor, and my desk are the contents of a gift box given to me by Lieutenant General Chalmers. The box also contained some personal items.

"Well, there you have it. We have to make that ship, the *Cortana* our top priority. Those solar kits mean civilization and the power necessary to fight off the darkness around us. Are we all in agreement?"

All heartily agreed, though Staff Sergeant Eldridge asked, "Sir, of course, I agree, but why am I included in this meeting? Should I excuse myself?"

"No Scott, you most certainly may not. You have been invited to this meeting because you are going to lead the mission to begin securing those kits."

"Me? But sir, this is an incredibly important mission, are you sure it's me you want to run it?"

The First Sergeant interrupted and asked, "Staff Sergeant Eldridge, are you suggesting that Colonel Levins has made a mistake as to your qualification for this mission? My bet is he knows a bit better than you who is best qualified. So, shut your pie hole and take some notes. Sorry sir, I just couldn't let that pass."

Smiling Levi said, "Top, I couldn't have said it better myself, though I was preparing to give it a try.

Now, Sergeant Eldridge if you don't mind, I'd kind of like to continue, I mean, with your permission of course."

"Sir, please accept my apologies, it's just that…"

"Didn't you hear the Top Sergeant of this fuster cluck tell you to shut your pie hole and takes notes?"

"Yes, sir."

Now, everyone but an embarrassed and red-faced Staff Sergeant Eldridge broke out laughing. Levi said, "It's okay Scott, relax, we're just pullin' your chain."

"Yes, sir."

"Ok, Ben, your task is to get thirty of those trucks unloaded ASAP, as in today. I want this mission on the road No Later Than 0600 tomorrow. Roger?"

Ben said, "Top, get the dozer fired up and let's move."

"Roger sir, I'll get on the berm prep right after this meeting. Then start a roster for guard duty."

"Good man," said an excited Levi.

"Mayor, do you think you can find sufficient electricians to put on a massive effort to get us up and running when the first trucks get back?"

The Mayor thought for a couple of seconds before saying, "Well, right now we do not have sufficient personnel for a massive effort. We'll see what we can find among the remaining walkers. I sure hope there are some electricians out there, 'cause the walker population is falling fast.

Levi, it was just a few days ago that you said we needed to find the skill positions early on. Man, were you right, but who could have guessed we'd need a large number of electricians so soon? I mean, I didn't even think we'd need more than three or four for another twenty-five years. Anyway, I'll see what we can find.

Can you spare four troopers for a shopping trip to get a gazillion deep cell batteries?"

"We're really tight with this new mission, so if it's okay with you, I would prefer to wait for the batteries until we know exactly what we need. Once we've got the kits, we'll have extra men for the batteries."

"Yes," said Mayor Bassett, "that does make more sense. Good plan, I'm in."

"Ben, work with Top for max effort to have the trucks and equipment ready for the 14th," said Levi.

"Yes, sir."

"Sergeant Eldridge, steal some of the XO's time so he can get everything you need ready. Men, and ammo heavy. The road's still a dangerous place. Roger?"

"Yes sir, Roger that."

Ralph became even more animated and exclaimed, "Hot damn, this is exciting, the return of electric power and hot showers."

Everyone agreed, and Levi added, "We'll call this Operation Bright Light. Any questions? Good then let's get to it. Ralph, would you remain a moment?"

"Sure thing."

After everyone had gone Ralph asked, "What'cha need partner?"

"Ralph, I'd like to place the flags and this letter in your possession for safe keeping. It must be a major piece of our history. Would you take on this mission?"

Ralph looked at the flags secured in the heavy plastic air tight containers and said, "Colonel Levins, I would be more than honored. I am, well, I just don't have the words right now, but yes sir, I've got this. Damn Levi, if I don't get out of here right now, I'm gonna' cry right in front of you."

"I know my friend, I feel exactly the same, so get the hell out of here before we both start blubbering," and with that Ralph nearly fled the tent after using great reverence to pick up the flags.

Levi then lay upon his cot for a while and did shed some tears for the demise of America's 9-1-1.

CHAPTER TWENTY-TWO

What is Money? Trust

27 April 0900
Bank Manager's Office
1ˢᵗ National Bank

Mr. Harold Kearns didn't look the part of Chairman of the Board of the 1ˢᵗ National Bank. After two months of no electricity, no car, no water, and no contact with the Federal Reserve Bank, Harold was frightened, and it made him realize that he was way, way out of his element.

Just two months ago Mr. Harold Kearns was a most respected man, and he knew it. His world was ordered just like the Teller's cash-on-hand sheets he personally reviewed at the end of each workday.

Suddenly, in a flash of light, he had become one of the lost. He no longer had funds, servants, a country club, or any of the position things that had so defined his life.

His wife, Eleanor was in San Francisco, California visiting her sister when the lights went out, and there had been no word from her.

Now, alone, totally lost, and defeated, he could not comprehend what to do, so he sat in his office waiting for contact from the Federal Reserve.

Knowing full well that his prayer would never be answered, it seemed at this moment that the .38 caliber Smith & Wesson Police Special short barreled revolver was his only exit from this unending torment of a nightmare. It lay on his desktop, and to Harold's mind, it was the only thing working in his world. He began to reach out for the pistol when he heard someone walking through the bank toward his office.

A week earlier and he could not have imagined the effrontery of some unknown person approaching his door without first passing through members of his managerial staff. Why; it had been unthinkable.

Now, Harold hoped it was a thief coming to rob the bank and kill its Chairman. Harold placed the revolver in his lap.

Mayor Ralph Bassett smiled as he entered the dimly lit inner office, illuminated only by a hissing Coleman lantern.

"Good morning, sir, my name is Mayor Ralph Bassett of the Township of Defiance. May I inquire as to your name?"

Harold did not bother to stand; he simply nodded for Ralph to sit down, though his curiosity was piqued. "My name is Mr. Harold Kearns, and until the lights went out, I was the Chairman of this bank and its largest stockholder. Since there is no more bank, and money is worthless, I must say that I cannot even begin to fathom what business we could possibly have to discuss, but in the interest of courtesy, and my lack of anything else to do, I am, as they say, all ears."

Ralph smiled in a most friendly manner and asked, "Harold, oh, may I call you Harold?"

Harold Kearns displayed the hint of a smile; the first in a month. "Before this damnable collapse, I would have had you thrown out, but now Harold seems entirely appropriate. What was it you came to see me about, Mr. uh, excuse me I do not recall your name? Please be kind enough to repeat it for me."

"Of course," said Ralph, "My name is Ralph Bassett, please call me Ralph, and I am the Mayor of Defiance.

"I have come to discuss a business proposition, no, perhaps that is an over simplification. What I want to discuss is a new beginning, to avoid a step into the abyss of civilization's demise. Would you like me to continue, or shall I leave you to your thoughts of what to do with that pistol in your lap?"

The Chairman of the Board of the 1st National Bank of North Carolina realized he was speaking to an educated and even cultured man. This man spoke most elegantly. A spark of hope was kindled in Harold Kearns…still… "Sir, I have never heard of your Defiance Township, so if this is a ruse to rob the bank, I can only say…have at it. Would you like me to open the vault for you? There is, of course, a way around the electronic locking mechanism when power is off for more than twenty-four hours. You may take what you wish, not that it will do you any good since the cash on hand is worthless."

Ralph sat back in his chair and said, "No Harold, robbing your bank is the furthest thing from my mind. Please bear with me, and I will tell you of our plan to create an oasis of civilization. We…"

When Ralph finished, he looked at Harold Kearns and said, "Sir, a huge piece of our little puzzle is the acquisition of precious metals to provide a new currency. With that, we can initiate trade, as opposed to the limitations of barter with other communities in our area, and beyond.

We need you, Harold, to be the Secretary of the Treasury of Defiance. So, the only question is, are you willing to take a chance on rebuilding America, or sit here and die of self-inflicted lead poisoning?"

Kearns took a few seconds before responding, "Ralph, on the surface this plan of yours seems totally insane, but in truth what have I got to lose other than my now worthless life? Is there room in your little birthplace of a new world for an old man who has nowhere else to go, except possibly to hell?"

Ralph stood and leaning over Harold's desk offered his hand and said, "Harold, there is a hot shower waiting for you, and hot food. I can't vouch for the taste factor, as our new community Mess Hall will not be online for another three or four days, but don't worry, food is plentiful."

Harold also stood to take Ralph's hand as his revolver slipped, forgotten, from his lap. "Ralph, I accept, and may I say your timing is impeccable, two minutes later and…well, let's just say your arrival was, indeed precipitous."

…so, this is how it feels to have a prayer answered in the last second, thought Harold Kearns. God had sent the Cavalry in the form of the Mayor of a new town.

Harold added, "Now I have a surprise for you, my new-found friend, there are two safes in this bank, one large vault for the cash to impress the account holders, and a second somewhat smaller hidden safe that currently holds two hundred pounds of gold, silver, and platinum.

I realize, of course, that two hundred pounds is not a huge quantity to fund a new currency, but I know where there is more, and I know how we can get to it, that is, if you think it would help," laughed Mr. Harold Kearns, Secretary of the Treasury of Defiance, "Come, let me show you."

CHAPTER TWENTY-THREE

Sunny Point

28 April 0600
Defiance War Room
Defiance

The convoy crossed the Line of Departure on time and made their way to Cherry Point along Hwy 64 Alt to US 258 S. This route would have been far more difficult before the CME, but now with so few vehicles on the road, the going was much faster.

The convoy consisted of 20 M-85, 5-Ton trucks with six machine-gun mounted jeeps. The lead jeep was the scout, followed by an M-85 with a dozer blade mounted to push aside stalled vehicles. Every fifth vehicle was an armed jeep, followed up by the tail gunner.

There had been far fewer walkers along this route, almost giving the appearance of what was once considered a normal day. Very few skeletal remains littered the road as the animals in the area had eaten the remains and scattered the bones.

The small towns were sparsely populated. The populations had dropped due to the lack of food being brought in. Those that remained were solidly self-sufficient and preferred the seclusion of the Inner Banks. Few people ran out to meet the convoy, and those that did were informed by the scout that they were not government assistance and could do nothing for them.

The only roadblock was just before the village of Leland, just outside of Wilmington. The scout observed the obstruction and waited for the convoy to catch up.

Staff Sergeant Eldridge climbed down from the cab of the five-Ton and walked to the scout.

The Corporal commanding the three-man scout jeep said, "Sarge, we got a roadblock about a quarter mile up ahead. It appears to be manned by a minimum of five men; two on each side of the road and one in the center. It is unknown if there are snipers on the flanks."

"Good sitrep Corp, what say we mosey on down there and see what they have to say."

"Ogden, hop on down here and take a break while we check things out."

The Private got down and decided to relieve himself while he waited.

The jeep drove slowly to within two hundred yards of the barrier and halted. "Driver, if you see me or the Corporal turn and point back to you, I want you to fire a short burst into the tree line to your right. You got that?"

"Sure Sarge, you or the Corp turn and point to me then I fire a short burst to the tree line to my right. Got it."

"Good man."

The driver took over the MG as Eldridge and the Corporal walked, carrying their M4A1's pointed down as they made their way to the barricade.

At about the fifty-foot mark, a voice said, "That's close enough. This road is closed, go back, turn around, and go away. This is fair warnin', so git afore we decide we really like your little jeep."

"Well, good morning to you too, sir. My name is Staff Sergeant Eldridge, and we mean you no harm. We have a convoy of twenty-six vehicles en route to the Military Ocean Terminal at Sunny Point.

We have no desire to take anything that you have. We only want safe passage through Leland. We can clear a path and when we are through, we will replace the vehicles we have moved, back into position."

"Say, does that pop gun your driver's aimin' our way work, or is it just for show, and what the hell kinda' uniform is that your wearin'?"

"Sir, instead of yelling at each other, how about you come down here, or I come up there, so we can talk face to face and get to know each other."

"Okay, but your man stays right there in our sights, so don't try nuthin stupid. Just lay your weapons on the ground and come on up."

"Fair enough," said Scott who laid his weapons on the ground and following the directions of the man on the barricade made his way to the rear.

The man on the right flank of the roadblock met Scott and patted him down before escorting him to the man in charge.

Scott held out his hand and said, "My name is Staff Sergeant Scott Eldridge. I'd be honored if y'all call me Scott."

Taking Scott's hand, the man said, "Lucas McRay. You say you mean us no harm and can move and replace the roadblock? All ya' want is a passage to Sunny Point. That about right?"

"That's it, Lucas. We are not looking for trouble. Oh, you did ask about the uniforms. We are the Security Force for Wilson County, working with the government there. These gray uniforms are government security contractor get-ups."

"That so? Well, tell me, what do you know about what the hell is goin' on?"

Scott told Lucas everything he knew about the world chaos.

Lucas said, "Well, kiss my ass. You mean to tell me that we're finally free of them blood suckin' thieves in DC? Hot damn. Hell, we doin' fine here, well, once Wilmington cleared out. No more taxes, huh? Okay, we'll let ya' through, but you gotta' stay with us until y'alls convoy clears the roadblock at the other end of town. Deal?"

Scott held out his hand to seal the deal and said, "Deal, Lucas, is it okay to start right now?"

Lucas agreed, and Scott walked with his escort back to the Corporal and explained that the convoy could pass through.

The Corporal picked up Scott's weapons and making sure he did not raise his hand walked back to the jeep.

They brought the convoy up, and the dozer truck cleared a path allowing the other vehicles to pass through.

After the convoy cleared the far side Roadblock and repaired the damage, Lucas said, "Scott, I wish you well, and Y'all come on back now, heah?"

They shook hands as Scott climbed back into his truck and departed for Sunny Point.

The driver looked at Scott and asked, "Hey, you okay boss? You look a little pale."

"Yeah, yeah, I'm fine now. That encounter had so many possibilities leading to disaster. I am just so relieved that nobody started shooting. There are enough dead folks now without killing anyone just trying to get by."

"I like your thinking Sarge. Say, are we coming back this same way?"

"Oh hell no. We'll go around…"

Scott was thrilled to find the main gate at Sunny Point still secured. He dismounted his truck and using the key unlocked the front gate. Once all of the convoy vehicles were safely through the gate, he relocked it and led the convoy to the dock.

The trip, which would normally take under four hours took nearly seven. Everyone was exhausted when they parked the trucks.

While the men from Troop A rested, Staff Sergeant Eldridge grabbed his megaphone and walked up to the *Cortana*; "Hello the ship. I am looking for Captain Aaron Reyes. I have a message from an old friend, Lieutenant General Paul Chalmers."

After a few seconds, Captain Reyes exited the Bridge and came to the railing. "Hello the dock. I am Captain Reyes. What message have you from General Chalmers?"

Scott asked permission to come aboard to show Captain Reyes the letter and identifying docs.

"Permission granted," and turning to his XO the Captain ordered him to lower the gangway to allow Staff Sergeant Eldridge to come aboard.

As he arrived at the top of the gangway the *Cortana's* XO offered his hand and welcomed him aboard as he turned to lead Scott to the Captain's Ready Room where Captain Reyes awaited him.

The galley sent coffee, which the XO poured. Once the pleasantries were formalized Scott handed the manila envelope holding the Chalmer's documents to the ship's Captain.

Captain Reyes read the letter and looked at the enclosed documents before returning them to Staff Sergeant Eldridge.

"I must say," said Captain Reyes, "that I am greatly surprised to see my old friend's ID card included here. I would feel much better had it not been here because it indicates that my friend is no longer among the living."

Staff Sergeant Eldridge looked to the Captain and said, "I have no knowledge of his current status, but upon reflection, I believe you may be correct. Sir, may I assume that you will turn over your cargo to me as is stated in the letter."

The Captain looked down at the table before saying, "No, I have no intention of turning my entire cargo to you. However, I will honor a portion of his request and give you the solar kits, and something he did not know is a part of my cargo; razor wire. We are carrying five thousand coils of it. I will also include one functioning semi-truck to carry them. They are in a container ready for loading. I cannot turn over my entire cargo to you, as we must use the remainder as barter for fuel. You see, it is my plan to continue plying the trade routes trading operational vehicles for oil, to power the *Cortana.*"

Staff Sergeant Eldridge asked him why the *Cortana* would not sail back to the Philippines and home.

Captain Reyes told Staff Sergeant Eldridge that it was a simple matter of economics. In the Philippines, he and his crew would only be additional mouths to feed, whereby continuing to sail the world would both feed his crew, but also give them a purpose. "We are deep water sailors," said the Captain, not coastal fishermen."

"Yes sir, but how long can you remain at sea?"

"Until the *Cortana* takes us to Davey Jones Locker, you see the price of oil has dropped to zero, and there are billions of barrels of it in tanks just waiting to fill us up.

"Our plan is to trade our cargo for fuel and supplies. Anyway, that is our plan."

"I see," Staff Sergeant Eldridge said, may I ask what cargo you are carrying?"

Reyes told him, "the primary cargo is cars and trucks, semis to be precise; one hundred and seventy-five of them, and over four hundred cars. We also have various other cargo in one hundred shipping containers.

"You see, the *Cortana* is not actually a RORO, but a ROLO, (Roll On/ Lift Off). She is considered a twin decker with a tween deck for autos and containers on deck. We have sufficient cargo to keep us afloat for years and, of course, in time we will also pick up additional cargo at our ports of call."

"Interesting," said Staff Sergeant Eldridge, "I like your plan, it seems most worthwhile. Oh, before I forget; I was told to ask if either you or your Chief Engineer would like to join our little village, which, thanks to you will soon have electricity. Should I assume that neither of you is interested in our offer?"

"For me, no, but Chief Adan Ramos is ready to return to the land, though for the life of me I cannot begin to fathom why," chuckled the Captain.

Captain Reyes introduced Staff Sergeant Eldridge to his Chief Engineer/Machinist, Adan Ramos. He was most pleased with the offer and readily accepted.

Staff Sergeant Eldridge then asked the Captain how he would handle the loss of such an important position. Reyes told Scott that Adan had been prepping his replacement for nearly a year.

"Scott, please come with me. I have something to show you." The Captain led Scott deep into the bowels of the ship until they came to a hatch that opened onto a very large room housing dozens of computer workstations and equipment that Scott could not even guess the function.

"Wait, you are a spy ship?"

Captain Reyes sighed and said, "We prefer the term intelligence gathering, and before you ask, yes we are Americans. The NSA personnel have all gone home since they no longer have a job.

He handed Scott his ID card, which identified him as a U.S. Naval Captain. "Adan is a retired Lieutenant Commander.

"We have served in this capacity for several years while functioning as a licensed cargo vessel. I must say that, when we get back out to sea, we'll dump all of this overboard."

Scott asked, "How is it that your trucks all run? Shouldn't they be dead?"

"We thought so too, but the containment area for vehicles is an enclosed watertight compartment, our guess is that this created a giant Faraday Cage. It is the only thing we can come up with.

"At first, we could not figure out why the NSA cabin's electronics all crashed, then Adan noticed there was a porthole in that compartment. Still, we aren't certain."

Scott felt certain that in this new world, some people were lucky, and some were not. The lucky survived while the unlucky died.

Chief Ramos was sent back to Defiance in one of the jeeps. He was to relate what was coming.

As Scott wandered through the rows of trucks stored below decks, he came upon a staggering find. It was a flatbed small cab semi bound for Lowes; complete with a portable forklift.

Over dinner that evening, Scott asked what the Captain would accept in trade for the Lowes truck. After much thought, Aron Reyes said, "Scott, you have been incredibly helpful to us, but more importantly you have offered a safe harbor for my old friend Adan. Therefore, you may take the truck as my gift to you."

Scott could not believe this gesture of friendship and reminded Aron that he would also always have that same safe harbor should he ever tire of the sea.

The following day was hectic with offloading and loading of the solar kits. Had the forklifts not been running, the job would have taken a week, with them it took only seven hours. Scott was truly happy that these forklifts did not have any circuit boards.

The last thing to be loaded on the trucks were four small forklifts onto the Lowes truck.

29 April 0600
Military Ocean Transport Command
Sunny Point

The morning dawned dark and rainy. Winds blew from the west bringing the promise of more rain to come.

On the Bridge of the *Cortana*, Aron and Scott finished their last cup of coffee together. As Aron peered at the screen of his radar, Scott said, "Captain will you sail today as planned or wait for better weather?"

Smiling, the Captain of the *Cortana* said, "We will sail this evening just prior to darkness to clear the port facilities. This rain will only last for perhaps another seven or so hours."

With the emotion of saying farewell to a friend, Scott said, "Captain, I hope you know how much the cargo you have given to us means to our little village. I will tell you, what Colonel Levins related to me; the return of electricity to Defiance will be the spark which keeps the flame of civilization from being completely snuffed out. Now, I know exactly how he felt when he told this to me. I wish you good sailing and safe harbors. May God Bless you and the *Cortana*," as he shook hands with the man who historians may say provided that spark.

"And may you go with the blessings of God. Good-bye my friend," replied Captain Aron Reyes.

-

Staff Sergeant Eldridge held a short briefing before leaving Sunny point and heading for home.

"Men, I know it looks nasty out there, but this front will only last for another six or seven hours, and for us that is truly a blessing. Bad guys tend to be fair weather crooks.

"We need to get every last piece of our cargo safely to Defiance, so stay sharp, maintain proper distance and let's get home without losing anything, or anyone.

"All right, let's make like the shepherd and get the flock out of here."

The rain did persist for seven hours and did not begin to clear until the convoy was only ten miles from home.

30 April 1700
Briefing Tent
Defiance

On site for the briefing were; Colonel Levins, Major Ben Smith, Mayor Ralph Bassett, and First Sergeant Bradley Cobb. There were also two new additions to this core group; Mr. Adan Ramos, and Ms. Coleen Biddle, a historian. Her job was to write the story and history of Defiance.

She was forty-eight years old and 5'2" tall with unruly mousy-colored hair she tried to keep in a tight bun…complete with a protruding pencil. She was every bit the epitome of the stereotypical College Professor. Though her duty as Defiance Historian was important, the critical piece granting her admittance to Defiance was the simple fact that she had learned shorthand as a young woman and she accurately recorded, verbatim, each meeting she attended.

Staff Sergeant Eldridge gave an excellent briefing, covering the entire trip, to include his encounter with Lucas in Leland. He added, "Yes, sir, all went well, but to be safe I chose a bit more roundabout path in returning to Defiance.

CHAPTER TWENTY-FOUR

White Supermen

3 May 1800 hours
Just outside of Roper, NC

Staff Sergeant Eldridge and his ambush patrol set out via truck and were taken four miles from the outskirts of Roper, a small town known to have been overrun by a criminal gang.

The patrol disembarked from their truck and watched as their transportation returned to Defiance. Each member of this patrol had experienced similar patrols in Berzerkistan. They took their assigned patrol positions and made their way to town.

At approximately ½ a kilometer (klick) from the town limit, the patrol point man spotted a manned roadblock just ahead. Staff Sergeant Eldridge conferred with the patrol and sent Corporals Daniels and Gentry to flank the position. Should they need help in eliminating the sentries, Gentry would return to brief Eldridge.

"Gentry, this can't be right. The only sentries I see appear to be passed out. If you look, you can see that all three of them have a bottle beside their chair."

"Roger that, no experience here. We can do this without going back for help. Agreed?"

"Yep, let's slip right up to 'em, take out the outside two and capture the dumbass in the center.

Hold on while I do an infrared survey to see if another has wandered off to take a dump."

"Roger, let's not get in too big of a hurry, go ahead."

As they climbed to the top of the barricade, they immediately discovered three bodies with bullet holes in their heads. They had been beaten and executed.

Finding no sign of anyone else providing over-watch to the sleeping guards the two moved to the passed-out guards, dispatched them, and took the third man prisoner.

Gentry returned to Staff Sergeant Eldridge to inform him the position was now in their hands.

Upon crossing the roadblock barrier, Eldridge said, "Good work, now let's see what this silly bastard has to say. Check for gang tats, maybe we can figure out who we are dealing with."

"Sarge, look at this, all three have W S, swastika and teardrop tats. So, we've got elements of the White Supermen who have all killed someone in prison.

"Oh, crap, how many of them do you think there are Sarge?

"Last I heard this bunch of skinheads had over 500 members, so yeah…oh, crap."

Staff Sergeant Eldridge was briefed and also said, "Oh, shit." He then said, "Okay, listen up; I want the three of you to ride their bikes back to HQ. Report to the Old Man what we've got here and ask him to send out the RF to pick up me and Tiny here.

I'll bring Tiny along with me and meet the Reaction Force on the way. I imagine that I'll be slow draggin' this tub of lard."

Sergeant Goldberg said, "Roger Sarge, I don't like the idea of leaving you here alone, but okay, we're on the way. All right men, grab a bike and let's go."

One of the privates yelled out to Staff Sergeant Eldridge, "Hey, Sergeant E, these ain't old bikes, they're almost brand new. How's that possible?"

"Yeah, okay, Sergeant Goldberg, I don't know either so don't forget to include that little tidbit in your brief to the Old Man."

"Roger that," and shaking hands, he turned to grab the one remaining bike and waved as they took off for Defiance HQ.

Scott used zip ties on the skinhead and then threw a cup of water onto his face.

Choking and blubbering he awoke with a start and tried to wipe his face. It took several seconds for him to realize that his hands were cuffed behind his back.

"What the hell?" asked the now furious biker as he looked around and saw both of his buddies covered in their own blood with slashed throats.

Scott looked down at his captive and said, "Hi Tiny, top of the evenin' to ya'."

Confused, still a bit lightheaded and in the massive throes of a killer hangover, he muttered, "What, top of what? Who the hell are you…oh, my aching head. Gimme a drink."

Then without warning, he threw a kick toward Staff Sergeant Eldridge who suspicioned Tiny would try something like that and effortlessly deflected the assault.

"Oh my, Tiny that was surely not your best move, now stand up…NOW, YOU PIECE OF SHIT!"

Tiny, with some difficulty, rose to his feet and as he stood there shaking with rage, watched as Scott stepped around behind this giant and punched him in the kidney. This sent him to his knees and put tears to his eyes.

"Now you just listen up Tiny; that was just a gentle prod. It would be best if you did not force me to take action that is way more painful.

Through his glassy eyes, he asked, "Why you keep callin' me Tiny. Can't you read the nametag on my vest? It's Bones."

Staff Sergeant E then walked to his side and said, "Gee, we already have a Doctor we sometimes call Bones, so from now on your name is Tiny Needle Dick, but for the most part we'll just call you Tiny."

Tiny looked up at Scott and said, "I am gonna' rip your head off, you little prick."

Without warning, Scott kicked Tiny in the nose knocking him backward onto the ground.

Tiny was screaming, but in pain rather than rage. Blood spewed from his nose and into his mouth causing him to choke and roll over onto his side.

Scott said, as he reached for Tiny's nose, "Aw man, your nose is flat against your cheek. I just know that's gotta' hurt, here, let me help you with that," and swiftly grabbed the bent nose and sharply straightened it."

Tiny let out a primal scream and began begging Scott to stop.

Scott grabbed Tiny by his right skull earring and jerked it off his ear. Tiny tried to grab his ear, but the cuffs held tight. Grabbing Tiny's bloody ear, Scott pulled him onto his knees and walked behind him saying, "You worthless sack of shit. How does it feel to hurt like you hurt the people you killed? Tell me, asshole, do you want to live through the night?"

"Let me loose! I'm gonna' rip your arms off your shoulders."

"Really? Man, I gotta' tell ya' that from where I stand that does not seem likely," and just to prove his point he savagely kicked Tiny in the genitals. This kick contained so much force that it not only took him onto his back but caused him to vomit. He tried without success to break the shackles, so he could hold his smashed genitalia.

Once Tiny finished his retching, Scott took hold of Tiny's other ear and pulled him to his knees, said, "Tell me Tiny, do you like receiving pain as much as dishing it out? Now, tell me your name."

Through sobs, Tiny said, "I already told ya', it's Bones."

This time Scott's boot again contacted Tiny's kidney with a powerful kick sending Tiny smashing his face into the dirt, then saying, "No, that's not right, now let's try again; what is your new full name?"

Tiny so wanted to bring his hands to his nose, kidney, and testicles, but the three zip ties would not give.

Through bloody lips, Tiny said, "I am so gonna' love killin' you."

"Damn Tiny, that was the wrong answer," said Scott, as he savagely kicked Tiny on the upper arm. giving him two elbows.

Again, Tiny screamed and through pain-filled sobs said, "Ok, ok, it's Tiny Needle Dick. Enough already. You broke my arm, you shit. You do know how to set it, right?"

Scott knelt down in front of Tiny and said with a smile, "Set it? Of course, I know how to set it, but Tiny you make such a fashion statement with two elbows on your right arm. Say, how about I do the left arm, and you'll have an even number on each side?"

Tiny began begging, "Oh, no, please. You win, no more, please."

Scott said, "There, now that wasn't so hard, was it? Ya' know, we have so much to talk about, but not here. So, drag your raggedy fat ass to your feet and let's get going."

"What? I can't go anywhere with a broken nose and arm. You need to get a doctor to me," pleaded Tiny.

"Oh Tiny, you are such a big wussie. I'll tell ya' what. You get your lard ass up, or I will lift you up by that second elbow. Can you feel me, asshole?"

Struggling mightily to rise; shackled and with a broken upper arm Tiny finally managed to get to his feet. Of course, Scott making a threatening move toward him did encourage him greatly.

Tying a noose around Tiny's neck, Scott began leading him back to Defiance. Every step caused Tiny to moan in pain until Scott turned to him and said, "Tiny, you are such a candy ass. Here's the deal, if I hear one more moan from you, I will take great pleasure in giving you something to whine about.

I gotta' tell ya,' Tiny, I am a bit concerned about you having one good arm as it is, so given the slightest excuse, I'll give you another elbow on your left forearm. They won't match, but it will be a hoot to see."

Tiny, in desperation, managed to sob out, "Why, why are you doin' this to me. I didn't do nuthin' to you."

"Tiny, I saw those three people you murdered after beating them. I guess you could say that you just pissed me off, and I thought you might like to understand how they felt. If you don't cooperate, I'm gonna' make what you've felt so far seem like tiptoeing through the tulips.

"What? No, that wasn't me. It was them, I…I wasn't even there when it happened. You gotta' believe me. I swear to God."

"Whoa, hoss, would you like for me to really hurt you?"

"Oh no, please no."

"Then leave God out of our little chat and no more lies. Lies equal pain; lots of pain, can you feel me?"

Tiny was too afraid to respond.

As they trod along Scott asked Tiny about the White Supermen, "Tiny, how exactly did a crybaby like you make it into the White Supermen? You're not an example of their courage, are you?"

Tiny was beginning to slip into shock, and he began to become a bit numb to the pain.

"Oh, never mind; tell me Tiny, is anything left of Roper?"

"Well, yeah, the buildings are still standing, and a few good lookin' bitches are alive, maybe a little worse for the wear, but alive for now."

"Have some fun with those gals, did ya' Tiny?"

"Of course, I did, we all did. I mean it's what they're for, ain't it?"

At that point, Staff Sergeant Eldridge saw two pickups coming toward them. He quickly recognized the Militia Reaction Force.

2 May 2300
Colonel Levins' Office
Defiance

Staff Sergeant Eldridge removed his hat and reported to Colonel Levins. He approached the desk and stopped 18" from the edge, came to attention and saluted, saying, "Sir Staff Sergeant Eldridge reporting as directed."

Colonel Levins returned his salute and directed him to a seat. Scott said hello to his First Sergeant then shook hands and said hello to Mayor Bassett.

Levi had requested coffee be brought in and after the Company Runner had poured a cup for everyone, he left the remaining coffee on his Colonel's desk and left the room.

Before Levi could even begin, Ralph said, "Levi, how did you do it? I mean, in only two months you have formed a militia that would stack up against anyone. How did you do it?"

First Sergeant Cobb asked if he could offer his two cents worth on that subject. Colonel Levins smiled and said, "Please Top, I'd kind of like to know your take on that myself."

"Thank you, sir. Mr. Mayor, remember the day when we were in that auto museum place?"

"Yes, of course."

"Well sir, that's where it started, Colonel Levins immediately took charge and gave us the opportunity to show what we knew from our active service days, which were only a couple of years ago for most of us.

He didn't pussyfoot around. He told us what he wanted and then let us do it. Shoot, each and every one of us just fell back on our training, and there was just something about the feeling that Colonel Levins knew what he was about and expected us to know also. He has also never once made any member of Troop A feel unimportant, down to the lowest recruit.

I'm telling you, sir, Colonel Levins knows and expects us to know how to train the new recruits until they know what to do. I mean, hell sir, we all go through PT every morning, and who is right there with us? The Old Man.

When we call Colonel Levins the Old Man, it is a term of endearment and deepest respect because that is what he gives to us.

There's not a man among us who wouldn't low crawl through two acres of broken glass and barbed wire just to ask if the Colonel has any further orders."

Levi interrupted, "Whoa, Top, you'll make my head swell. Now Ralph, let me add to that. You gave me the reins, and I used the 13th rule of leadership; when in charge, take charge.

So, the ultimate question is why these men are willing to live under the rather rigorous rules of an old black boot army? Well, I have the answer, and it is really simple…purpose. Before the lights went out, they all just had jobs, but none of them ever forgot the sense of comradeship that military service gave them.

There is also the simple fact that every man jack of them is a Sheepdog."

"A what?" asked Ralph. "Not very nice to call them dogs, is it?"

"No, not at all, you see there are three kinds of people; Sheepdogs, Sheeple, and Wolves. Now, don't be offended because I'm calling those people who just want to live their lives Sheeple. We mean no disrespect and it is just a term to describe those we want to protect.

The Sheeple are, by definition, those who only want to earn a living, raise a family and be, for the most part just left alone, and that's exactly what we want for them.

It must be something in the deepest recesses of our DNA because we Sheepdogs are compelled to run *to* the sound of gunfire to protect our flock. Without Sheeple to protect we would have no purpose. So, as Sheepdogs, we only want to protect our flock from the wolves. Ultimately it comes down to our being a part of something that is bigger than we are as individuals…purpose, the pride of membership in a very select fraternity, and I guess lastly would be the fact that each member of Troop A will always run to the sound of that gunfire. They can't tell you why, hell, I don't know either.

Now me, I'm just a rallying point, the Old Man. By this October Scott will be ready to take over, and the men will show him the same respect because he has been where they are. Yes, I am danged proud of them, but I'm just the Old Man. Show them respect Ralph, and they will find the way to save Defiance whatever comes, well, short of fighting a Tank Battalion."

Ben looked to Ralph and whispered, "Don't you believe that he is just a rallying point crap. He took a bunch of prior service civilians and believed in us. Yeah, he's the Old Man, and the very heart of Troop A. We respect him and follow him because he respects and believes in us."

Ralph looked at Levi and said, "Okay, I think I get it now, and Levi, I thank God that we found each other."

Levi brought them back to the agenda by asking, "Okay, now let's talk about Tiny. Sergeant Eldridge, what have you learned?"

"Sir, it ain't good. Roughly, seventy-five members of a skinhead gang are holding Roper. They have murdered everyone but a few young women they use as their personal slaves, and some of the older women to cook and clean.

These assholes are called the White Supermen. What they are is a bunch of Neo-Nazis out to cleanse America of any person of color and turn the rest of us into slaves. They are tough and mean, and love to fight, but they have no inkling of security or tactics. They just ride into town and abuse and kill everyone.

Oh, there is one other thing we noticed. The motorcycles they are riding are new. Now they do have kick-starters attached, but other than that they are brand new. The ones we brought in are Star Cruisers made by Yamaha.

My guess, sir, is that they have one hell of a good mechanic with them. If we are lucky, he'll be a captive, and we might be able to put him to work for us in some mechanical capacity working for Adan Ramos."

First Sergeant Cobb asked, "Is all of the gang in Roper?"

"No, Top, the whole gang has around five hundred members and growing."

Cobb looked at his Colonel and said, "Sir, we have to whittle them down a bit. If we can take out seventy-five then I believe we should do it, anyway, sir, that's my recommendation."

The Mayor chimed in, seventy-five, why we barely have seventy-five in Troop A and another forty in B Troop. Is that enough? Levi, do you really think we can take them out and be ready to stop over four hundred more?"

Levi smiled and said, "Ralph, they are drunks and dopers. We are a well-trained and highly motivated military unit. Oh, hell yes, we can do it.

Sergeant Eldridge, did Tiny admit to his participation in murder?"

"Yes, sir he did."

Colonel Levins looked to the assemblage and asked for everyone except the Mayor to step outside for a few minutes.

When only Levi and Ralph remained, Levi said, "Mr. Mayor, as this Tiny fellow was captured in a lawful military operation, he is subject to a military tribunal. I hope you do not feel the need to try him yourself."

"Hang him high, Levi, you are right, he's a murdering bastard guilty by his own admission of high crimes against humanity. I have no desire to soil a civilian court with him."

"Thank you, Mr. Mayor, I will have him brought before me this night. I will read the charges and find him guilty. We will hang him in the center of Roper after his pals are dead."

"Fair enough, but why the Mr. Mayor stuff Levi?"

"Official business calls for proper protocol… Ralph."

Both turned and smiled at the Defiance Historian.

4 May 2000 hours
Roadblock outside of Roper, NC

Three motorcycles came roaring up to the roadblock. As they dismounted their bikes, one shouted, "Wake up you lazy bums," They laughed as they walked to the chairs where two of the guards sat in the chairs, dead.

"What the hell? Demon, get over here, they're dead!"

5 May 0200
Colonel Levins Office
Defiance

The prisoner known as Tiny was brought before Colonel Levins for a Military Tribunal. He was accused of the murder of the residents of Roper, North Carolina.

Levi said, "State your full name for the court."

Tiny's arm was in a wooden splint. His broken nose had caused his eyes to begin to turn purple. He started to respond when Staff Sergeant Eldridge coughed. Tiny looked at him and cringed. He said, "Tiny Needle Dick."

Levi tried, but could not fully stifle a smile and said, "Are you sure that is the name you want to be recorded in the record of this Tribunal?"

Staff Sergeant Eldridge again coughed, and Tiny said, "Yes."

"You have been arraigned to this Tribunal on the charges of murder. How do you plea?"

Gathering just a bit of bluster, Tiny said, "Yeah, I done that, so what? And where's my lawyer? I got rights. I am so gonna sue you."

Levi's eyes turned steel gray as he said, "Yes, Mr. Dick you do have rights. You have met your Defense Counsel, Staff Sergeant Eldridge.

Sergeant, do you have a defense to present to this court?"

"Sir, if he hadn't already admitted his crimes to you, I might have said something, probably, well maybe…um, no, I guess not."

Tiny looked at Levi and said, "Hey, what is this? This ain't no trial."

Levi looked Tiny right in the eye and said, "Actually, it is, and I find you guilty. The punishment is that you shall be hanged by the neck until you are dead, sentence to be carried out three days hence at the time and place of my choosing. First Sergeant, see that he is shackled and secured in one of the empty Root Cellars. Since he is so fat, he shall be placed on a bread and water diet until the sentence is carried out."

First Sergeant Cobb said, "Yes sir, right away sir.

"Get up Mr. Dick, let's go to your new quarters."

As they got just outside, everyone in attendance heard the Top Sergeant say, "Don't worry, Mr. Dick, I'll make sure your full name is spelled right on the sign around your neck, let's see, that was Tiny Needle Dick, two ees in Needle, right?"

Tiny's reply was lost to the night.

CHAPTER TWENTY-FIVE

The Cavalry Report on the Double R

5 May 1000
Colonel Levins Office
Defiance

A Troop B scout came riding fast to the gate of Defiance. He said, "I've got an important message for Colonel Levins from Lieutenant Pickett." He was quickly passed through the gate and rode to the hitching post in front of the new Orderly Room.

Dismounting, he ran into the Orderly Room and told Corporal Jones that he had an important message for Colonel Levins.

Levi heard the commotion of the horse charging up to the Orderly Room and upon entering the main office area said, "Jonesy, get Major Smith, Staff Sergeant Eldridge, Top and the Mayor in here…skosh."

"Yes sir, on the way."

Seeing the three upside down yellow stripes sewn to the rider's shirt Levi asked, "Your name, Sergeant?"

"Sergeant Bruno Tolan, sir."

"Well Sergeant, it's good to meet you. Please feel free to grab a cup of coffee if you like while we wait for our First Sergeant. and the Mayor. Then come on back to my office."

"Thank you, sir; I would like some coffee."

The First Sergeant and the Mayor came rushing in, followed by his XO and Staff Sergeant Eldridge, just as Levi was escorting the Cavalry Trooper to his office."

After everyone was seated Levi asked, "All right Sergeant, what word do you have for us from Lieutenant Pickett?"

"Yes sir, the LT told me to give you this message." Tolan reached into his dispatch case, produced a letter, and handed it to the First Sergeant. who passed it on to Levi.

Levi read the letter aloud;

Colonel Levins,

For the last five days, one of our four man scouting patrols has been surveilling a large group of people making their way directly toward Roper. They call themselves the Army of the Double R.

They are currently bivouacked in Robersonville which is forty miles from Roper, and thirty-two miles from Defiance.

Upon notification of this development, I immediately reinforced the patrol with an additional eight men, plus myself.

We have discovered that they started out as an inner-city Latino gang from Raleigh. They have added others to their gang who are predominantly Black and Latino.

They are armed but have few military-style long guns.

Their numbers are well over two hundred but roughly half of them appear to be slaves.

On a more tragic note, we have observed that the gang murders several people each day, slaughters them and feeds the meat to the slaves.

We were able to capture and interrogate one of the scouts to obtain this information. Our captive had an RR brand on his forehead. He did not come to a good end.

Beginning three days ago, in an effort to slow their progress we have begun sniping at the gang members and executing any of the RR scouts we track down.

We have also been warning those in the path of these animals, so they may avoid being captured, or killed.

Sir, this gang must be destroyed to the last breathing soul.

The burning question is; should you agree with my analysis, what do we do with the slaves who are now cannibals.

These slaves each carry the C brand on their foreheads.

I await your orders via my rider, Sergeant Tolan.

Leon Pickett
1LT, Troop B,
Commanding

Everyone let out a breath as the seriousness of this message sank in. Levi broke the silence by saying, "Sergeant Tolan, please wait in the outer office for our reply."

Sergeant Tolan stood, saluted and said, "Yes sir, I will await your orders." He then did an about face and left the office.

"Whew," said Levi, "this is a pickle. We have this Latino Gang thirty or so miles away in Robersonville, and the White Supermen in Roper. Ok, here is my operational guidance on this conundrum; we destroy the White Supermen first then begin to march toward Robersonville. Lieutenant Pickett is to increase his hit and run attacks to slow the Double R down and reduce their combat effectiveness. Assuming we can satisfactorily eliminate the White Supermen, we must still leave, say twenty-five troopers here as a Defensive Force. Tolan can stop by Fort Pickett, pick up all but twenty-five, and then rush back to Pickett. That will give us a force totaling no more than sixty-five effectives to take on the Double R. Discussion?"

Ralph said, "No, I can't say that I like the plan, but it does seem the logical thing to do. I must say that I am glad we were able to get razor wire around the settlement area. I vote to go."

First Sergeant Cobb said, "Sir, I feel comfortable that the 60mm M-224 mortars from Lejeune will be a major force multiplier for the defense of Defiance, and the more mobile 40 mm automatic grenade launchers will do the same on the Roper and Robersonville bunch. I would also recommend that we use the 60 mm on those Robersonville devils."

"Good thinkin' Top. Those 40s, being shoulder fired with five rounds per cylinder should really help with the odds. Ben, your thoughts?" asked Levi.

Major Smith sat up straight in his chair and said, "I agree, absolutely. I will get the auto grenade launchers online and with your approval, we can be prepared to attack tonight at 0400 hrs. We will then return here and exchange our troopers for fresh faces before we take off for Robersonville after a few hours rest."

"Thank you, Ben, but I intend to lead these attacks."

Ralph, Ben, and the First Sergeant all shook their heads, and in near unison said, "The hell you will!"

Levi looked at each of them and replied, "Funny, but I thought I was the ramrod of this outfit. I say I go, and that is that."

Ralph said, "No, that is not final. This is a big operation for us, and Scott must be the one to lead it."

Before Levi could object, the First Sergeant. added, "The Mayor's right Colonel. You once told me that every young officer must earn his collar points by leading a force across a creek against a hostile force. Well, this is that creek the young Sergeant must cross."

"Oh, all right, Scott, you're the man, let's do it. Ben?"

"Don't worry sir; I'll have everything he needs together by 1800. Colonel, I know that Scott can do this, and I will make sure he has the men and equipment he needs. You have given us your concept of the campaign, and as always, I know you will let us do our jobs. Roger, sir?"

"Yeah, yeah, Roger that. Since I'm needed around here, about as much as a boar hog needs teats I might just as well go take a nap."

Ralph piped in with, "Yes, you do that; I'll have my clerk bring you some warm milk and a couple of Fig Newtons."

"Funny man, Ralph, real funny…smartass.

Ben, Scott, I want to see your Roper plan of attack in two hours, Roger?"

"Yes sir, shall we have lunch delivered here?"

"Oh, good grief, make it 1300, okay?"

Ben said, "Absolutely sir, will there be anything else?"

"Heaven help me I'm in the hands of maniacs. Don't you think that's enough for now?" said Levi as he tried to hide a smile.

Ralph hung back after everyone had gone and asked, "Levi, you're not mad, are you?"

"Yeah, a little bit, but not at anyone in particular. Truth is, I just don't like being the one who sends these fine men out to do battle while I sit here all warm and toasty with my milk and Fig Newtons."

"I know my friend, I know."

CHAPTER TWENTY-SIX

Battle of Roper

5 May 1300
Defiance War Room
Defiance

Ben and Scott entered the War Room. Ben said, "Colonel, we are prepared to brief you on our concept of the battle as per your guidance."

"Fine, let's hear it."

"Yes sir," said Ben, approaching the map hanging from the wall opposite Levi's desk, "first I will provide you with our recommended equipment requirements. We believe the enemy force can be eliminated utilizing the following:

- Night vision helmet-mounted monocle
- Standard issue M4-A1 Assault Rifle w/suppressor and Rifle Combat Optic (RCO)
- Standard basic load of ammunition with reserve of second basic load totaling fourteen twenty round magazines for each M4-A1
- Four each M-32A2 Automatic Grenade Launchers (40 mm) w / 20 rounds each
- Eight each M-27 IAR Squad Machine Guns w / 500 rounds each

This completes my portion of this briefing. Staff Sergeant Eldridge will present the concept of attack."

Levi asked about the 60 mm M-224 mortars and was told that in their considered opinions they would not be needed and should remain for the defense of Defiance.

"Thank you, Major Smith. Colonel Levins, my concept of attack is as follows:

- Enemy force is currently under observation

- Attacking force will cross the Line of Departure No Later Than 2400, and be transported to three miles of the target to be in position by 0345
- Attack to commence at 0400
- Scouts have been monitoring the sleeping patterns and arrangements of the enemy force and have found they have taken up residence in the immediate area surrounding the Dew Drop Inn
- Manpower requirements include sixty-one personnel, fifty combat effectives, two medical doctors, four 5-Ton drivers, four assistant drivers, and commander
- One man per SAW, total eight
- One man per Grenade Launcher, total four
- Thirty-Three Infantrymen encircling the enemy encampment
- All M4-A1 rifles to be set on semi-automatic
- Five men reserved to eliminate any enemy opting for separate sleeping quarters, as required
- The Dew Drop Inn along with surrounding buildings will be encircled prior to the attack
- Force makeup to include:
- Eight SAW squad machine gun emplacements in an equilateral position formation around the kill zone
- Four 40 mm Automatic Grenade Launchers will be placed equilaterally around the kill zone

"The initial assault will consist of 40 mm grenade launcher bombardment into the sleeping quarters forcing those inside to exit the buildings. Once out in the open, overwhelming fire will be placed upon the enemy to eliminate them all.

"Once all visible personnel are down, a second grenade launcher bombardment on the same buildings, or any others with hostiles, will commence followed by a ground assault, using overwatch, to secure the area.

"The estimated time of engagement is anticipated to be no more than ten minutes. There shall be no prisoners taken. Upon mission completion, sufficient bodies will be hung at strategic locations around our twenty-mile perimeter to deter future hostile forces. Mr. Tiny N. Dick will be hanged with the other bodies ringing our perimeter. Sir, this concludes my portion of this briefing. Questions?"

"Have you made allowances to minimize collateral damage?"

"No sir, we have not. We do not have sufficient forces to trade Trooper lives for civilian casualties. Such a mission would greatly increase the potential for Troop A casualties. We are at war with numerically superior hostile forces that have invaded our established borders."

"Gentlemen, I can find no fault with your battle plan. You are a go. Dismissed."

When Levi and Ralph were alone, Ralph asked, "Levi, are you sure that we can't find a way to save the civilians?"

"Ralph, we don't even know if any civilians are still alive. I *am* sorry but, as the man said, we are at war and as sad as it is, there is always collateral damage."

6 May 2330
Main Gate (LOD)
Defiance

Levi walked amongst the troopers offering encouragement to these men about to go into battle.

Morale was high, each man was well trained and knew the stakes involved in their mission. He was most impressed with the way the NCOs interacted with their charges. Equipment was given a final check just prior to climbing aboard the trucks.

At 2355 hours, Staff Sergeant Eldridge reported to Levi that the convoy would cross the Line of Departure on time at 2400 hours.

Levi wished him luck, shook his hand and returned his salute before Staff Sergeant Eldridge mounted the second transport and signaled for the convoy to move out. The first truck crossed the Line of Departure at exactly 2400 hours.

26 May 0030
Three miles from Roper, NC

The Defiance troopers dismounted; formed in their squads and began the trek through the pine forest to within visual range of the mission objective.

At 0350 hours the assault force was in position and ready to begin the 0400 assault.

At precisely 0400, the first whumpf of the automatic grenade launcher was heard followed immediately by the other three launchers. The rounds struck, in and around, the target area and quickly adjusted onto the targets.

Windows blew out and 40 mm grenades detonated inside the selected buildings. The barrage kept up until each launcher had fired all five rounds in the weapon's cylinder.

Within seconds, a few hostiles in other surrounding buildings began firing wildly from the windows.

Staff Sergeant Eldridge, using his megaphone, called for the enemy to cease fire and surrender. There was no response, so he ordered one more 40 mm grenade to be launched through the window of one of the occupied buildings. This action immediately brought a shout to stop shooting, "We surrender."

Staff Sergeant Eldridge ordered the hostiles to come out unarmed and place their hands over their heads. There were seven uninjured "Supermen" out of seventy-four, twenty-two wounded to various degrees, and forty-four dead.

Upon entering the targeted buildings, troopers found that the predominance of the hostiles were passed out in the Dew Drop Inn and were killed or wounded in the grenade assault.

Of the ten civilians in the targeted buildings, none were killed as they were chained and locked in the supply room. In fact, one Trey Dillon, the missing master motorcycle mechanic, was among the chained.

The mission succeeded without firing a single rifle shot…well, except for dispatching those who were wounded. The uninjured were hanged along with Tiny.

The battle for Roper was over.

06 May 0865
War Room
Defiance

The senior staff and the Mayor were seated around the conference table to hear the after-action report from Staff Sergeant Eldridge.

He reported on the mission events, complimented his men and said, "Sir, it was too easy. It was like fishing with dynamite. I am concerned that the troopers all think they are *The A-Team*. When we actually see real combat, I fear they are in for a very rude awakening. On the other hand, the operation went off without a hitch. All in all, I am extremely proud of them."

Levi thanked Scott for his briefing and said, "Staff Sergeant, we train hard every day. I am a firm believer in 'train hard, win easy'. I just hope we never have to face a competent hostile force. I have just two more things, Staff Sergeant Eldridge please come to me."

Eldridge stood and walked to his commander and said, "Sir, how may I be of assistance?"

Levi smiled and said, "Well, first we must remove these Staff Sergeant collar pins and replace them with Captain's Bars. In the Army, we call this a frocking. You wear the rank and have all of the responsibility, but you don't get the pay."

Those around the table chuckled, and Captain Eldridge said, "Well dang, sir, that would have been a pretty good pay raise. Seriously, sir, are you sure? Am I really ready?"

"You know Scott that is the second time you have questioned my senility. Yes, I am sure, and you are as ready as anyone of us…me included. Now it is my turn to be serious. If you do not know that I have tremendous faith in your ability, then maybe I was wrong, but then we all know that I am never wrong. We will be having a promotion party in early to mid-May, and your promotion will become official then. I have advanced your promotion because of the upcoming Robersonville attack. This will be a valuable experience for you.

"I will also be frocking Lieutenant Pickett to Captain. He will be in overall command of the attack, and you will work both for and with him. Following our success, you will take your place as my Aide. In that capacity, I task you to learn from Major Smith. You will profit greatly by what he has to teach.

"Any questions, young Captain?"

"Sir, right now I'm not sure I know enough to ask any questions. Sir, from my heart, thank you for this trust. I will not let Defiance or you down."

"I know you won't. All right, the last thing is simply commander's guidance. Give me an attack plan for the Army of the Double R. Captain Eldridge, you will leave immediately following this meeting for Robersonville to see what Leon can teach you. Now, take off those bars. You can pin them on again when I frock Leon. You good with that?"

"Yes, sir, of course."

Levi then adjourned the meeting.

CHAPTER TWENTY-SEVEN

Dealing with the Double R

6 May 1000
Robersonville Encampment

Pablo went to Romeo Cruz, the Jefe of the former Rican Rogues and now the Generalissimo of The Army of the Double R. Pablo was not happy out in such open country. His complaint was that all the Double R members had spent their lives in the canyons of a city. They were very uncomfortable and felt very vulnerable out in this open country with only pine trees along the road.

"Romeo, I got to tell ju that many of our army are unhappy being out of the city, and I muss agree. Do ju really plan to stay out in thees wide open country. Jefe, it geeve me the creeps."

Romeo felt the same but wasn't sure what to do. The larger cities were mostly burned down, and by his own kind...gangs. Now, what had been home was mostly burned out shells, more like deserts than home.

"Jayss, Pablo, I unnerstan, but what can we do? The cities have nothing to support us now. At least here we have food and slaves to do the work; still, I unnerstan what ju are saying. Perhaps after we reach the ocean, we can go north to find a city by the ocean where we can live and fish. Perhaps there we can finally live in the style we deserve. It will be Bueno."

"Si, Romeo, I tell the others..."

A shot rang out, and another of the army's men fell dead from a 7.62 NATO round in his chest. Pablo threw himself over Romeo to shield him, and when no other shots were fired, he stood up and said, "Mi Amigo, thees ees happening four or five times a day now. We muss do sonthing about these cowards who will not fight, but only shoot and run away."

"Si, Pablo, form a group of four men from the crypts; they peess me off anyway, and have them ready to run toward the next shot as the shooter runs away. They will not be seen and then we can perhaps catch one of thees murderers. ¿entender?"

Pablo did understand and left to organize the reaction force.

-

A seething ember becomes a flame

6 May 1200
Robersonville Encampment

A shot rang out, and another Double R soldier died. The Crypt reaction force immediately ran to the sound of the shot hoping to enter the forest without being seen. As they entered the tree line, the four men spread out about five feet apart and began crashing through the forest. After moving approximately three hundred yards into the pines, they found themselves surrounded by men in gray uniforms telling them to drop their weapons and to lie down face first on the pine-needled forest floor.

The Crypts were shackled and tied to a tree.

The irony of the men dressed in gray was lost on them.

The sergeant in charge of the ambush approached and picked up the weapons. "Corporal Wilkes, will you look at these weapons, why are they carryin' two Glock 17s and…holy shit this is an old ass Mac 10…this goes in my saddlebag. I cannot believe that there is not an AR or an AK here. Hell, they might's well be comin' at us with dildos and bongs.

Boys, y'all picked a bad day ta' go walkin' in the woods.

"Who you callin' boy?" the Crypt leader said,

The sergeant smiled and said, "Oh, hell, we call everbody boy, hit don't mean nuthin. Here's your sign." The patrol had come with signs saying:

WE MURDERED, ABUSED, STOLE, AND TURNED
GOOD FOLKS INTO SLAVES AND CANNIBALS.

FOR THAT, WE WERE EXECUTED.

JUSTICE HAS BEEN SERVED…COLD

COURTESY OF B TROOP,
1ST CAVALRY (MOUNTED)

The men were offered hoods, but these gangstas were not cowards and all refused. They did die bravely.

Romeo heard the shots and jumped for joy thinking his force had killed the sniper. After ten minutes no one had exited the forest. Pablo sent four more Crypts to find out what had happened. The reaction force took several slaves with them to lead the way. It took only a few minutes to find the bodies…and the signs.

They cut the dead men from the trees and ordered the slaves to carry them back to camp.

Romeo read the signs and went into a rage walking among the slaves and randomly shooting twenty in the stomach. The remaining slaves were ordered not to touch the dying. They were to die where they lay. An inner seething rage began to spark into a flame among the slaves…the screams of the dying pierced the nerve endings of every gang member except for Romeo and Pablo. Those screams also added fuel to the ember of revolt among the slaves.

Romeo decided to lay low and had everyone move into the East End Elementary School on E Third St. The decision was made to remain in Robersonville until the threat was dealt with.

6 May 1800
Troop B, 1st Cavalry (Mounted)
Defiance Militia Encampment

Lieutenant Pickett, the Troop B Commander sat in the Command tent speaking with the Troop First Sergeant, Harley Hatch. They discussed the day's events and were pleased to find that the Double R was settling in. The tactic of sniping and ambush had worked well in forcing the enemy to cease his advance and take up a holding position.

Harley Hatch was raised near Robersonville and said, "I feel really bad for this little burg. Just three weeks ago the population was around fourteen hundred, and now it's completely deserted. When this is over, I bet there ain't a hundred who'll be back. Probly the folks from the Scattered Acres Farm, but whoever does come back will be here with their ass in the wind for many years with no protection. It just makes me so sad, because this is a lovely little town that in six months will be a weedy ghost town.

He and Hatch discussed the letter from Colonel Levins and were confident they would soon have sufficient reinforcements to seal the enemy into their neighborhood encampment. While Robersonville is really just a small community, the Double R had settled into an area with roughly a two-hundred-yard perimeter.

The slaves had been set to work digging a moat around their camp. From the rate of progress, the moat would be finished in about two years.

The two discussed the slaves forced into cannibalism. "What should be done about them, sir?" asked the First Sergeant.

"I don't know Top, but just between you, me and the fencepost; I think they have to be put down. I tell ya', I am really glad that decision belongs squarely on the back of Colonel Levins. This is one time I'm glad it's not on me and I sure as hell hope he does not ask me for any input."

"I hear ya', sir, whew I hope God tells him the right thing to do…whatever that is," said the First Sergeant.

"Sir, I just have to tell you that I cannot believe how stupid the boss man of that bunch of crap is. Why; he's done penned himself up. How long you figger before his rations begin to run low?"

"Top, my guess is that they already are. They don't seem ever to have a plan other than taking other people's stuff, and that stuff in Robersonville is probably already gone. I figure they will begin sending scavenging parties soon, maybe even tomorrow and when they do, we'll kill 'em and take their vehicles…simple."

"Well, sir, I sure hope you are right, and yeah, it does sound simple at that."

They continued to discuss the cannibal problem for a few minutes more before getting down to business with the Senior NCOs concerning the next day's move to encircle the Double R.

With only twelve men in the saddle, encircling the Double R was, of course not possible, but by establishing observation posts around their camp, a force of six troopers could rapidly respond to anyone leaving their self-imposed prison.

7 May 0600
Robersonville

Pablo came to Romeo Cruz and told him that the food situation was bad. He suggested sending out foraging parties to the Robersonville grocery stores. They decided on the Food Lion on Main Street near the Bojangles chicken place to find food. He thought sending ten men would be a good way to go. They could take three carriages and twelve slaves."

"Thass a good plan, Pablo, go ahead and do eet. Juss don't forget to tell the team to be careful of those fockin' snipers."

Pablo immediately got with his lieutenants and tasked them to provide the manpower and slaves. Everyone agreed, but Madre de Dios, the Crypts were cranky about their losses yesterday. They wanted to go out and hunt down the murderers who killed their gang brothers to make them pay.

Around 1100 hours the team set out for the Food Lion.

The OPs reported the movement and Corporal Wilkes took six men to ambush them. The ambush party trailed the hostiles to the Food Lion and began setting up firing positions to cover the entrance. Corporal Wilkes thought it a good idea to let them do the shopping and then take the food.

The Food Lion hadn't really had much of a chance to be looted, but the pickings were still meager. The carriages were soon stacked with the available canned meats and a lot of Sauer kraut.

Once the task was complete, the slaves prepared to begin pulling the carts back to the camp at the Elementary School.

Just as they began to pull away, shots rang out dropping six members of the gang. Almost immediately the slaves lashed out at the four remaining tormentors by throwing cans at them, then smothering them to the ground where they began to bite large chunks of flesh from these men who had forced them to become cannibals.

The screaming lasted for several minutes as the troopers approached and watched as the slaves finished biting and spitting, biting and spitting, leaving no gang member alive.

At this point one of the slaves stood, his face and mouth covered in blood and asked if he could borrow a pistol. "We do not want to live after what we have been forced to do, and we do not want you to be responsible for our deaths. Please, you have freed us, so now let us end this torment, please."

Without saying a word, Corporal Wilkes went to his saddle bag to retrieve his Marine issue 9 mil. He then walked up to the saddest man he had ever seen in his life and handed him the pistol.

Each of the slaves said, "Thank you, may God Bless your soul, and may He find it in His heart to forgive us. Then each man knelt in prayer as the sad man shot them in the back of the head.

He then looked to heaven and prayed, "Dear Heavenly Father, I beg Your indulgence, and Your forgiveness, but I simply can no longer live with the evil I have done," and he then placed the barrel in his mouth and quickly pulled the trigger, ending his life.

Wilkes and every man jack of them had tears flowing down their cheeks as he retrieved his weapon. He then led these Southern Baptists in prayer asking God to forgive these poor people forced into slavery and cannibalism, "Please just forgive them, and let their souls find peace."

They left the food in the carts for a truck to pick up later. Then, they mounted up and rode in absolute silence back to camp.

Once back in camp Corporal Wilkes told the First Sergeant where the carts were and asked if he could go to his tent for a while. "Top, I'll give a full report later if that will be ok, but right now I just need to be alone and cry myself to sleep."

Seeing the honest need in his eyes, the Troop Top Sergeant said, "Go ahead son, come back when you are ready, it's okay, I think I understand."

Of course, he did not understand; he could not…until he led the detail to the Food Lion and saw what had happened. Then he understood, and he too wept. The troopers on the detail did not have to be told to bury the slaves. It seemed like the thing to do…an honorable thing to help ease the horror each felt in his own heart.

Each trooper swore a silent and personal vow that those monsters would pay for what they had done to these people.

CHAPTER TWENTY-EIGHT

"Only the Dead Know the End of War" - Plato

7 May 1015
Troop B Encampment
Outside Robersonville, NC

The convoy from Defiance pulled into Troop B's perimeter and immediately began, again, to clean weapons and check all gear for combat by the fifty combat effectives of Troop A. On 7 May, Troop B had arrived with another three troopers bringing the total Defiance Militia numbers to sixty-five.

Levi met with Lieutenant Pickett in his Orderly Room tent where he presented his battle plan. "Sir, my recommendation for this mission calls for surrounding the elementary school where the Double R has decided to hole up and make a fight of it. Once the cordon is established, we place the 60 mm mortar one thousand yards from the target area. The mortar teams will place their aiming stakes and prepare for a twenty-round bombardment of the enemy positions. Two 40 mm auto grenade launchers placed in front of the main entrance and two covering the rear of the building.

"Our infantry force is to remain in place and firing only when a target presents itself, and in general, conduct a siege. They are already short of food and will soon become desperate. I would recommend to you that we demand their surrender prior to engaging the enemy with mortars in an effort to save a potentially valuable asset like a functional school. Failing this we should fire one mortar round onto the area immediately in front of the main entrance and again demand their surrender."

Colonel Levins felt the plan was sound but was concerned about the fate of the slaves.

"Sir, the slaves have been forced into cannibalism. We have had some interaction with several of them, and there is no question that they have no desire to survive this engagement. Fear of beatings and torture has kept them from defying their tormentors. My concept of the attack has no plan for freeing these people into the community. Perhaps if they had not been branded with a C, but sir, they have no desire for anything but a quick death."

"I see; all right Captain, I believe you are correct, but first tell me about this interaction with slaves."

"Excuse me, sir, did you say Captain?" asked Troop B's Commander.

"Why, yes I did. The Troop A 1st Sergeant had the orders typed up last night, congratulations Captain.

Pinning Captain's bars onto the collar points of Lieutenant Pickett's uniform, Levi said, "Leon, this will become permanent at the promotion ceremony upon our return to Defiance. I also want you to know how much I appreciate your mentoring Captain Eldridge during this campaign.

Once this campaign is put to bed there will be a number of additional promotions, so please prepare your recommendations for Platoon Leader and any NCO positions not yet filled.

Captain Pickett explained the action of the day before, and Levi agreed with his recommendation.

At 1500 hours the encirclement was complete. The first in place were troop sharpshooters whose mission was to keep the enemy's heads down, chip away at their combat effectives, and ruin morale.

Principal's Office
Eastside Elementary School
Robersonville NC

Pablo sat across from Romeo as they talked about what was going on around them.

"Who are these people? Why attack us? We didn't do nothing to them."

"Relax Pablo, what can they do? If they attack, we will kill them all. We are well protected behind our walls. Een fact, I wish they would hurry up and make their rush. I am tired of thees place."

Little did Romeo know that he was about to get his wish and he failed to feel the 7.62x.51 NATO round enter his body. Pablo followed his boss a split second later as a second sniper took him out as well. The remaining thugs were stupefied by loss of their gang leader and they surrendered on demand. Immediately after placing their weapons on the ground and following orders to back away from their weapons, they were attacked by the entire slave population as the seething ember of hatred became a raging pyre of revenge.

They fell upon their captors *en masse* and some even began feeding on their remains.

Captains Pickett and Eldridge watched the scene in horror of the savagery taking place in front of them.

Captain Eldridge turned and walked to the auto grenade launcher and taking one from the designated user placed the weapon to his shoulder and fired all five rounds into the heart of what could only be described as a Hieronymus Bosch painting of Hell.

Then, in a quiet voice, he whispered, "May God forgive them and give them peace." He then took a ten-man squad and with pistols in hand applied the *coup de grace* to those still alive.

The tragedy of Robersonville was over, and a silence fell upon this field as the troops, using a backhoe, began the process of digging a mass grave to bury the slaves.

Everyone there knew that there was no honor, or glory there and none would ever speak of it again…even among themselves.

CHAPTER TWENTY-NINE

The Widow's Sons

17 May 1000
Defiance

The three weeks following the horror of Robersonville flew by, well, there were still the critter plagues of Levi's prediction, but by this time everyone was used to the situation and considered it just an irritant…except for the grass and wolf spiders…they were truly disgusting irritants.

Troop A was well on the way to ridding a twenty-mile radius of criminal elements. Most of the larger neighboring communities had found a Dodge City type of Town Marshall to keep the peace.

Defiance, however, had decided through a vote to allow the militia to continue in its role of keeping the peace. In fact, things were going so well that only three citizens of Defiance had been forced to hit the road.

Word had gotten around that the twenty or so miles around Defiance were not safe places for any criminal group.

Three weeks after the victory at Robersonville another motorcycle group rode through and sent three representatives to meet with Mayor Ralph, as he had come to be called and Colonel Levins.

The three reps arrived at the gate at the agreed upon time and after being searched and relieved of their weapons were shown to the Mayor's new office where they were met by Ralph and Levi. The mayor deferred to Levi who bluntly demanded, "What do you want here?"

The leader of the bikers said, "Colonel, our motorcycle club is called *'The Widow's Sons.'* We are a Masonic group that has no ill intentions toward anyone unless we are endangered and make no mistake, we will defend what little we have.

We decided that Defiance was the place to come to introduce ourselves and let you know that we are not a threat. Should we be allowed to settle in this area we will make good friends and true allies."

Ralph said, "Then you are a traveling man."

Jordan Daniels, the leader of The Widow's Sons Motorcycle Club looked at Ralph and smiled, "Yes, I am a Mason and am currently in the East."

Ralph asked, "How do I know you to be a Mason?"

Jordan asked for a private moment with Ralph, who asked Levi to step outside for a moment.

Levi asked, "Why? I am also a traveling man, though I have not been to the east."

After certain rights of passage to prove membership in the Masonic Family, all five of them sat down to talk about The Widow's Sons introduction into the community at large.

As they got to know each other, the Widow's Sons relayed that their club was affiliated with a Blue Lodge in Punta Gorda, Florida.

In addition, all thirty of them were 32nd degree York Rite Masons and were members of the Knights Templar. Each of them was a veteran.

After the meeting, Levi asked Ralph, "Did you know about a Masonic Motorcycle Club called The Widow's Sons?"

"Sure, they are a Blue Lodge group of Masons who like to ride motorcycles. When I lived in Killeen, there was a Chapter in our Blue Lodge."

"Levi, how is it I didn't know you to be a Mason?"

Levi smiled and replied, "You never asked. By the way are you also a York Rite? I'm Scottish Rite myself."

Sharing the ritual handshake Ralph said, "Am as I, Levi, am as I, and yes, I have been to the east."

The Masons settled on three nearby abandoned farms, and did, in fact become good friends, and trusted allies.

CHAPTER THIRTY

Return to Camp Lejeune

14 May 0800
Defiance War Room
Defiance

At the morning meeting Levi welcomed everyone and announced that he had only two items on his agenda; begin to consider a name for our new nation, and to begin the planning phase of the return to Lejeune to open some of the Armories and bring their contents back to Defiance.

Levi put his foot down and made it absolutely clear to everyone in attendance that he intended to lead this mission, with Captain Eldridge as his Deputy and Staff Sergeant Guyardo as the NCOIC (Sergeant in charge). Though there were objections, everyone realized that the Colonel was going to win this one.

A number of names were discussed, but no agreement was reached until Major Ben Smith suggested the new nation be named The Republic of America. All agreed that this name would be friendly and familiar in the collective memory of the survivors. Being called Americans could become a rallying call to never give up.

At any rate, the name of a new nation was far too important to be decided in one short meeting, so the members were tasked to get feedback from the community, both inside and out of Defiance proper. The decision was tabled until members of the community could, both mull over the name, or suggest another.

It was decided that the new name would be a ballot referendum, voted upon not by just the settlers living in the village of Defiance, but everyone within the stated boundary of this new nation.

Ralph believed this to be a wonderful idea that would give those living outside of Defiance proper a sense of belonging, a sense of community.

The second of Levi's agenda items, concerning a return to Camp Lejeune, was unanimously approved. Major Smith and Captain Eldridge, along with First Sergeant Cobb would work out the plan of action and the logistic concerns of such a major undertaking.

Ralph's agenda input consisted of four items. Of great importance was the progress of the building projects. He said, "I am very pleased to announce that the new Government House and the 1st Squadron Regimental Headquarters are estimated to be completed within the next thirty days.

He also announced that the first solar electric project; the Dining Facility should see completion within the next two days.

His third agenda item for this meeting was to announce that the Secretary of the Treasury reported that his efforts to fund a gold backed currency now had hard assets of nearly one thousand pounds of gold, one thousand four hundred pounds of silver along with other precious metals.

He also recommended that the initial price of gold should be set at $18 per ounce and silver at $3.00 per ounce and that all monies would be issued in hard currencies. The Secretary had also asked Ralph if he should plan on melting down gold and silver jewelry to create ingots for the treasury. Ralph told the group that he would suggest to this group a plan which would keep eighteen karat gold up to twenty-four karat intact and melt down those items of lesser quality.

The members of this governmental grouping agreed with the Mayor's recommendation. Now the task was to find a metallurgist capable of accomplishing this monumental task.

The Mayor's last agenda was to announce that the spring planting was complete and that the first sprouts were popping up everywhere.

The news of a successful first planting caused a loud approval from everyone, except the Historian who said in a very low murmur, "Oh, my, fresh veggies."

With the agenda covered, and committees established, the meeting was adjourned at 0925.

14 May 0930
Defiance War Room
Defiance

The Lejeune Committee, as they called themselves, met to prepare for, and execute a mission to add additional arms and ammunition from the Armories at Camp Lejeune.

Major Smith opened the planning session with his definition and concept of the operation.

"This mission objective is to acquire as much of the arms and munitions as our vehicle resources will allow, and then return safely to Defiance. The lead vehicle (jeep) will scout one tenth of a mile ahead of the main body to warn of blockages, ambushes, or any situation which may cause the convoy to be halted.

Up-gunned jeeps will be evenly spaced throughout the convoy providing alternating flanking coverage.

The trailing jeep will hold position one hundred yards to the rear of the main body to warn of any approaching danger.

My concept of the operation will be to travel vehicle heavy, double basic ammo load, standard LBE (load bearing equipment), vest, helmet, two-day supply of water, and MRE's for four days.

"The vehicle requirements are, as I see them;

- thirty-five of our truck fleet in 2 ½ and 5-Ton trucks,
- six up-gunned jeeps,
- our lone Lowe's truck,
- one medical,
- one maintenance truck
- All other vehicles will carry three men each.
- This will allow the third man to rest and hopefully preclude mass casualties should a truck carrying many troopers be hit or destroyed.

"As you can see, this will strain our home defense, but, if we have insufficient personnel to complete the mission, well, we just cannot fail to retrieve what is there, if anything. I anticipate crossing the LOD No Later Than 0600 hours on 16 May. Command and Control will consist of Colonel Levins, Captain Eldridge, Captain Pickett, and Staff Sergeant Guyardo."

Major Smith then opened the meeting up for discussion.

Captain Pickett said, "Major, I would like to recommend that elements of B Troop be sent out two days in advance of the convoy to recon the route and provide flanking support as may be required. I propose two ten-man teams flanking the road. Should a danger present itself, we shall either eliminate the threat, or await the convoy should more firepower be needed."

Major Smith said, "Leon, that is an excellent plan, but can you be on the road today?"

"Yes, sir, we can. I have discussed just such a mission with my NCO's, and they assure me the mission can commence with two hours notice. That being the case I would say we could be on the move No Later Than1400 hours today."

"Very well, Captain, you have my blessing; Colonel Levins, do you have any input on this?"

Levi shook his head and made it clear he approved the plan. When the plan was agreed upon the individual requirements for preparation of mission success were established. After much discussion of the minute details, the meeting was adjourned at 1005. Following the meeting, Colonel Levins spoke with Major Ben Smith. "Ben, you did a great job, now tell me; just how long have you been planning this mission?"

Ben smiled and said, "Since the day Scott returned from Lejeune. I regret that I didn't include the use of our cavalry. That was foolish of me, but I am very pleased you liked the overall plan."

"Liked? Ben, that was as good a mission guidance briefing as I have ever attended. Ya' dun good, son. Ya' dun good.

I have to tell you my friend that I may be a rallying point, but you are the glue that keeps us on the right path. Say, do you remember the old sci-fi series called, Star Trek the Next Generation?"

"Yes, sir, of course."

"In that series, the XO, Riker, was the template for you. The only difference, Number One, is that your work doesn't take place on a movie set. You are the best, Ben. Keep up the good work."

Levi shook Ben's hand and left him speechless. As Levi left the room, he muttered to himself, just loud enough for Ben to hear, "Damn, how lucky can a Commander get?"

Leon drove his jeep back to Fort Pickett and began preparing for a dangerous mission. They crossed their Line of Departure at exactly 1400 hours.

Once arriving at the route, LOD, the convoy would take Leon's divided force of twenty mounted cavalry into two ten-man squads on each side of the roadway. Two scouts on each team eased along the flanks of the road followed at two hundred yards by the main bodies.

At dark, the units made a dry camp, and after placing OPs, and tin cans filled with rocks hung on wire around the camp, everyone settled in for some cold MREs and sleep. At first light, the scout set out on their recon mission, followed ten minutes later by the main bodies.

At thirty miles from their last camp, the scouts spotted a roadblock. After ascertaining that the blockage was manned by six men at the blockade and a sniper on each flank, one of the scouts rode back to the main body to report. Captain Pickett ordered a halt and after hearing the report decided to advance, on foot, with ten men to within one hundred yards of the roadblock. The thick pine forest concealed the troopers.

Leon sent one scout to each flank to get a closer look before considering his next move. The scouts easily spotted the men playing sniper, both sound asleep. They made their way around them to investigate the position from the rear. What they saw were five heavily armed men and seven naked women in chains performing cooking duties.

The scouts clearly heard one of the men on the roadblock saying, "Man, this job sucks. Do you think Ike really believes we can stop that Defiance outfit? Remember what they done to Snake and a lot of our boys? Well, if he does, he's nuts, but I ain't gonna' be the one to tell him that.

The man then turned around, and the scout saw the logo on the back of the man's vest. It read "Death Dealers."

At this point, both scouts slipped back to Captain Pickett and reported that there were still Death Dealers around.

"Sir, we have a total of seven of the Death Dealer's motorcycle gang. Remember that group that Troop A took out in Kill Devil Hills last month? Apparently, we didn't get them all."

"Yeah," said Captain Pickett, "my guess is the rest are enjoying the pleasures of Washington Park. It is a lovely little town right on the Pamlico River. Ok, we need info on this bunch of scumbags, so that means we need a prisoner, so here's what we're gonna' do.

Ted, you take three troopers to the left flank, and Joe, you do the same on the right flank. Now, do not forget the snipers. I'm going to give you thirty minutes to get into position. Let's see, right now it's quarter to, so at exactly twenty minutes past I will fire a shot. You will quickly follow suit and take all save one of these big bad Death Dealers out…but remember I want one prisoner, so we don't shoot the man nearest to the slaves. We clear on this?"

"Yes, sir, at twenty past, you fire one round we shoot all the males, save the one closest to the slaves, and take that bastard alive. Yes, sir, we're good."

"Well, all right, get your teams ready for silent movement and get your asses movin'."

The NCOs grabbed their fire teams, removed any noise making equipment, and made their way through the forest. At fifteen minutes past the hour, everyone was in place, targets assigned and awaiting the signal to open fire.

At twenty past Leon fired one round into the air and a second later rifle thunder roared through the trees, leaving only one bewildered man standing in the open throwing his hands high and screaming, "Don't shoot, I'm unarmed."

Ted took the scoped Remington 22 LR and placed a well-aimed round into the meaty portion of the man's right calf, taking him to the ground, and leaving him screaming in pain. Ted then instructed the trooper nearest him to ease on down and make sure the survivor was in fact unarmed, and that the others were dead.

The women sat huddled together fearing that another horror might now be coming into their lives. Once the entire force had arrived at the roadblock, Leon asked the women, "Which of these assholes has the key to your chains?"

They all pointed to the man still screaming in pain on the ground. A Sergeant went to the downed man and said, "Fish out them keys dickweed, and be quick."

The man said, "They're in my right pocket. I need a doctor, ya' shot me, damn it."

The Sergeant gently kicked the wounded calf and said, "I didn't ask y'all where they wuz. I told ya' to git 'em."

When the Sergeant touched the wound, the man screamed and scrambled to get the keys, then handed them to his tormentor.

Leon had him unlock the chains around the ankles of the women. As he freed them, Leon asked, "Ladies, do you have any clothes, here?"

Without looking in Leon's eyes, one said, ye… yes, sir, over in their truck."

Leon smiled his most charming smile and said, "Thank the Lord, please go over there and get dressed. We mean you no harm, and I suspicion you have had enough harm for this lifetime."

While the ladies were dressing Leon knelt down beside the wounded Death Dealer, and said, "Well, well, well, how the worm has turned. Now here's the deal. Just so you know who we are I will tell you. We are Troop B, Defiance Militia, and you are nothing.

Let's make this easy, I ask, you answer. If I like what you say, then when we leave I won't let these ladies care for you. I imagine that leaving you with them would not be a good thing…well, for you anyway.

So, here goes; how many of you pricks are there?"

"You get me to a doc, and I'll tell."

Making a wrong answer buzzer sound, Levi said, "Nope, not the right answer." He called the woman who seemed to be the oldest of her group and asked her, "Ma'am, if I were to leave this maggot in your care what would you do?"

Feeling the power of freedom, the woman, named Alice said, "Strip him naked, stake him to the ground by one of these red ant nests, then cut off his balls to attract the ants."

"Hmmm," said Leon as he looked down at the man on the ground now begging not to be left to the women.

"Ma'am, would you like to demonstrate a small token of your love of this man?"

"Oh, yes. Would you loan me your knife?"

"Alice, I would love to do that, but we need him alive for now, so maybe just a swift kick?" and Leon whispered into her ear.

"Well, okay, that'll work, for now, I guess."

The screaming from pain now turned to pleas for help.

Leon thought that maybe she was getting into this just a bit too much, but he did have two troopers hold the man's legs open by the ankles and she kicked him squarely on the bullet wound in his calf.

The man screamed from the pain, which was severe, but probably not as debilitating as where he had anticipated the kick.

"All right," said Leon. "Now you had best listen up if you want to avoid these ladies. I'll ask one more time, and if I don't like the answer, well, you get staked to the ground, oh, and naked. One more time, how many of you pricks are there?"

"Twenty-two," answered the defeated gangbanger.

Now, making a pinging sound, Leon said, "Oh, yeah, I like that answer. Question two: where are they?"

"They're in Washington Park, over by the river."

"Did you kill anyone in the town?"

"Well, duh, we had to, didn't we? How else were we goin' to take over?"

"Why were these women naked?"

"If they're naked they cain't be hiden no weapons, and 'sides they look better that way, right?"

"Of course, what else are they good for, besides cookin' and shit?"

Leon then turned to his troopers and said, "Would any of you like to offer anything in this man's defense?"

Almost to a man, the troopers just spit on the ground.

Turning back to the wounded man, Leon said, "What's your name?"

"Bull."

"Well, Bull I needed your name to put on the sign. I find you guilty of murder. The penalty for these crimes is hanging by the neck until you are dead."

"What? No, you can't do that, hell you ain't even read me my rights. This is bullshit. I want a lawyer."

"Oh, Bull, you are such a whiner…"

Suddenly, the rumble of motorcycles could be heard approaching. Leon ordered his troopers to take up positions on each side of the road. He also promised to let the women have Bull if he made one single sound. Leon sat in a nearby chair and waited for the arrival of the bikers who seconds later came riding in.

As they put down their kickstands and started to get off the bikes, Leon shouted, "Gentlemen, please stay seated. You are covered from each side of the road, and you will be shot if you get off your bike.

The men were surprised to hear Leon but decided not to get off the bikes.

The leader said, "Who are you?"

"My name is Captain Leon Pickett, commander of B Troop, 1st Squadron, 1st Cavalry Regiment of Defiance."

The leader reached for his gun but was thrown to the ground from the impacts of a dozen caliber 30-30 rounds slamming into his body knocking him from his ride.

The others seven riders froze in place and raised their hands.

"All right now boys, go ahead and get off those bikes. Using only two fingers, take your weapons very carefully and put them on the ground. You will then back away from those weapons by taking three steps. Do it now, please."

With great slowness, the bikers removed their weapons, dropped them to the ground, and took three steps back.

"Well done. Now drop to your knees and keep your hands on your head."

Leon then signaled his men to zip-tie the biker's hand behind their backs."

Signs were then made and tied around the prisoner's necks, then with signs in place they were each hanged by the neck until they were dead.

The signs read:

TO WHOM IT MAY CONCERN:
I WAS GUILTY OF MURDER AND KIDNAPPING
THE PUNISHMENT FOR ANY OF THESE CRIMES IS DEATH.

TO MEMBERS OF MY BROTHERHOOD;
THE DEATH DEALERS;
WHEN THEY CAPTURE YOU,
THEY WILL HANG YOU.

THIS IS A PUBLIC SERVICE ANNOUNCEMENT COURTESY OF:

B TROOP, 1ST CAVALRY (MOUNTED)
LEON PICKETT
CAPTAIN, CAVALRY
COMMANDING

Leon then ordered the bikes destroyed by draining their fuel onto the ground and setting them afire.

The women were given weapons from the dead, and the keys to their old pickup, used to transport food, and such things that the bikes could not carry. Captain Pickett left a short after-action report attached to the center of the roadblock. He ended it with;

We anticipate making another forty miles before you catch up to us. Perhaps more if you take out the remaining bikers in Washington Park. They are along the riverbank. I think there are fourteen left. If we'd had the time, we'd have taken care of them ourselves. Godspeed, sir.

"Sergeant Ted!" shouted Leon, "We're burnin' daylight."

18 May 1000
Forty miles beyond
Washington Park

The convoy caught up with the Cavalry just over forty miles from the roadblock near Washington Park.

Colonel Levins met with Captain Pickett and instructed him to return to Fort Pickett, but to detour to Washington Park to eliminate the gang threat.

"That was a fine job you did back a ways. I do believe that word will get around that this dog will bite when bad boys rattle our cage.

Oh, Leon, save a few of the leather vests, we'll add one for the museum and others as mementos."

"Roger that, sir. I'll make sure you get the big dog's vest."

After this short meeting, the Cavalry made its way back to Washington Park and home, while Troop A continued to Lejeune.

The remainder of the trip went without incident until they arrived at the gate and found the lock missing and the gate slightly ajar. A man in Marine Corps BDUs stepped from the guard shack and waited for Captain Eldridge to approach him before saying, "I'm sorry sir, but the base is closed."

"Is that so?" asked Scott Eldridge.

"Yes sir, it is, so if you will please return to your vehicles and vacate the premises."

Scott politely asked, "Would you please ask your commander to speak with us."

"Well, I gotta' tell ya' that I have no communication with him until I get relieved, you know, from whatever it was that knocked out the lights. You see, right now it's just me, and the sniper that has you in his crosshairs."

"Ah, yes, that would make sense to have an overwatch. How about calling your sniper down and asking him to get your commander?"

"Look, Doc, just get your ass back in your trucks and get the hell out of here."

"Well," said Scott, "if you feel that strongly about it, I'll go, but you should know that if I turn around you die."

A shout from the lead jeep said, "Captain, we have the sniper located, shall I take him out?"

Looking at the guard, Scott said, "Well, Doc, the ball is now squarely back in your court. You have five seconds."

The guard didn't know what to say or do and let the five seconds slip by before he began his reply. The old M-60 rattled and chewed up the window, which provided insufficient cover for the sniper who fell dead. By the time the M-60 stopped firing, Scott had his pistol out and aimed squarely at the chest of the gate guard.

Upon seeing the gun pointed at his chest the guard raised his hands in surrender. It didn't take much to get the guard to tell Scott everything he knew about the whereabouts of the squatters…locals who planned to carve out their own little kingdom.

As the troopers advanced to the squatter's headquarters, they came under fire from a first-floor barracks window. Private Henderson took a 7.62 NATO round squarely in the chest. He was quickly dragged to cover as more fire rained down onto the Troop A skirmishers.

Two troopers made their way around the building and gained entry by smashing a window in the rear. They slowly advanced in overwatch until they reached the room occupied by three shooters.

One quick burst from an M4-A1 dropped the ambushers. The troopers made sure the hostiles were dead before collecting their weapons and exiting the building, to rejoin their fellow troopers.

Colonel Levins told Captain E that he was glad that different uniforms were in use.

Private Henderson suffered a broken rib, but was saved by his vest. He was helped to the ambulance for medical treatment.

More fire erupted from the Company's Orderly Room, but it only took a demand for their surrender to end hostilities. Three more emerged with hands raised. Upon questioning it was discovered that the squatters were locals who had nowhere to go and thought they would have a better chance to survive here, rather than outside the gate.

"Well, Colonel, what do we do with them?"

Colonel Levins said, "Shit, I wish they had fought it out rather than surrender. Oh, hell, dress 'em in civvies, give 'em each three MREs, a sidearm one mag with twelve rounds, then drive 'em fifteen miles down the road and turn those young fools loose. Let the road deal with them."

Levi was thrilled to find that the Armories throughout the Camp were still secure. Using his keys and combinations, the treasures hidden in these crypts yielded valuable weapon and ammo caches.

Camp Lejeune was home to the 2nd Marine Division which consisted of twelve Battalions of Infantry. This MarDiv consisted of 90 companies. Each of these companies held its own armory. Just this singular Division could take years to empty.

The second Armory yielded a vast number of Claymore and anti-vehicle mines, along with case after case of hand grenades.

The fifth Armory yielded tons of C-4 explosives, fuses, det-cord and blasting caps. Levi inwardly chuckled at the thought that in the past, these items would have never been stored together…oh well, that was then, this is now.

There were many more Armories to raid, and the operation took nearly three days to load the trucks.

On the morning of the third day, Levi made his way to the Camp Headquarters Building. Going to General Chalmers' office was not a trip he wanted to make because he feared what may lay there. Still, he had to see for himself.

Using his key, he unlocked the main entrance and entered the dark and now dusty alcove. The building had the feeling of a dark mausoleum, a foreboding thought of the ghosts of the thousands of men and women who had worked here since 1941.

As he made his way down the hallway, he passed the office of Captain Wainwright, the General's Aide de Camp. Peering in through the door he saw that the office was neat and tidy.

Standing outside the office of General Chalmers, Levi hesitated before opening the door, not sure he wanted to enter. After a few seconds, he turned the knob and opened the door. There, with what remained of his skull thrown back from the impact of the bullet sat his friend, Lieutenant General Paul Chalmers.

As an act of sincere admiration for General Chalmers, Levi saluted and said, "Thank you, sir, I promise that the world will one day know the contribution you, and The United States Marine Corps have made to preclude a thousand year Dark Age.

Levi entered the office and under the General's hat found a note addressed to him. The note asked that this building be turned into a future museum, should it survive.

He replaced the note to its resting place and nearly tiptoed out of the office, not wishing to disturb the General who sat at his desk; forever on duty.

As Levi walked down the hall to the main entrance, he felt that if he could turn quickly enough, he would see ghosts of better days watching as he left the building.

CHAPTER THIRTY-ONE

Unity Day

```
6 May 1000
Village Green
Defiance
```

Captain Pickett brought three gutted cows and two pigs to be spit roasted on the Village Green to celebrate a spate of peace, military promotions, and a village party. A two-day holiday was proclaimed by Mayor Ralph Bassett.

Roasting a cow or large pig takes a minimum of twenty to twenty-four hours, so when the pits were dug, they added two extra pits for cooking lambs to feed those volunteers who would tend the fire during the nighttime hours.

A Carnival atmosphere began to build among the citizens of Defiance as cooks began the preparations for the massive amounts of side dishes needed to feed nearly three hundred people.

The newly arrived Widow's Sons were invited to the festivities. In an effort to become a part of the community, they volunteered to spread the word, but most of the folks were not yet comfortable with motorcycles approaching their home. Ultimately, it was the Cavalry that was chosen to pass the word and to let everyone who had no way to get to the party know that a bus would come by their home to get them. This would be a party for the ages.

New clothing hung on racks and tables free to anyone needing them. The Doctors and Dentists set up booths to give quickie exams for later treatment as needed. The Dentists even passed out free toothbrushes and paste.

There were classes on personal health, planned to make sure everyone had the skills to filter and purify their home water. So far, Typhoid, Dysentery, and other antihygienic or waterborne diseases had not visited them, and with proper care, they might be kept away. The village carpenters even built several Johnnie Houses in various phases of construction to show how to build them.

Games for the children and toys for the smaller children were to be given out, and drawings for thirty bicycles, one per family, were planned. Booths for exchanging recipes, pots, and pans, simply everything imaginable. There was even a booth with a fortune teller.

The betting odds on the sack race gave Adan Ramos and Miss Mary Collins the early edge. They had been seen walking hand in hand along the village green on several occasions lately…good-natured rumors were flying.

There was already talk of getting a school up and running, and much excitement at the thought of building an open-air stage and putting a band together for next year's festivities. The air was electric with excitement after so much fear and dread…why some people even spoke of getting electricity. Surprisingly, no one over the age of twenty-five wanted a return of TV or the Internet.

7 May 0800
Defiance

People from all over the twenty-mile border of Defiance came streaming into the village. All were dressed in their finest clothing although for many the clothes seemed a bit too baggy as so many had lost weight.

The smell from the spits had everyone's mouths watering, even with another five hours for the meat to be ready. Today, there would be no talk of the dead still lying on the streets, or murderous gangs attacking the outliers of the community. No talk of the terrors that lay ahead. Today was a day of celebration, of community, and the emotional bonding of a new nation.

Oh, everyone knew that the ugly world outside of their little twenty-mile border held horrors beyond description, but not today. Many asked if they could move into Defiance. The Mayor said he would address that issue during his speech.

MAYOR'S SPEECH:

"I want to welcome each and every one of you to this the celebration that has grown from a military promotion and block party to a gathering of all the citizens of Defiance, which, at present includes anyone living within a twenty-mile radius from this spot.

There is no more United States. It has gone the way of Rome, and countless other civilizations into the dustbin of history.

We will be taking suggestions…in writing, to be placed in our suggestion box for a name for our new nation. Yes, I know, the term Nation sounds like a Delusion of Grandeur, but even Rome began as a tiny village on the Tiber River in what was, until a mere six weeks ago Italy.

Many of you have asked to move into Defiance Proper. I am sorry to say that our goal from this point forward is to expand outward. There are many farms with lands now lying fallow that will, after resting for a year, be ready in year one for renewed plantings. Farmhouses need cleaning out and repairs need to be made.

Newcomers to our land will be welcomed but will also be thoroughly vetted. We are a Conservative Constitutional Republic, and our Constitution is that of the Founding Fathers of the United States of America. We will adhere to that document and the Bill of Rights.

We are a young nation of those willing to work for a better future. We have no time, resources, or inclination toward the liberal socialist views which had the United States nearly on its knees before the Coronal Mass Ejection from our star, and guided by the hand of God, to miss us, and we have been given a chance for a new and better tomorrow.

We will also be running a new flag up the pole in the near future. It will have one bright white five-pointed star with a red backing centered on a sky-blue field. It is simple and humble and will fly to remind us of our beginnings.

Here in Defiance, we stand as a proud group of people…survivors made up of White's, Black's, Latino's and a few Native Americans. Yes, we once were divided against each other by race, but no longer. Today and forever more we are one, WE ARE DEFIANCE!"

The crowd erupted in applause of approval. After thirty seconds, the Mayor raised his hand to silence the crowd allowing him to continue.

"We cannot and will not tolerate the old tribal hatreds that kept us apart. Therefore, having said that, I give each of you this warning; if you feel differently, then you must leave Defiance. There simply will never be room for you here. The history of our new nation begins here, today and we will call this day, Unity Day, to be celebrated each year on this day, 7 May."

Again, the crowd broke into loud applause, and once more, after thirty seconds, the Mayor raised his hand to silence the crowd allowing him to continue.

Our language is English, and anyone who does not speak our language may not reside inside the borders of Defiance, no exceptions.

Once the crops are in, school will commence. The curriculum will be heavy on the three R's. I fear, however, that for, at least a few years, a college education will elude us.

We will also be striking a new currency of both gold and silver. If you currently have gold and silver, I ask but do not insist, that when our new coins are minted you will trade in your gold and silver in exchange for the new currency. Any coin minted in the old U.S. prior to 1965 will be accepted for purchases at face value. Gold will be valued at $18 an ounce. Yes, I do feel your pain as I also have some gold coins, but that currency is now worthless. As an example; the cost of a loaf of bread should not be more than a nickel.

My friends, there is so much to do that it will take years to fully establish a working government of the people, for the people, and by the people, and there will be no career politicians in our new nation.

I have been asked how we will support our military force once we have established a currency and have gone through those resources currently being utilized. I fear that now is the time to inform you that, yes, you will be taxed at a rate of 10% on all goods purchased, and rounded down to the lower penny. For example, a five cent loaf of bread will have no tax. There will be no end of year tax documents to file as the tax will be collected at the point of purchase. We anticipate the new tax will begin on the first day of year one and will coincide with the introduction of our new currency.

Applause again erupted when the Mayor said, "Thank you, and now I would like to introduce someone you all know, Colonel Levi Levins."

The crowd stood in ovation following Levi's introduction. Levi was obviously embarrassed to receive such accolades and several times raised his hand to quiet the crowd. The ovation lasted for three minutes, and many thought that Levi's face got so red they feared he might have a heart attack had it gone on much longer. Finally, he was able to speak.

"Wow, this is amazing and really scary. My friends, we have in a very short time come a very long way in preparing a path for us to remain above the New Dark Age, which has gripped the rest of the world. Here, we have been very lucky, and many things have fallen our way. I surely hope that trend continues, but I am not holding my breath. Oh, I don't mean to say that we will not be successful because we will be, but there will also be many setbacks, missteps, and disasters ahead of us, but through it all, we will prevail.

As you may know, our militia has had several successful operations to destroy those criminal elements that have come our way. There will be more. I have also just made a proposal to our Mayor Ralph that since we are now a new nation; calling us a militia is a misnomer.

We are the infant Regular Army and from this day shall no longer be referred to as a militia. We are now officially Troop A and B of the 1st Squadron, 1st Cavalry Regiment. Yes, I know, it sounds a bit grandiose for such a small force, but we must not assume that our current force is sufficient to deliver us from all the evils outside of our borders.

Our force has grown to the point that we now have two troops, one of Mobile Infantry and one of Mounted Cavalry. The Mobile Infantry located here, and the Mounted Cavalry at what was once called the Lykes Brothers Ranch and is now renamed Fort Pickett in honor of its founder, Captain Leon Pickett.

The Defiance military must continue to grow and train hard to be prepared and able to fend off those criminal bands who want to destroy us and take what little we have.

We must also realize that we cannot become a successful and prosperous nation with only a twenty-mile border. No, Defiance must expand her borders to bring law and order, but more importantly…peace for those living within our borders.

We shall not seek expansion through aggression or war. We intend to build a nation that others will seek out to join."

Levi then named those Troop A & B personnel being promoted and presented each of them with the new insignia of rank before saying, "And that, my friends will take us to the fun time. Lunch will be served around 1300, but the booths are open for your enjoyment immediately after I quit yappin', thank you."

CHAPTER THIRTY-TWO

Levi Gets Restless

10 June 2300
Levi's Quarters
Defiance

The weeks since Unity Day had passed with a disarming calm sameness that left Levi feeling antsy. His dreams were filled with visions of Sarah, but occasionally those dreams took a darker turn. He would often awaken with a start and in a cold sweat after reliving the trauma of discovering her lifeless body on the second-floor landing.

These dreams took on a more sinister tone as the suppressed rage rekindled like the stacked coals of a banked fire.

Levi began taking his jeep outside of the accepted borders of The Republic of America as the vote had overwhelmingly decided to name the new nation.

While on these excursions he carried an upgraded M-14 which had been scoped, carefully sighted in and silenced. Levi had become an expert with this weapon out to one thousand yards. He also carried his sidearm and an M4-A1 along with a double issue of fully loaded magazines. No one in Defiance knew that Levi often left America to prowl the roads leading to towns known to have been taken over by invading gangs.

A few days back, on 8 June, two miles from the little town of Miller's Ford, Levi had parked and covered his jeep with a camo net. He took his M-14, sidearm, a basic load of ammo and slowly made his way to within five hundred yards of the village.

It soon became obvious that Miller's Ford was now in the hands of a very bad bunch of red neck bullies. Finding the highest piece of ground allowing him an unrestricted view of the happenings around one of the local bars, Levi prepared a sniper's nest and through his rifle's scope, waited until he saw one of the red necks strike a young girl.

The man held a Jack Daniel's whiskey bottle in his right hand while he struck her with his left. As the man took a pull on the whiskey, Levi's rifle made a soft pop, and the man dropped the bottle to the ground. The NATO round had passed directly through the heart of the drunk and came out of his back leaving an exit hole the size of Levi's fist.

The man was knocked back and off his feet, dead before his brain could even register that he had been shot. The girl screamed once before jumping to her feet and running away. No one had heard the shot that killed one of the brutal animals of this new world outside of Defiance.

Levi then took out a few pieces of jerky and lay there awaiting his next target. His wait was nearly ten minutes before two other men exited the bar dragging two women by the hair.

Levi stopped chewing, sighted in on the man in the rear, took a deep breath before releasing half, and with the pad of his index finger squeezed off a round that struck his target directly in his genital sack. The man screamed and grabbed his balls as he fell to the ground. The front man turned to see his friend was in terrible pain. He pushed the girl down and ran the four steps to his brother.

Again, the silencer made no noise whatsoever to a target five hundred yards away. Levi shot the third man two times, once in each leg. The two men screaming in pain finally drew the attention of those inside of the bar. The first three men who came through the door were dropped in rapid succession.

Those inside the bar stopped at the door as they saw their mates fall to the ground screaming in agony. Levi did not shoot these men to kill them immediately, but to cause serious wounds that would lead to a lingering death. His goal was to cause them pain and fear.

The screaming lasted for roughly twenty minutes until the last man bled out. Levi picked up his brass and poncho, then returned to his jeep and home. Those inside the bar waited, afraid to come out for three hours. When they did emerge from the bar, they saw the carnage as six members of their tribe lay dead. No one had heard a shot. No one had any idea how this had happened.

By the time the drunks found the courage to exit the bar, Levi had been looking over the training schedule and was on the way to the range to observe sharpshooter training. While there he joined the men for some target practice before cleaning his weapon.

That night Sarah came to him and cautioned him to be very careful. She said, "Levi, I love you. Please be aware that I do not require you to go hunting evil men. Perhaps you should consider staying on in Defiance." When he awoke, he knew that remaining in Defiance was not in the cards, at least for the foreseeable future.

Today, Levi was back in his sniper's nest patiently waiting for another of these evil men to emerge from the bar. His wait wasn't long as two men emerged from the bar and went to the side of the building to relieve themselves. Levi figured the smell in the bar toilet must be too foul for even these men.

As they were relieving themselves, Levi placed a round squarely into the back of the man on the left and squarely in the kidney of the other. The first round passed through the lungs and exited just to the right of the left breast. The man shot in the kidney began to scream in pain. This time, however, no one deemed it a good idea to run out to help.

Levi packed up and went home.

Now, at 2300 Levi lay in his bed wondering how long it took the kidney shot to kill that man. He also wondered if he was becoming a monster just like those he killed. He quickly decided that he was not becoming a monster. He was becoming an avenging Vigilante…

CHAPTER THIRTY-THREE

Katie Jarvis

3 July 1230
Just outside of Miller's Creek

Levi rode Scar to the outskirts of Miller's Creek. He wanted to see how the tiny community was getting along. He tied Scar to a tree and put on a feedbag of oats.

He made his way quietly around the extreme edge of the village when he came upon three laughing men who stood over a poor skinny young woman who did not look like she was happy with the attention being given her by the three drunks who hemmed her in against the outside wall of an old building and she told them so, not sparing any words.

Spunky, thought Levi.

Drawing his Beretta M-9A1 nine millimeter pistol he walked up behind the three men and said, "Howdy boys, havin' a bit of fun are ya'?"

The three men spun around and started for their guns, until they saw they were looking down the barrel of Levi's Beretta. This fact changed their demeanor immediately as they moved their hands away from their weapons and smiled through rotting teeth.

Levi said, "Peace boys, I'm lookin' for a meth dealer I heard had a lab around here. You got any idea where I might find the Chemist?"

The leader of this group said, "Oh hell yeah, you come to the right place. I'm the Chemist, and I make the best meth you ever smoked."

"Well," said a smiling Levi, "just as soon as you are finished with your little party, let's talk."

All three men were smiling now as the Chemist said, "Good idea, why not join us?"

Now, for the first time Levi could see that this was not just a skinny young woman, but a child no more than sixteen.

"I think we should do our business first. Young'un you might just want to stand up and come over here behind me. Do it! Now!"

The girl scrambled to safety behind Levi just as he shot the two outside morons in the chest. The Chemist looked on not believing what just happened.

"What fer you dun that? We ain't dun nuthin' to Y'all. We juss havin' a li'l fun. Now, look at my brothers?

The man was high on Meth, and the realization of what had just happened was only slowly sinking in. "I guess you gonna' rob me of my meth and that li'l gal I dun bought for three grams uh perfectly good product."

Levi didn't want to hear anymore and fired another round that dropped the man to the ground… permanently.

Levi took the weapons and said, "These are filthy, just like the animals who owned them." He then turned to the girl who looked at him and said, "I guess now you figger on doin' to me what they wanted to do, huh?"

He looked back at the building and said, "Nope. Do you know where his meth lab is?"

"Of course, I do, come on, and I'll show ya'." Levi followed her into the building as she took him to the lab. He then poured kerosene on the floor from the chemist's cooking fuel and lit it as they backed out of the room.

As they returned to the three men, Levi was somewhat surprised to find the chemist still alive, and without a second's thought, shot him in the head as he walked by. Levi then asked the girl where her parents were.

"Hell, I don't know, dead I guess somewhere up in Delaware."

"Delaware? How did you get clear down here? Or do I not want to know?"

"No, you don't want to know, and I don't want to say."

"Okay, how about your name?"

"Katie Jarvis, what's yours?"

"Levi Levins, and how old are you?"

"I'm 22, is that a good age?"

"Well, it would be if you were 22, now, how old are you? The truth this time."

"Oh, okay, I'm sixteen, that is if it's past July 1st."

"Well then you must be sixteen since it's now July 3rd. Come on; my horse is just up ahead. You can ride behind me back to Defiance."

"Whoa, mister, what makes you think I'm going anywhere with you? – 'cause I ain't. I know what the hell you want to do as soon as you get me over in them trees. Well, you best understand, I'm done with that. I'll fight ya' till you have to kill me before I let you do what they was gonna do."

"'Whoa' is the right word, little miss. First of all, I am no rapist, and second of all, I'm not interested in forcing myself on anyone, especially children. Now come on. I'll get you back to Defiance and get some food into you, and you can get a bath…don't say it. There are lots of mothers in Defiance that will protect you from me," smiled Levi.

"Okay, but you been warned. You gonna' bury 'em?"

"Nope, buzzards gotta' eat same as the worms, besides what difference could three more bodies make to a world that is one big open graveyard?"

"Good, let's go, but don't you try nothin'. You really got a horse around here?"

Levi looked at her and said, "Okay, I'll somehow manage to restrain myself, and yes his name is Scar."

As they walked back to Scar Katie suddenly stopped, looked at Levi and asked, "Wait a minute, how did you know he ran a meth lab?"

He laughed and said, "Aw, that was easy, remember how they all had rotted teeth?"

"Yeah, so?"

"Well, if just one had had bad teeth I wouldn't have known for sure, but not all three, well, that's a dead giveaway. Ya' see, long time meth users usually develop rotting teeth, I don't know why, I just know that they do."

"…and their breath, whew, nasty," added Katie.

3 July
Defiance

As they rode into Defiance Katie looked around at all the clean, happy people and said, "Holy shit, just look at this place. I didn't think there was anywhere that looked this nice anymore."

Levi helped her down, and as he placed his hands on her shoulders, she suddenly shook them off and stepped back, ready to fight.

"Easy girl, I just wanted to tell you that you will no longer be living with animals, so I'd appreciate it if you'd watch your language and speak with a civil tongue in your head."

Relaxing somewhat, but with her back still up she said, "Oh, so now I can't say what I want, huh?"

Levi smiled and said, "Not if you want to stay in Defiance. Now come on, I want to introduce you to the Mayor of our little village."

Trust came hard for Katie, but it was understandable since she had been treated so badly, abused and traded among evil men, but she decided to give Levi a chance and said, "Well, okay, I'll try."

"Fair enough kiddo, now let's go meet Ralph."

Ralph had been told of Levi's return and was on the way when they met on the Village Green.

"Levi, what have you got here, picking up strays now, are you?"

"Ralph, I'd like you to meet Katie, Katie Jarvis. She's had a rough time since the lights went out and it's about time something good happened to her. Think we could get one of the ladies to get her cleaned up and something to eat?"

"Of course, come on Katie," said Ralph as he took her hand.

She jerked away and took two running steps to Levi. She threw her arms around him and said, "No, please. Let me stay with you."

Levi tried to pry her off him to no avail. He finally said, "It's okay sweetie, Ralph is a good guy, I promise. Won't you please go with him, so he can find one of the ladies to get you a bath?"

"No, Levi, please come with us. Don't leave me." Tears began to run down her cheeks for the first time in, well, a long time.

"All right Katie, I'll go along with you, but I can't be with you while you are taking your bath. Tell ya' what, as soon as you are all cleaned up, we'll have lunch together. Okay?"

Her tears slowed, and she said, "Not really, but I guess it'll have to be okay. You won't be far though, right?"

"Katie, I promise I'll be close enough that you can hear my voice."

"Okay then, let's go. I ain't had a bath in a long time."

"Oh my, we'd better get to it then. Lead the way, Ralph."

Ralph led them to the home of Mary Collins, the Supply Officer for Defiance. She was thrilled to help and took charge.

As Katie was getting her shower, Levi filled Ralph in on the day's events. "…then we burned down the lab and since it was bring her back here or leave her out there alone…well, the only thing to do was bring her back with me.

"You know, I'd planned to look over Miller's Creek, but I didn't get close enough to see anything but the meth lab."

Katie shouted to Levi as she was drying off and putting on clean clothes, "Oh, there's folks there all right, but they got a new Sheriff. They didn't elect him, he just showed and took over. He ain't nuthin' but a big bully and everbody is just way too scared to try anything. The folks got it bad there."

Levi asked, "Katie, how many deputies does he have?"

"Nine and they are some kinda' mean bastar…oops sorry, I meant to say, mean men."

Levi smiled and whispered to Ralph, "She's tryin' to clean up her language among civilized people."

"Oh, I see," smiled Ralph.

Katie said, "Hey, you two know I can hear you, right? I hear real good."

Levi began to laugh and said, "I guess we'll have to keep that in mind. How much longer are you gonna' be, I'm hungry?"

Mary and Katie came out and Katie said "Thanks for not leaving me, now can we get something to eat, it's been a while?"

Ralph stopped one of the young fella's passing by and asked him if he would go to the mess hall and tell the cooks that they would be over shortly for a bite.

"Yes sir," said the boy who looked kindly at Katie before running off to the mess hall. Katie wasn't really what anyone would call a real beauty. She was about average height for her age, but downright scrawny. She had sort of mousy brown hair, but good features to her face, Levi thought she looked like what he would have liked if he'd had a daughter.

Ralph started to say something about how young Ted had looked at Katie, but a sharp shake of Levi's head caused him to change the subject. Later Levi told him about how she had been continuously abused and beaten over the last few months.

Ralph said, "Thanks, old buddy, I'm sure glad you stopped me. You know, sometimes I forget how bad the world is outside our gate."

After lunch, Levi, Ralph and Katie went to Levi's office. Katie was so tired she could barely keep her eyes open. Levi convinced her to lie down on his cot while he and Ralph had a meeting in Levi's Office, which was in the next room. He had to promise her that he would not go anywhere else until she woke up.

As they sat down to talk about the day's events Ralph said, "Oh, and that reminds me, just what in the hell was our Regimental Commander doing wandering around the countryside all by himself."

He looked to Ralph and said, "Do you remember the day we met, and I told you that I would stay for maybe one year because my path was elsewhere?"

"Well, yeah, sure I remember, but that was then, surely you don't still plan to leave, do you?"

"Yes, Ralph I do. In fact, I'm going to leave in October and head south."

"But Levi, you can't just leave us. Why, without you to lead the troops, we won't be safe. Come on; you can't just leave us."

"Well Ralph, I guess this is as good a time as any to discuss Troop A's future leadership."

"No Levi, I won't hear of it."

"Ralph, it's not up to you. Now let's talk about the leadership roles. We need Ben here because he has a big part in what I need to say." Levi rose and opened the door calling for the First Sergeant to send a runner to get Major Smith for a meeting.

"Ralph," said Levi, as he sat back down, "we need to discuss Ben before he gets here."

"Yes, okay, what?"

"Ben is the perfect XO, but he does not have either the experience or the temperament to Command. When we had the last promotion ceremony, making Ben a Major, Sergeants Guy to Lieutenant and Eldridge to Captain I have been grooming Scott Eldridge to take command. He is a natural leader; an excellent tactician and the Troop supports him all the way. When Ben comes in, I'm going to have to tell him that he won't be my replacement.

"I hope you will agree to two promotions today, Guy to Captain and Scott to Major. Scott will remain my Aide. Pretty soon people will see him as the heir apparent and will more easily accept the change."

Ralph's demeanor turned sad as he said, "Levi, of course, I'll agree to promote anyone you say, but I have to tell you that I am opposed to this whole thing.

Office of the Commander
Defiance Military, HQ

"Come on in Ben, we have some things to talk over with Ralph," said Levi.

"Sure thing boss, what's up?"

"Ben, how do you like being the XO?"

"Why Levi, are you planning to get rid of me?"

"Oh, hell no, Ben you are the best XO I have ever had the pleasure to work with. No, there is no plan or even consideration of replacing you. Still, I do need an answer."

"Well," said Ben, "This has been the best job I've ever had. I love being the XO. In fact, I wouldn't have it any other way. If you're happy with me, then here is where I plan to stay."

Levi looked at Major Ben Smith and said, "Ben, that is really good news, because we would be lost without the job you do. I know I can depend on you to always carry out your mission, big or small."

Ben looked back at Levi and said, "Levi, what the hell is going on here? Why are you blowing so much smoke up my ass? You didn't ask me to come here to make me blush like a school girl who just got kissed at the Prom."

Levi smiled, but Ralph remained stoic. "Yeah, Ben you are right. Tell me, if I died do you think you could take the reins and command this outfit?"

"Ralph, is Levi sick?"

"No, not in the traditional way, but yeah I think he's sick in the head."

"Okay, the answer is no. I mean I'd have to take over until we found someone better suited to the job. If we are being brutally honest here, I have to tell you that I do not have the necessary experience for command. I'm a born logistics guy, but I am not a tactician. The job of Commander is something that a person is born with. Oh, he needs years of leadership training and a desire to lead troops in combat as well. Levi, I am sad to have to say it, but I don't have any of that.

"I mean, yeah, I'm second fiddle, but I like being second fiddle to someone who knows what they're about. So, no, I do not think I would be a very good commander simply because I have neither the experience, nor the necessary training.

"I'm sorry Levi, but I don't want to tell a soldier to secure that rock, and he gets shot. That's bad enough, but the thought of having to tell the next man to take that rock is not something I want to do. That's not saying I wouldn't or couldn't do it, but it goes against my nature…am I rambling here?"

"Yeah Ben, just a little bit, but that's okay because I think you are 100% right, and now I have something to say to you that many men would feel like they had just been kicked in the gut.

"My friend, I plan to leave in October, and I intend to promote Captain Eldridge to Major and groom him to take my place."

Ben was shaken to the core and said, "Leaving, why Levi, that's crazy!"

Ralph interrupted saying, "Exactly what I said."

Ben continued, "Levi, are you really serious? We need you. You can't just ride off into the sunset like some singing cowboy."

"Actually Ben, I can, and I intend to do exactly that, well, without the singing part. My personal path has not changed. I am only here on a detour. This was a chance to help this community get started and a place for me to lay low until the bodies stopped stinking, and the diseases and plagues of critters had passed.

"Well, those things have mostly all happened, and now I have to get on with my personal mission.

"Defiance is doing great, the village is secure, the farms look super, the bodies have stopped stinking, and the plagues of critters are just about over.

So, here's the bottom line, I'm promoting Eldridge and keeping him as my Aide. We'll be telling everyone that I offered the job to you and you turned it down because you just don't yet have the experience to take on the job. The word will be that you recommended Scott for the job and I agreed that he would be an excellent choice.

"Ben, I gotta' know; can you live with this?"

"Well, if you mean can I live with you leaving, then I ain't so sure, but if you mean can I be Scott's XO, well I did tell you that I'm a born logistician. So yeah, of course, I can live with that. I can't think of anyone better than Scott, I mean he has that Ranger experience and to tell the truth Levi, he really reminds me of you. So yeah, if he wants me as his XO then I'm in, and thanks for that saving face thing."

"Ben, I don't think I could ever tell you how much I respect you and that I don't believe things could have ever worked out so well for Defiance without you. Thank you, Ben, I really do mean it."

Ralph stood up to leave saying, "Well, I'm not hanging around for any more of this love fest because I don't understand why you have to leave or why you would even want to. I got to tell you, Levi, I am pissed, but I'll get over it…someday…you prick," and all burst out laughing.

Levi said, "Hang on a minute Ralph, just one more thing.

Ben, I think it would work out best if you were to go to Scott and tell him that if anything should happen to me that you do not want the job of Commander because you just don't have the background.

Coming from you, I believe the community will appreciate your honesty and more fully realize your value to Defiance and its military by remaining where you are happiest, as XO."

Ralph nodded his approval and simply said, "Good thinking Levi, I like it. How about you, Ben?"

"Well, everything you said here is true, but it wasn't my idea…exactly."

Levi interjected, "Oh, now I'm not so sure of that since you are the one who told us you wanted to remain as XO, as opposed to Commander, I simply made a suggestion."

"Yeah, sure I can live with that, but there is one thing you should know, I would love to be the commander of Troop A, but I am also a realist and know my limitations. I mean, really, wouldn't anyone prefer to be the CO rather than the XO?

"Don't be concerned though, because I know I don't have the training or history to be as good at the top job as I am as XO. It also helps that I do love my job.

"Now, just to be clear; I don't tell Scott that you are stepping down, right?"

"Right, we don't want that rumor to get out there. Okay, let's get to work."

After the men had left Katie came in and asked, "So, when are we leaving?"

"Huh, what? Whoa, you just listen up; *we* are not leaving. I am leaving and how did you know? Wait a minute, you listened through the wall, right?"

"Yep, did you know that a drinking glass makes a pretty good stethoscope? Now you listen up. If *you* go, *I* go. I ain't safe with nobody but you, and I like this feelin' safe shi…sorry…stuff. If you leave without me, I'll just follow you on foot. Like it or not, we are a team now."

"Katie, what I have to do just can't include you. It's not that I don't want you to come along but what I have to do will not be good for you. You have to stay here to finish your education and live in safety. I cannot offer either of those things. Being out there with me would make you just like me; way too hard and maybe way too mean."

"Levi…I'm already too hard and just as mean as you. You are the only person I could ever care about and trust…as a Dad I mean. Don't you understand, we are family now, and I just can't lose you. I just can't…"

"Katie, let's not make any promises right now. I'm not planning to leave for a couple of months."

"Okay, but my mind will not change, if you leave, I leave; end of discussion," and with that, she stepped away from Levi and began to wipe the tears from her eyes. "Damn you, Levi, I swore I would never ever cry again, and look what you've done. Ya' got me cryin' like some teenage girly girl. It's all your fault ya' know."

"Really? All my fault? Well, just look at me sittin' here cryin' like some teenage girly girl," and they both started laughing.

Later that night another battle royal raged between Levi and Katie. She absolutely refused to sleep anywhere but close to Levi and spent the night in a sleeping bag outside his tent. Bright and early the next morning, ten carpenters were brought in and with only a, *"Mornin' sir,"* went to work on adding a room addition to Levi's shed. It was finished and furnished by nightfall.

Ben looked at his handiwork and said to himself, *Levi, I'll do just about anything to try to make you stay,* as he walked to the new all ranks club to serve those carpenters a beer.

CHAPTER THIRTY-FOUR

Levi and Mike Go Hunting

```
8 July 1030
1ˢᵗ Squadron, Cavalry HQ
Office of the Cdr.
Defiance, America
```

Captain Mike Guyardo was ushered into Colonel Levins' office by SGM Cobb.

"Oh, good morning Mike, how they hangin' this morning? Please have a seat."

Before leaving the SGM asked if he should have some coffee and muffins sent in. "Great idea, Sergeant Major, thank you."

"Sergeant Jones…"

"I'm already on it," shouted the newly promoted Sergeant Jones.

After the door was closed and Levi came around his desk to sit in a chair across from Captain Guyardo, Levi said, "Mike, the reason I've asked you in this morning is to discuss the problem with the self-proclaimed Sheriff and his nine Deputies over in Miller's Creek."

"Yes, sir."

Levi told Mike that the situation there could not continue and that he was going to put an end to the Sheriff's tyrannical rule and restore some law and order to that little village.

"Mike, I don't think we need to take a sizeable force in there and shoot up the place. I also think that you and I might be able to handle this ourselves.

"Oh, by the way, how's the foot these days, or should I say, the lack thereof?"

Mike chuckled and said, "Sir, over the last four years since it was blown off in Berzerkistan, I've gotten so that I don't even realize that it's gone. Really, sir, I'm fine and as you see every morning during PT that it is not a hindrance in any way."

Levi smiled and said, "Yes, Mike I have noticed that you seem to do very well, but I just wanted to hear you say it.

"Would you be interested in a little clandestine operation to rid Miller's Creek of the criminals who think they have taken over?"

"Yes, sir, of course, what do you have in mind?"

Levi explained how Katie had told him that ten men arrived in town and said that they were the law from then on. A couple of men objected and were murdered on the spot.

"Since then the folks have lived in tyranny and fear of these bullies who do what they want, to whoever they want, and I intend to put a stop to it. They are inside the border of America, and they must go. You interested?"

"Of course, I am. What's the plan, sir?"

Levi told Mike about his foray to Miller's Ford where he was slowly whittling down the criminal element there, and how he thought they might use the same tactic at Miller's Creek.

"We set up two sniper's nests and when the self-proclaimed Sheriff and his Deputies show themselves, well, to put it simply; we shoot 'em. No big gunfight, just a couple of snipers with upgraded scoped and silenced M-14s."

Mike looked at Levi, smiled and said, "Sir, I like the plan. Have you run it by anyone else?"

"Nope, and I don't plan to. If you don't want to participate, I understand and no hard feelings, but I do require your discretion."

Mike said, "Sir, of course, you have my discretion, but I would like to ask why you are doing this instead of creating a small team to do the job."

Levi told him that he had asked a fair question and his answer was, "Mike, I'm bored, and past the point of being useful as anything other than a rallying point. This place is running just fine without me, and in truth, I am sick of these four walls. I need to get back to being productive by ridding the world of those who would murder and abuse others.

"Yes, I know, high ideals with no chance of being more than a drop in the bucket considering the size of the North American bucket. Still, if I can help one single person, I will have made a difference for the better in that one person's life."

Mike liked the idea but questioned Levi's rationale concerning his belief that he was nothing more than just a rallying point, though in the back of his mind Mike agreed that the current command structure did have things well in hand.

"All right, sir, I'm in. When do we start?"

Levi instructed Mike to draw one of the upgraded sharpshooter M-14s and take it to the range to get it fine-tuned and zeroed in, and today would be good if his schedule allowed for it."

Mike now commanded Troop A and his First Sergeant could handle anything that would come up for the next few days.

"Mike, that sounds good, get it done today and we start cleanin' up Dodge City tomorrow morning. Let's shoot for a 1000 hours departure."

"Roger that, sir. Is there anything else for me?"

"No, Mike, just get ready and let's set some people free."

Mike stood, saluted and departed for the Arms Room…muffin in hand.

7 July 0900
1ˢᵗ Squadron, 1ˢᵗ Cavalry HQ
Conference Room,
Defiance, ROA

The morning meetings left little for the military Commander to do other than saying "good idea, good work, good plan, or yes, let's do it." Levi was nearing his wit's end.

When the meeting broke up, Levi asked Ralph to stay for a few moments.

"Ralph, we have reached a point where we have to expand our borders. We are growing too comfortable and complacent in our little twenty-mile enclave.

"Mark my words; if America does not grow, America dies. Others will grow and eventually surround and absorb us. I would like for you to consider sending out reps to those communities just outside our borders, for, oh maybe another ten miles.

"Lay out the advantages of being a part of something other than just surviving, and when you say the magic word "electricity", they'll come begging to join up.

"We should also do a recon of Raleigh to see if those solar panels that Dannen told us about are really there, and what condition they're in."

"Levi, those are wonderful ideas, and I am in complete agreement. I'll take care of the diplomatic stuff, and you recon Raleigh. I've also got to tell you that I am absolutely thrilled to hear you talking about what *we* need. May I assume that you have decided to stay?"

"Sorry, old friend, but no, my plans have not changed. Just because I still plan to leave around 1 September does not mean that I am becoming uninvolved in Defiance. Besides, who knows, I may just turn around and come back one of these days, if you'll have me, of course."

"Don't be silly, you know this is your home, but speaking of home, what about Katie? Did you know that young Ted Wilson is teaching her how to shoot? That boy may only be fifteen, but he is without a doubt, one of our best marksmen.

"I just hope he doesn't get fresh with her, because I think Katie might just kick his butt. I was just speaking with her Karate instructor, and he told me that he has never seen anyone learn so fast.

"Now, I don't mean to get into your business, but I think she's working so hard because she plans on going with you."

"Damn, if I didn't think those were skills we must all have, I'd put a stop to that right now. No, she's not going, this is where Kate belongs."

"Yeah, well you know I agree with you, but does she think this is where she belongs if you are gone? You just might want to cogitate on that for a bit, ya' ole fart."

"Oh, Ralph, one other thing before you go. Captain Guyardo and I will be out of pocket today. We are going to do some recon work over near Miller's Creek…wait, don't say it. Mike will be my babysitter, and yes, we will be very careful Daddy-o."

Ralph was not happy and left mumbling something to himself about doddering old fools.

-

Levi shouted, "Sergeant Major Cobb!"

As always, he stuck his head in the door and said, "Yes, sir, what'cha need?"

Levi asked him to schedule a meeting with Major Smith and Major Eldridge for 1900 hours tonight to be briefed on their plan to reconnoiter Raleigh and see if they can find those solar panels Mr. Dannen told them about.

"Will do, sir, 1900. Captain Guy is here with your jeep all ready for your *recon* of Miller's Creek, bag one for me, sir," said a smiling Sergeant Major.

"Ayup, will do."

Picking up his hat, Levi walked out of the office with his weapons of the day and together, he and Mike went hunting.

As they drove the thirteen miles to the drop off point Levi told Mike that the plan was to kill the Sheriff, then severely wound his deputies. "Maybe, with the brains of the outfit dead, and some others slowly dying, maybe they'll just pack up and skedaddle. Hell, it's worth a shot," both men chuckled at his pun.

Mike agreed that the plan sounded solid and was eager to run with it.

Together they camouflaged the jeep, checked their gear, painted their faces and began the trek to find their ideal firing positions.

8 July 1305
Sniper nests
Overlooking Miller's Creek

The waiting is always the hard part; time crawls at a snail's pace when you have to just sit tight.

Levi thought that the Sheriff must have been having his lunch when he and Mike took up positions around four hundred yards from the front of the building used by the Sheriff as his office.

Finally, at 1355 hours the Sheriff and four of his henchmen exited a small café and began working their way back to the office. The Sheriff did wear a uniform, well, sort of a uniform. He reminded Levi of a 1930's politician, three hundred pounds, dark suit pants, white shirt, and to complete the ensemble, wide dark green suspenders with a belt.

His Deputies were more scruffy looking with longer stringy hair and a bully's swagger. He wondered if they were all family members.

The signal to fire on the Deputies was Levi's shot to kill the Sheriff, which is exactly what happened; from four hundred yards the bullet hit the Sheriff squarely in the spinal cord, severing it at the seventh vertebrae. Before he hit the ground both Levi and Mike were firing shots to create lingering and painful wounds. Within five seconds all were down and screaming, well all but the Sheriff who died instantly.

Only the other Deputies came running to see who their boss had shot. All five of them were dropped before any of them had a chance to find cover.

After gathering up their gear, they walked together to the men who lay dying on the ground. Pools of blood were soaking into the ground. With no further need to try to frighten the Deputies into leaving, Levi and Mike put them out of their misery with a shot to the head.

Levi then called out to the residents of Miller's Creek and ordered them to congregate around the bodies.

Once all of the remaining residents had arrived Levi reminded them of their responsibility to try to police their own ranks. He also reminded them that American's help each other.

"Tomorrow," Levi said, "we will return with weapons and ammo for each of you. If you do not know how to use them, training will be arranged for everyone, to include children ten and older.

Now, I recommend that you bury the trash, start cleaning this place up and get back to your crops. If you want to eat this winter, you had better tend to your farm work. This place is a pigsty. I highly recommend that we see an improvement tomorrow.

CHAPTER THIRTY-FIVE

The Road to Civilization goes through Defiance, The Republic of America

1 September
Defiance, America

Defiance was growing fast; the total population of the area controlled by America was now in excess of one thousand.

A new currency was in the works. The Secretary of the Treasury was finding precious metals at many nearby banks. He knew where to look because he had been on the Board of Directors for ten Coastal North Carolina Banks.

Jewelry and other precious metals appeared in the Defiance Treasury on an almost daily basis. A new value to gold was established that one ounce of gold would be valued at around $18 Patriot dollars.

Rudimentary trade through barter was growing. Several citizens were looking forward to starting small businesses once a monetary system was accepted throughout America. Tool repair and feed stores were those most commonly mentioned as true necessities.

The Army of the Republic of America would add a third Troop in another week bringing the force to nearly four hundred men, and borders that now stretched outward to forty miles. The army was now sending out small units to attack and destroy those evil forces well outside of America's forty-mile border. Those people living in areas policed by the 1st Cavalry Squadron now knew life without fear of being murdered in their homes.

The acreage under cultivation was impressive as The Republic of America now covered forty miles in all directions and boasted fifty farming families responsible for 10 acres each. Crops were assigned by a farming committee of those same families to insure the proper amount of staples were grown.

Buildings were going up fast and it appeared that everyone would be in a cozy wooden structure before winter, and all with some level of electricity.

Levi decided to continue residing in his Ted's Shed. It was actually designed as a horse stall complete with a tack and storage room. He had it insulated, wired and prepped for winter. The tack room became his sleeping quarters and the storage room his office. The Defiance carpenters had added an additional room for Katie. He had it placed next to the new Orderly Room. It was nothing fancy, but much more comfortable than the GP Medium tent he had been occupying in the early days. Ralph fussed, but Levi would have none of it.

Katie had begun to smooth out after a few days in Defiance, but she was never far from Levi. Their relationship began to grow daily and she began to see him as a surrogate father. One day, she asked if it was ok to call him Dad.

"Katie, there is nothing that would please me more. I am honored that you would want to call me, Dad. Actually I was thinking last night that next week we could arrange for Mayor Ralph to make you legally my daughter. Would you consider changing your last name to mine?"

She immediately teared up and began sobbing out, "I love you Dad. My first Dad was a drug user and dealer. He smacked Mom and me around a lot. Do you still want me to be your daughter?"

Levi hugged her tightly and said, "More than ever Katie, more than ever. In fact, let's go see Ralph about it right now."

For the first time in a long time, Katie seemed genuinely happy and likewise, Levi had not felt such happiness since the day before Sarah's murder.

Levi and Katie arrived at Ralph's office and asked his secretary if he was available. She got up and knocked on the Mayor's door, then opened it just enough to place her head inside and said; "Mr. Mayor, Colonel Levins and Miss Katie would like a moment of your time."

Ralph got to his feet and came out to usher his visitors into his office. "Please, sit. Barbara would you please send in some coffee, and something for Katie?"

"Of course, Mr. Mayor, I'll be right back."

All three sat in chairs around a coffee table before Ralph asked what he could do for them.

Katie jumped in and said, "He wants to be my Dad, and I want to be his daughter. I'm so excited I could bust."

Ralph looked questioningly at Levi, who said, "Ralph, we figured that you being the Mayor and all, that you might have our historian enter into the official history of Defiance that on this day Katie Jarvis became the daughter of Levi Levins, or some such words."

Ralph relaxed and said, "Wow! I am thrilled at this news. Of course, we can get that done, in fact as Mayor of Defiance I now officially make the pronouncement that Colonel Levi Levins, Commander of the Military Forces of the Republic of America is now and forever the father of Katie Levins.

I'll have Barbara make up a certificate and we'll post a copy on the Village Green bulletin board.

So, tell me Katie, how does it feel to now be Katie Levins, daughter of Colonel Levi Levins?"

Tears streamed down Katie's face as she ran to Ralph and gave him a huge hug before running back to Levi hugging his neck and crying tears of joy…yep, they matched Levi's tears.

That very night the Dining Facility had a special cake made for Katie and Levi. Levi was so proud and happy that he very nearly popped the buttons off his shirt. Levi put his arms around Katie and felt the warm tears of a fatherly love slip out of his eyes, roll over his cheeks and onto the top of Katie's head. In only a day Levi became the loving parent he always wanted to be. Katie needed a father, Levi needed a daughter, and it had been that kind of love at nearly first sight.

EPILOGUE

Master, all glory is fleeting

1 September 0900 hours
Troop Formation
Village Green,
Defiance, America

Colonel Levins watched as the NCO's organized the formation before Sergeant Major Cobb and newly promoted Lieutenant Colonel Scott Eldridge commanding the 1st Squadron, 1st Cavalry Regiment.

These formations were held daily, though normally at 0600 and were followed by morning PT; the old style daily dozen and a two-mile run before breakfast. Following breakfast, the Troopers showered and shaved before going to daily tactical and rifle practice. Some of the older NCOs called it *Colonel Levins black boot Army.* The army had grown from just forty members on 29 March, 00 to nearly five hundred well trained Mobile Infantry and Horse Mounted Cavalry.

Following the destruction of The Death Dealer gang, The Double R Latino Gang, The White Supermen, and many other small unnamed groups of murderers and rapists, the Squadron troopers were exuberant and felt they could not be defeated.

Colonel Levins, now on extended leave had turned over the reins of leadership to younger, competent men. On this, Levi Levins last formal formation he decided to give them a lesson about glory.

Levi ordered the Troops to form an arc formation around him and then had them sit on the warm summer grass. The Historian recorded his words:

"I fear that we may believe that things will always go right for us. If we will just remain faithful to our training, and we all must never forget that when we stop earning what we get, we shall surely fall apart just as did the Romans.

Rome was victorious and ruled most of the known world for roughly five hundred years, but in the end, they became very liberal and bought the vote just as the American liberals had done before the collapse.

Cradle to grave entitlements made for a lack of desire to pull one's own weight, thus the Roman Empire eventually became a hollow shell of its former greatness and when the Huns were at the gates of Rome there was no well-trained army to protect the city.

We must always remain vigilant and never become complacent, nor be willing to let others carry our water.

Following a long campaign to conquer and plunder other nations, Caesar, returning from great victories in Africa, stood tall and proud as he rode in his war chariot.

Caesar led the victory parade through the ancient cobbled streets of Rome, trailed by thousands of slaves, elephants, lions, bears, and unimaginable riches plundered from the conquered peoples.

The crowds lining his path cheered and screamed their eternal love with passionate joy as he passed.

Yet at the height of his glory, the moment he was to become the master of the known world, the slave standing behind him, holding his crown and spear whispered in his ear, *"Master, all glory is fleeting."*

We must never forget that all glory is indeed fleeting if we are to stave off the New Dark Age which has overtaken the world around us."

Of course, no one really liked the daily PT and the various classes, both formal and tactical, but there were very few complaints because everyone in the Squadron felt an immense pride of belonging to a group that had the responsibility to protect Defiance and its people. Today's formation was to be both a farewell to the founder of this fighting force, and a training holiday...

THE END

Please look for my next book

in the Vigilante series:

VIGILANTE: INTO THE FRAY

ABOUT THE AUTHOR

Cliff Deane grew up in South Charleston, West Virginia. At 17, he left school and joined the U.S. Cavalry, as a Private. 35 years later, he retired as a Lt. Colonel, spending 10 years Enlisted, and 25 years Commissioned.

Cliff holds a High School G.E.D., a Bachelor of Science Degree in Elementary Education and English, a Master's Degree in Education Administration and Management from West Virginia and is a graduate of the U.S. Army Command & General Staff College.

After retirement, a love of the American West took Cliff to Prescott, Arizona, which he has called home for many years.

Today, Cliff and his dog Katie reside full time in his 44' Toy Hauler. He and Katie just go where the wind blows, as long as the wind blows them to Sturgis, SD in August.

THANK YOU FOR READING!

If you enjoyed this book, we would appreciate your customer review on your book seller's website or on Goodreads.

Also, we would like for you to know that you can find more great books like this one at www.CreativeTexts.com

BOOKS BY CLIFF DEANE

The Vigilante Series
Vigilante: Into the Darkness
Book one
Post-Apocalyptic Justice
Vigilante: Into the Fray
Book two
Post-Apocalyptic Justice
Vigilante: The Pale Horse
Book three
Post-Apocalyptic Justice
Vigilante: No Quarter
Book four
Post-Apocalyptic Justice
Vigilante: The Way West
Book five
Post-Apocalyptic Justice
Vigilante: Indian Territory
Book six
Post-Apocalyptic Justice

The Oort Chronicles Series
Red Alert: Missiles Inbound
A Prelude to Apocalypse
Book 1
The Oort Plague
The Pandemic Apocalypse
Book 2
America Fights Back
The Mag Apocalypse
Book 3